A SEASON IN PARIS

AN HISTORICAL ANTHOLOGY

GIRL ON A SOAPBOX PRESS

A Season in Paris: An Historical Anthology

First published 2021

Bows, Beaus and Sweet Chapeaus! © 2021 Ava January

The Toymaker © 2021 Clare Griffin

The Secret Artist of Paris © 2021 Sarah Fiddelaers

The Sparrow and the Tin Man © 2021 Nancy Cunningham

The moral rights of the authors have been asserted.

Except for use in any review, the reproduction or utilisation of this work in whole or in part in any form by any electronic, mechanical or other means, now known or hereafter invented, including xerography, photocopying and recording, or in any information storage or retrieval system is forbidden without the permission of the publisher.

This book is sold subject to the condition that it shall not, by way of trade or otherwise, be lent, resold, hired out or otherwise circulated without the prior consent of the publisher in any form of binding or cover other than that in which it is published and without a similar condition including this condition being imposed on the subsequent purchaser.

All rights reserved including the right of reproduction in whole or in part in any form.

Published by

Girl On A Soapbox Press

BAYSWATER VIC 3153

AUSTRALIA

Cover image from Arcangel Images Ltd (UK)

Designed by Nancy Cunningham

Paperback ISBN: 978-0-994-5333-6-4

Digital ISBN: 978-0-994-5333-7-1

❦ Created with Vellum

To all our loved ones.

∽

"Breathe Paris in. It nourishes the soul."
– Victor Hugo

"Just add three letters to Paris, and you have paradise."
– Jules Renard

"A walk about Paris will provide lessons in history, beauty, and in the point of life."
– Thomas Jefferson

"There is only one happiness in life, to love"
– George Sand

BOWS, BEAUS AND SWEET CHAPEAUS

By Ava January

CHAPTER 1

PARIS, SPRING 1909

Delphine Altraine had done many regrettable things in her life, but the dampness of her palms told her this very well might be the pinnacle.

The tall, lean man paused at the edge of the makeshift stage, smiling blindly into the crowd as the shouts and hollers drowned out the voice of the emcee. The man laughed as the crescendo of whistling increased and gave a sweeping bow toward the audience.

'The bidding will begin at twenty francs,' the emcee announced.

Hands immediately shot into the air, and he began his work of increasing the bidding.

Delphine ran her palms along the seams of her skirt and swallowed hard. Her mouth became drier with every number called aloud.

The frenzied air that had accompanied the start of the auction began to slow. It appeared the battle was now being waged between a tall, elegant redhead and a dowager whose hand could barely support the weight of the jewels that crowded her fingers.

'One hundred francs.' Good lord, was that strong, confident voice hers? Delphine was glad she was sitting as her knees had begun knocking together so violently, she feared the entire room could hear.

She had known this was going to be an expensive exercise, but one hundred francs was her entire life savings. If this gamble didn't pay off, she was sunk. Not only would her dreams be dashed, but she would be penniless. Destitute. On the streets. Delphine bit her lip; she couldn't think like that. She had to believe this plan, no matter how outrageous, would work.

A murmur flowed through the crowd as heads turned to see who was the owner of the bold offer. Delphine lifted her chin and one corner of her mouth in what she hoped was an enigmatic smile, and crossed her fingers tightly in her lap. She couldn't afford to pay any higher than one hundred francs *and* eat for the rest of the week. Her entire plan depended on winning this one-on-one date with Paris's wealthiest businessman, Gabriel Lapouge.

'One hundred francs,' the emcee repeated, pointing toward Delphine with his mahogany gavel.

Gabriel lifted a hand to his forehead, shielding his eyes from the glare of the spotlight as he gazed out toward her. Although Delphine was certain she was too far for him to see, as she was at the back of the room in one of the cheapest ticketed seats. Her breath still hitched at the intensity of his gaze.

'Going once.'

Gooseflesh erupted on her arms as her heart beat wildly. Her dream was within reach. She could feel it.

'Going twice.'

Delphine screwed her eyes closed tightly and fought the urge to press her hand to her chest. Her plan was foolish, that much she knew, but there had been innumerable times people had told her that her dreams were impossible. If only they could see her now, here, making them happen.

'Sold. To number twenty-seven, the beautiful *mademoiselle* in the purple.'

The crowd erupted into a cacophony of cheers and whistles, and faces turned toward Delphine in varying stages of pleasure, confusion and curiosity.

Delphine ran her eyes around the crowd, meeting the stony gaze of the underbidder.

The redhead was staring at her with a frosty glare and a slightly upturned lip. Delphine held her gaze and smiled in return. The redhead looked away without returning her smile.

Oh dear. It appeared she had offended Gabriel's date.

'*Mademoiselle*, you may meet Mr Lapouge at the side of the stage here to make your arrangements. Next, we have a generous offer from a Mr Pablo Ruiz y Picasso, who will paint some brave person's portrait.'

Delphine was grateful for the change of focus to the painter. She stood and inhaled deeply, fighting the urge to adjust her dress. This was a business transaction, and it made no difference how she looked. Although it didn't help that Gabriel was immaculate in a jet-black tuxedo, all sharp angles and masculinity. Even from this distance, Delphine could tell he would smell as good as he looked. And he looked good. Very good.

He weaved through the crowd, shaking hands and laughing with the people as they reached out to him. It appeared as if he knew every person in the room. Given his reputation as *the* party man of Paris, she was not surprised. He was rumoured to work as hard as he played, and if the social pages were right, he played very hard.

Delphine slipped between two tables and made her way toward Gabriel. The last thing she wanted was for the table of snobs who had looked her up and down and decided she was not worth their time, to overhear their conversation.

Her belly fluttered madly as she neared Gabriel, but she inhaled a deep breath to steel herself. She was her papa's daughter. Brave, bold and quite possibly, judging by this transaction, a little mad. When she reached Gabriel, she held out her hand.

'*Bonsoir, Monsieur* Lapouge. I am Delphine Altraine.' Again, Delphine was surprised at how strong and clear her voice sounded. Inside she was a quivering mess.

Gabriel gazed wordlessly at her for a moment before taking her hand in his and raising it to his lips instead of shaking it.

'*Enchanté*. Thank you for your generous contribution.' He released her hand and gave her a slow smile. Even in the dim, smoky light, his eyes were the brightest blue she had ever seen. They crinkled at the sides as he smiled, giving him a charming boyish air that was at odds with his height and the breadth of his shoulders.

Delphine bit her lip to steady herself, and his electric gaze followed the movement. An unwanted heat flooded her cheeks. *Mince!* Was she going to make a fool of herself in front of this man? She had just made a large investment in her future, the largest she could afford. She had spent her entire life savings on this man; she could not let it go to waste by falling apart like a schoolgirl. It wasn't his looks she was interested in; it was what he could do to further her career.

'I thought we could come back here for our date—'

'I know where I would like to go.'

His eyebrows rose. 'I like a woman who knows what she wants.'

Oh, Delphine knew what she wanted alright.

'Let me know which dates suit you and your address, and I will arrange for a taxi to collect you.'

Delphine almost laughed. She could imagine what her neighbours would think if a car, of the standard she imagined Gabriel Lapouge would have, came to collect her from her dingy, little bedsit. No, the old women in her building already looked down upon her with her modern ways. She would not give them anything else to gossip about.

'Tomorrow is good for me. I will meet you at 26 rue de Charonne at seven o'clock.'

The charming smile froze slightly on Gabriel's face. He was obviously unused to women making the decisions. Well, if he spent any time with her, and if her plan worked he would be, he needed to know he was dealing with a woman who made bold decisions.

'*Oui*, tomorrow at seven is fine by me,' he said slowly, rocking back on his heels as he considered her.

'Perfect. See you then.'

Delphine turned and walked the edge of the room towards the exit, painfully aware of the curious gazes that followed her. When she reached the door, she turned to look back, surprised to find Gabriel watching her with a cool, considered gaze.

Good, let him watch. Her future depended on it.

~

THE PARIS GAZETTE, *March 1909*

It simply isn't springtime in Paris until the Orphans and Widows Association has had its yearly auction.

It's a worthy cause, my dear readers, with all proceeds going to the foundling hospice, but between you me and the lamp post, I don't attend for the privilege of drinking lukewarm champagne, perspiring into my silk, and fighting for mirror space to fix my rouge. I am happy to admit that I only attend for a glimpse of France's most eligible, and elusive, bachelor Gabriel Lapouge, and to secretly gawp at whatever lucky woman has found herself on his arm for the night.

This year it was silent screen star Bridgette Vidal, and someone very close to this reporter can attest that she is as flawless in person as she appears on screen, and just as cold. Although perhaps the chill was due to the fact that her current amour was auctioned to the highest bidder, just as he is every year.

However, this year, instead of the fawning, fur covered dowagers (not you, Penelope, you're as exquisite as the day the count passed into the nether and left you all that delicious money) that regularly bid, the room, and this very reporter, were all shocked into silence (and if you've ever been in a room full of Paris's richest people, you'll know how difficult that is) when the highest bidder was an awfully attractive, if not a touch dowdily dressed, unknown woman who bid, won, and left, much like Cinderella.

Like little Cendrillon, our secret bidder has left us with more questions than answers.

Who is she? Where did she scuttle off to after winning the date with Lapouge? And more importantly, where did she get the stunning creation she wore on her head? A thoroughly modern lilac and cream lace creation that sat at just the perfect angle to both hide her eyes and enhance her exquisite cheekbones.

It is this reporter's business to know exactly where one can have such a creation made.

If you have any information that would shed light on this deliciously intriguing situation, do drop me a line here at the Gazette, but please remember – discretion may be my middle name, but I never answer to it.

CHAPTER 2

The cool evening air was thick with the spring scents that, for Delphine, were quintessentially Paris.

Tobacco, chickens roasting in the open-air market in the fifth arrondissement, the smell of the Seine as it stole and delivered a thousand romantic dreams. Of which, Delphine was sure, hers was but one. She inhaled deeply in a futile attempt to calm the butterflies in her stomach. The church bells of Saint-Séverin began their hourly chime. It was seven o'clock, but Gabriel was nowhere to be seen.

The butterflies tightened into a knot. She had handed over her wad of francs the night of the auction, albeit with a shaking hand. Surely he couldn't stand her up?

Movement on the road caught her attention. An olive-coloured Gregoire automobile moved along the road, the unmistakable shape of Gabriel behind the wheel. He lifted a hand in greeting as he pulled the car to a stop beside her. Delphine's pulse raced as he alit. More casually dressed than last night, he was still the smartest dressed man she had ever seen. A dark grey bowler covered his hair, and he wore a matching coloured suit that fit his broad shoulders with such perfection it would make a tailor weep.

'Good evening,' he said, walking around and opening the car door for her.

Delphine didn't move from the doorway.

Speak for goodness sake.

Here she was, on the threshold of making all her dreams come true, and she was as mute as Hesychia, the silent goddess.

'Good evening,' she finally croaked.

Mince! She cleared her throat and tried again, conjuring the clear and confident tone from last night. 'We will not need your vehicle. We are already at our location.'

She gestured to the small, cobbled passage that cut between the two buildings she stood in front of. Gabriel stared at her with narrowed eyes, his gaze flitting between the cobblestone path and her face. She smiled, although certain her terror was written all over it.

Gabriel closed the car door with a thud. 'This is where you wish to conduct our date?'

His tone was wary, and Delphine didn't blame him. She had purchased a date with France's richest man and instead of requesting he take her to the hottest nightclubs or most expensive bistro, she was standing outside a shadowy laneway in Bastille. Delphine studied his face to determine if he had made the connection yet. His gaze never left hers, and she was certain he hadn't.

'Not here exactly.' She licked her lips, which were suddenly dry. 'A little further down.'

Gabriel's gaze moved from her to the blank windows above. He took a step backward. 'Forgive me but I,' he paused, blinking into the dimming light, 'I am in a relationship.'

Delphine's heart sank. He thought she was inviting him

into her apartment? Could this have started any more badly? She scrubbed at her eyes. Of course, he thought she was propositioning him. He was France's most eligible bachelor, and she was trying to entice him into an unlit alley.

'I... I...' She forced herself to take a calming breath. She wouldn't fall at the first hurdle. 'I can assure you that is not what I intend for this evening.' He raised an eyebrow. 'Or any evening to be frank.'

The mocking eyebrow lowered. 'I can't tell if I am relieved or you have damaged my sensitivities.'

Her gaze flew to his, and she was grateful to find a smile playing along his lips.

'I imagine you'll survive either way.' Delphine paused, unsure how to begin. She sucked in a deep breath and licked her lips. She had practised her speech every night since the idea had taken shape in her mind. By this stage, she should be able to repeat it backwards.

Turning to Gabriel, she was surprised to find he was not, as she had expected him to be, looking at their surroundings but at her. His blue gaze was sharp and searching, and there was something in the way he looked at her that made her skin tingle. The well-practised words died on her lips, and she looked away. A white pigeon sat on the clay guttering of the building across from them, watching her with a judgemental air.

Losing courage? Its beady black eye seemed to mock. *Over a pair of blue eyes?* Delphine bared her teeth at the bird and turned back to Gabriel, whose gaze swung to where she had been staring. The bird lifted into the air, hovering for a moment before performing an expressive loop de-loop.

Typical. The man was so good looking that even birds performed for him. Well, not this bird.

Delphine began her speech, not waiting for Gabriel to turn back to her.

'I am sure I do not need to tell you what a superior position this street holds.'

Gabriel's arctic gaze landed on her, and a furrow appeared between his perfectly arched brows. 'You don't?'

The words stumbled on Delphine's lips. She hadn't expected that. 'Well. No. You must know how desirable this area is...' She gestured around the bustling street. A car honked and a young man stood on the passenger seat, waving his hat. 'Gabriel! *Ça va!*'

Gabriel smiled and lifted a hand in return. He swung back around to Delphine with a grimace. 'Apologies. I have no idea who that was.'

'I believe that was your brother.'

'Ah. Is that who that is? I had wondered why I keep seeing him around.' Gabriel winked, and her breath froze in her chest. 'Now, as you were saying. Rental prices around here are...' he gestured for her to go on.

'I wasn't speaking about rental prices.' Had she? Damn the man, he had her so flummoxed. She rubbed her eyes and ran through the speech in her head... desirable area...

'As the landlord of this particular building—'

'I am?' Gabriel's lip curled in derision as he took in the grimy windows of the empty storefront. The awning hung limply on one side, the canvas ripped and mouldy.

Did the man have so many properties he wasn't even aware of what he did and didn't own? Delphine ground her back teeth together. For over a year she had gone without nearly every pleasure. Her biggest pleasure was using a tea bag that hadn't already been used thrice and here she was, about to go cap in hand to a man who had the power to make or break her dreams, and he didn't even know if he owned the property she had dreamt about every night for the last three months.

'I believe so.'

Gabriel huffed a breath as if to say, if you say so. 'Well, I really should do something about it. No wonder it is sitting empty. Not a splendid investment if I do say so myself.'

And there it was. Her chance. Delphine's fingertips tingled. 'That is what I wish to speak to you about. I am a milliner. A very good one. And I wish to make you a business proposition.'

Gabriel's eyes widened. 'Ah, so I get my proposition after all.'

Heat flooded Delphine's cheeks. The infuriating man was so used to having women throw themselves at him that he couldn't believe when it didn't happen. Well, it would never happen with her. There was only one thing she wanted from Gabriel Lapouge and it was this property.

He continued to stare at her, a delicious half-smile on his face that sent her stomach flipping.

She cleared her throat and restarted her speech. 'I am a milliner, and I wish to make you a business proposition. If you will walk this way, I can tell you about it.'

Gesturing down the cobbled laneway to their destination, she began to walk through Passage Lhomme.

She cast a glance over her shoulder at him. He remained standing on the footpath. 'Well? *Allons-y.*'

His laughter echoed in the low ceiling covering the entrance to the lane, and the timbre of it sent a delightful shiver along her spine.

The thump of his footfalls sounded as he caught up with her.

'*Mademoiselle* Twenty-Seven, if you are trying to intrigue me, you have succeeded.'

Delphine kept her gaze trained on the uneven cobbles of the street in front of them. Was she trying to intrigue him? The idea of it hadn't occurred to her until now, but the very mention of it bought an unfamiliar heat to her chest.

What else would it take to intrigue a man like Gabriel Lapouge? She shot a furtive glance at him.

He was impossibly handsome, but as was too often the case in Delphine's experience, did not carry himself with the air of arrogance or entitlement of so many of the men she had encountered. He noticed her looking at him and smiled, his teeth shining white in the golden light of dusk.

She swallowed and looked away. His type of woman would be a glamorous and flawless woman like Bridgette Vidal. Delphine, like everyone else in the room, hadn't been able to tear her eyes from the woman. Everything about her was perfection. The set of her shoulders, the way her hair was held in the low chignon, her laugh the clear tinkle of a crystal bell being touched lightly with a knife edge of silver.

That would be the type of woman who intrigued Gabriel Lapouge. Not a country bumpkin from Auvergne, known for her big feet and even bigger dreams, with only a papa to steer her into the perilous abyss of womanhood. Her tomboy habits had made her popular with the boys in town, but only ever as a friend. And now there wasn't even papa. The thought brought a hot rod of steel to her back. It made no difference to her if there was anyone to help or not. She was more than capable of helping herself. She had her dreams and would do anything it took to see them realized.

They came to a stop in front of a door where the numbers 675 hung drunkenly on the jamb.

'You are the landlord of this property and I wish to rent it from you.'

Gabriel gazed at the windows, so covered in grime it was almost impossible to see in. There was a small patch on the lower left corner that, if you bent down and pressed your face, allowed you to see in. The stone floors were bare and filthy, the walls marred by mould and rising damp. But from the very moment Delphine had laid eyes on the timber-framed window, she had known this was the spot for her store. It had called to her.

'*Salut*, Monsieur Lapouge.' A well-dressed couple walking a small fluffy dog strolled by. The woman gazed at Delphine, raising her eyebrows as if to say she'd seen women like her before and good luck, dear, you'll need it. Delphine focussed her gaze on the split timber of the door to the store.

Gabriel raised his finger to his hat and nodded. '*Bonsoir*.'

The couple stopped, and the man began to question Gabriel heatedly about the recent Paris Film Congress.

'We can discuss this over a coffee, another time.' Gabriel made a movement toward Delphine to indicate he wanted to get moving again. The man continued his diatribe as they passed through the small tunnel back to rue de Charonne, his ire increasing as they walked.

'Garros, please. Let us speak about this another time.'

The man peered at Delphine as if seeing her for the first time, and nodded. 'Tomorrow, then.'

Gabriel and Delphine watched as the couple continued along the street, stopping while their dog relieved itself on every available surface.

Delphine opened her mouth to speak again when another voice rang out.

'Lapouge! I have a new model of automobile, just arrived! I just sold one to Max Decugis. A man like you might want to come and look I think, yes? Can't let that little upstart beat you in the tour!'

Neither Gabriel nor Delphine turned their head toward the speaker, their gazed remaining locked on each other.

The man neared, spouting stats and horsepower figures, but Gabriel held up a quelling hand.

'Shall we find somewhere quieter to discuss this...' a corner of his mouth lifted, 'proposition?'

Delphine's stomach flipped. For a moment she couldn't

do anything but think about what it would be like if Gabriel were smiling at her in that way in earnest, rather than sport. Her gaze fell to the patch of skin jutting from underneath his jacket sleeve. For some reason the sight of his tanned skin, and the smattering of dark hair along it, made her insides feel molten. He was an extraordinarily good-looking man. Not for the likes of her, was he. A sigh escaped before she had a chance to contain it.

Gabriel cocked his head and stared at her quizzically. There was something about his gaze that made her feel utterly exposed. Brushing her hands along her skirt, she gestured at a restaurant on the corner across from where they stood. 'Shall we try there?'

Gabriel followed her gesture with his eyes and grimaced. 'No.'

A hot wave of shame washed over Delphine. Of course not; that restaurant appeared to have been where all his friends had come from. The last thing he would want would be to be seen with someone like her. She tried not to adjust her clothing. She was painfully aware that her homemade skirt, while smart, was two years from the height of fashion.

'Come, I know a place.' Gabriel's warm hand encircled her arm, and they had set off at a trot before Delphine could consider whether it was wise for her to be alone with him or not.

Oh, who was she kidding? It was far from wise.

CHAPTER 3

Gabriel's long stride made it challenging for Delphine to keep up. Forced to take two steps to his one, she felt as if she were almost running to keep up with him and she disliked the feeling of being at a disadvantage enormously. She tugged on his arm, too out of breath to speak.

He looked down at her, his eyes widening in contrition as he took in her red face. 'My apologies. I'm not used to...' His gaze dropped to her feet and travelled back to her face, taking in her height. Heat moved along her chest. He was probably used to walking with the gazelle-like Bridgette. Not that it mattered to her anyway, she told herself fiercely. This was a strictly business arrangement.

Gabriel slowed his pace to match hers, and they ambled along the busy road until they came to a mahogany door. The scent of oxtail hotpot sent Delphine's stomach rumbling and transported her back to her childhood on the farm. When maman was still alive. What would she have had to say about this scheme of hers?

Delphine pressed her wrist against her chest. The slow

beating of the pulse against her heart dulled the ache that appeared every time she thought about her parents.

'After you.'

Delphine jolted back to the present as Gabriel held the door to the bistro open for her.

His brow furrowed as their eyes met. 'Are you alright?'

Delphine blinked. It had been a long time since anyone had asked her that and for the briefest of moments, she wavered on the knife's edge of an honest answer. What would that feel like? Her eyes wandered over the planes of Gabriel's face, avoiding his sharp gaze that felt like it saw too much. His skin was tanned and smooth, freshly shaved. The slight nick at his ear caused her heart to flutter wildly. Perhaps it was the image it conjured of him as a person, not a hero or god-like figure. A mere mortal who shaved, like every other beardless man. For a moment she imagined him, shirtless in a fog-filled bathroom, a towel low on his hips. Did Bridgette wind her arms around his torso, pressing herself to him while he shaved? Delphine could almost feel the soft skin of his back against her cheek. The thud of her heart against his.

This was insanity. She couldn't think about him like that, not only because a lowly commoner like her stood no chance with him, but she wanted one thing and one thing only from him and it was the shop in Passage Lhomme.

'*Oui*. Never better.' She forced her lips into a bright smile. Cool, calm, and collected and utterly capable of running a successful business.

She paused for a moment on the threshold of the bistro, blinking as her eyes adjusted to the dim lighting. A sharp-shouldered, grey-haired lady walked toward them, wiping her hands on her apron. Her face lit up when she noticed Gabriel standing behind Delphine.

Delphine stood awkwardly to the side as exclamations

were exchanged and cheeks kissed. Gabriel introduced the lady. The older woman offered Delphine a tight smile and ran her gaze in disapproving assessment along her outfit so quickly it was barely noticeable, but Delphine felt it like a slap. She was well aware she was not the usual woman Gabriel would be seen out and about with, which was clearly why he had chosen this tiny, dim bistro where they were unlikely to be seen by anyone who knew him. Pride straightened her shoulders. It didn't matter a jot to her what people thought of her. She only needed to have Gabriel's undivided attention for thirty minutes. Her proposal was good, the business idea sound. Her belief in herself was not the problem, simply her access to people with the business and financial acumen.

'Your usual table, Gabriel?'

He nodded in response, and she ushered them to a small table positioned under the shuttered window. A jar of freshly picked lavender sat in the centre of the cream linen-covered table. His usual table, the woman— the owner? — had said. So, this wasn't just some place to avoid being seen with her.

Delphine looked around the bistro. Small and cosy, it was reminiscent of a traditional bistro rather than the flashy continental cafés that had become so popular around Paris.

Peasant fare. The thought flashed through her mind before she could help herself. The type of food she had grown up on. It was surprising to her that someone like Gabriel would choose to eat the sort of simple dishes that a place like this served. She couldn't imagine Bridgette enjoying herself here. The lighting was dim, and the windows facing the street were too small and low to allow passers-by to see who, or what, was within.

Gabriel drew the rustic wooden chair from beneath the table for her. He sat and steepled his hands on the table between them, studying her over the top of his long, lean fingers.

'So, is now a good time to discuss this proposition?'

Delphine nodded briskly. 'I purchased this date with you because I have a business proposal for you. You are the owner and landlord of 675 Passage Lhomme and I wish to rent the property from you to start my millinery business. As I mentioned earlier, I am a very good milliner.'

Gabriel's brows nestled together in confusion. 'You could have just spoken to my agent and rented the property. Why spend one hundred francs on a date with me?'

Delphine forced a smile. She had spoken to his agent, an odious man who had all but laughed at her when she had tried to rent the property.

'I wanted to speak with you, and you are harder to get an audience with than the pope.'

They shared a smile across the table.

'I am a popular man but not quite as popular as the pope.'

She gestured to the street outside the window. 'I saw, and heard, differently.'

He grimaced. 'My apologies about that.'

She smiled at his bashful expression. He seemed genuinely embarrassed 'You can't help being popular.'

'So, why spend one hundred francs on a date with me?'

Delphine took a deep breath to steady herself. 'I would like you to be a partner in my business.'

Gabriel remained silent.

'I could rent your shop and start my own business but the rent in this area is prohibitive.'

'Less than one hundred francs, surely?' he interjected.

'Yes, but then I am making a name for myself, and that takes time. I need to buy high quality materials and pay rent. It would be easier to do that if Paris's most discussed man had reason to encourage his friends and *amoureux*, to wear my creations. Which you would do if there were financial reasons to do so.'

Delphine gulped another breath and forced herself to slow down.

'You are a business man and this is an excellent business opportunity. I am good, a very good milliner, but it is impossible to make a name in a city this large. Quickly at any rate. I am ambitious.'

A corner of Gabriel's mouth lifted, and he glanced down at the table between them. She couldn't read his expression. Was he impressed at her tenacity or terrified? A wave of self-doubt washed over her. Was this idea crazy? Surrounded by the warm and homely surroundings of the bistro, the street noises dimmed, she saw how crazy this idea had been after all. Her stomach twisted as the woman bustled out from the kitchen, a steaming pot in her hands. Gabriel pushed his seat back a little as she placed the food on the table. The silence between them seemed to take on a life of its own as he served her *en famille*.

Her stomach growled. It had been a long time since she had eaten anything that smelled this good. She'd chosen to save her francs for her business dreams, saving every centime she could. Hot tears pricked behind her eyes. Paris had made her believe her dreams were within reach. That all she had to do was hold her vision and take small steps toward it and she would have her own shop. She had been a fool. Somewhere along the line her dream of having her own millinery shop had morphed into something bigger and brighter than she could've imagined, and now she was paying the price. All her hard-earned and long-saved francs had been spent on a ridiculous notion of getting a private conversation with the richest man in France.

Delphine forked a piece of the meal into her mouth, the

buttery fish melting as it hit her tongue. Thank god it was delicious; it had cost her life's savings.

'Tell me more.' Gabriel's rich voice broke the silence.

She swallowed hard, not daring to meet his gaze. Was he really interested? She placed her cutlery beside her plate with care.

Forcing herself to choose her words carefully, she told him about her training under François Allard in Marseilles, omitting the worst parts but leaving him in no doubt that ending her employment with him had been the right thing to do.

'My vision is to have a reputation for quality and craftsmanship that is second to none, and then, to hire women and pay them decent wages, wages that are enough to keep themselves and their families fed and comfortably housed.'

She paused to take a breath, and Gabriel's gaze slid from his now empty plate to hers, still full. She had been too busy talking to eat. Had she said too much? Not enough? She turned her attention to her cooling meal. There was nothing else she could say. The decision was in his hands now.

She just hoped he could see the possibilities of her crazy idea.

~

THEY FINISHED their dinner in silence, and the longer it went on, the more convinced Delphine became that he thought her some kind of lunatic.

'About this business idea,' Gabriel prompted. 'I must admit, I am intrigued. One hundred francs is surely enough to rent the shop and just get started. And yet here we are.'

The note of scepticism in his voice brought her eyes to his. Arrogant man, he seemed to believe this was some sort of attempt to get close to him. She fought the urge to roll her eyes.

'Your agent demanded a year's rent up front. That would have left me with barely enough to purchase material to make one hat.'

She had done the figures, staying up into the gloomy hours of morning trying to make the numbers show something other than impossibility. It was perhaps possible if she gave up her tiny flat and slept on the floor of the shop, or if she worked evenings to supplement her income. But there were advertising costs, the costs of materials to make hats to display in the window to entice customers, not to mention the hours it took for her to make hats of the quality she did. No, it was impossible to start the type of business she wanted on one hundred francs. This had felt like the best way to spend that money.

She inhaled a deep breath. 'There are many hat shops in Paris. Nearly all of them are owned by men. The workers are expected to work long hours for very little pay. Our names are never synonymous with the craftsmanship of the product. It is always the name of the shop owner who takes the credit. The conditions are,' she paused, fighting the unwelcome memories of her previous employer. How his hot breath had crept along the back of her neck, how he had pressed his belly against her back as she worked. How he had screamed and yelled at the women, how he had grabbed at them. Until the day she had spoken back and she had been out of a job.

'I don't want to eke out a living, hand to mouth. I want my designs to be worn by the *crème de la crème* of society. And I want it to be my name they say when people ask who they are wearing, not someone else's. Someone who had nothing to do with the making of it.'

She slumped into the chair, embarrassed at how her voice had risen with passion as she spoke.

Gabriel considered her, that strange half smile still affixed to his face. 'I appreciate your ambition, but I don't think I am the man for you. I know nothing of women's fashion and often find myself utterly bemused by the contraptions I see on the heads of ladies.'

'You know business, though.' Delphine kept her voice calm and level. 'And you know very important people in Paris society.'

Gabriel nodded slowly, and a current of energy moved up her arms. Could it be that he was considering her proposal? She pushed on. 'I have some sample products to show you. You can inspect the quality. You know quality when you see it.' His shoes were of high quality, buffed to a glimmering shine, and his suit fit like a glove in a manner that only the best tailor could achieve. He was clearly a man that appreciated both high-quality goods and the efforts that went into making them.

'What do you see as my role in this?'

'My proposal is this. You allow me to work from your shop rent-free for twelve months. During this time I will pay you fifty per cent of all my profits. After twelve months we will part ways, and I will pay you rent on the shop should I choose to remain on.'

This time Gabriel laughed. And what a laugh. He sat back in his chair and threw his head back, his chest rising and falling. '*Mon Dieu.*'

'What you will earn from my fifty per cent during the rent-free period is far above and beyond what you can expect to earn from renting that poky little store.'

He raised a single doubting eyebrow. 'That poky little store, as you call it, is just off one the best streets in Paris.'

And didn't she know it. That was exactly why she wanted

to rent it. Why she needed to rent it. The foot traffic alone would be enough to bring her new customers, but combined with Gabriel's powerful reputation, she imagined the shop would be so busy. Of course, the more people visited and were seen visiting, the more people would want to. She dreamed of a queue on the street, of a group of women working behind the scenes bringing her designs to life. Well paid of course, in well-ventilated premises, with good lighting, and breaks for toilet and food. And above all else, safety. Safety from men who preyed on women's desperation, or love for their family in the way François did.

'Six.'

Delphine startled back to the present. 'I beg your pardon?'

'I will give you six months.'

A moment passed, an entirety, a lifetime, before Delphine's mind could grasp Gabriel's words. He was agreeing?

'Six months it is, then.' She tucked her fingers between her leg and the chair to stop herself from reaching across the table and grasping his face between her hands and kissing him with all the joy and passion that was surging through her body. While she had prayed and dreamed, she had never truly imagined that this moment would come.

'On one condition.' His bright blue eyes narrowed at hers, his tone cool. Her blood chilled. Was this when he proved himself to be a man of François's ilk? His open and friendly demeanour had lulled her into a sense of security. Was it to be proven fake now?

'You must allow me to repay you the one hundred francs for this date.'

This time her heart really did stop for a beat or two. If he repaid her the cost for the date, she could get the store up and running within six months, and that would allow her to purchase better fabric and hire someone straight away to do the beading rather than do it all herself as she had intended. It also meant she could stay in her apartment, as tiny and cockroach infested as it may be. It was certainly better than sleeping on the cold, tiled floor in the shop.

She knew it would be polite to refuse, but it was so much money and meant so much to her, and to Gabriel it was probably loose change.

Pretending to consider, she tapped a finger against her lip. 'Is that your only condition?'

His gaze followed her finger on her lip, and he looked away with an expression that almost looked like pain. 'Of course not, but we can have our lawyers discuss the rest.'

Her stomach flipped. She hadn't thought much past getting in front of him and discussing her proposal. That he may have accepted was too good to be true. She forked the remainder of her meal into her mouth and took her time chewing.

Should she ask him what his other conditions were? There were some non-negotiables for her, of course, but she wasn't certain if she could trust him. No, it was better to keep her cards close to her chest until she had regained some power.

'Dessert?'

Her plate was scraped clean. She placed a hand on her stomach. The meal had been the best thing she had eaten in a long time. Longer than she cared to remember.

'I will be ordering both the desserts they offer for myself. I find it hard to choose between two delicious things, so I never see why I should restrict myself to just one delicious thing when I can sample both.'

Delphine swallowed hard. Were they still talking about dessert?

'I have a number of hats I can show you. To prove to you

that I am capable,' she blurted out, desperate to get back on stable footing.

'I would like to see your hats. But purely out of interest. I have already told you I accept your offer.'

'You will accept my offer without seeing my hats?'

'Is this one of your designs?' He angled his chin toward her head.

Her hands lifted to her hat. She had worked on this piece every night since the idea to approach Gabriel had come to her, with the aim of impressing him. It was one of her best pieces of work.

Sliding the hat pins from the crown, she handed the hat across the table for Gabriel to inspect.

Although it was the hat his hands stroked and his eyes studied, Delphine felt as if she had laid herself bare before him. She twisted her hands together, fighting the urge to explain her stitches, and her decision to use tulle instead of feather plumes, as was the current trend.

His touch was gentle as he turned the hat around in his hands, softly caressing the petals of the candy-pink peony she'd picked along the way to their meeting.

'You made this?'

'Of course.' Her heart in her mouth prevented her from saying anything further.

With a little shrug, Gabriel handed the hat back to her. 'I think it looks great.' He gave her a boyish grin that sent her insides fluttering like crazy. 'Is it enough to say it is eye-catching? That when I pulled up in the car earlier and caught sight of you, I was unable to tear my eyes from you?'

Delphine blinked rapidly.

'But I feel that has little to do with your hat, as beautiful as it is, and more to do with you.'

Oh, but he was a silver-tongued devil. A master with words, a sorcerer, a spell weaver. Well, she wanted nothing to do with that. She wanted one thing, and that was her hat shop.

'I can make your *petite amie* one that will be even more eye-catching.' If he heard the catch in her voice, she hoped it made no sense to him.

He watched her for a long moment through sleepy eyes, the way a lion watches its prey.

At exactly the same moment as he burst into a smile that seemed to bring the stars from the sky, the door from the kitchen swung open and the owner walked toward them bearing a tray laden with dessert.

'Will you come and look at my designs?' She had promised herself that she wouldn't take more than one spoonful of the decadent chocolate mousse, but as soon as the thick and creamy mousse hit her tongue, she knew she was sunk.

Gabriel shook his head. 'I don't need to. As I said, I know nothing about hats. But I do know what it takes to be successful in business. It took real guts to approach me like this.' He shook his head in what she hoped was admiration. 'Crazy, but guts. If you approach business with that kind of tenacity, you're sure to be a success. And what do I have to lose? The shop is just sitting there empty anyway. You share the profits of what you make in six months, and even if it's a couple of francs, it's more than I would have had.'

It wasn't more than he had, not by a long shot, but Delphine supposed when you were that rich what did one little shop's rent mean to you? To Delphine, it was everything, the entire meaning of her life. To Gabriel, it was an amusing anecdote over a delicious chocolate mousse.

'Good, well if it's alright with you I would like to get started as soon as possible.'

'Let's meet with the rental agent. I haven't the faintest idea when that shop was last rented and how much work it might need.' At her raised eyebrows he explained. 'It was attached to the building I purchased on rue de Charonne. It was never something I needed.'

That explained why it was still vacant. That, and the sleazy rental agent who seemed to care more about what was under Delphine's skirt than in her pocketbook.

Gabriel glanced at his watch and blanched. 'May I drop you back to your apartment?'

Delphine lifted her handbag from the small table provided for it. 'Thank you, but no. I have a date myself. Just...around the corner, as it happens.' There was no way she was having The Paris Playboy drop her to her apartment. Not only because it was shabby part of town, but a car like his would get tongues wagging.

Gabriel stood. 'I must go, but we will speak about the shop. Soon.'

When? She wanted to ask but didn't have the courage. He was now technically her landlord and temporary business partner. She was perfectly entitled to ask him to clarify the time of a meeting. Her lips parted and she drew a breath, but the words died on her lips as he stood from his chair and gestured to the owner. 'Put it on my bill, Suzanne. I will see you Thursday.'

He turned to Delphine and they stared at each other for a moment. 'This was... unexpected. You are an intriguing lady, Mademoiselle Twenty-seven. My apologies, but I really need to go.'

The door had swung closed before Delphine realised her mouth was still hanging open.

So much for strong, powerful businesswoman's communication.

Perhaps next time.

CHAPTER 4

*D*elphine had always prided herself on being someone who made things happen, but the speed with which Gabriel had the hat store open spun her head.

It had been two weeks of endless work. Delphine had spent entire days on her hands and knees scrubbing the floors and walls, and then painting them both the same shade of fresh, crisp white. Her vision for her store had always been a blank canvas where the light, shade and texture were only provided by her hats. Unlike the trend for most milliners and modistes to have showrooms laden with fabric and samples, she wanted elegant simplicity where women could come and feel they were seen as they had a fitting with her.

Delphine had worked in the shop during the day, and then spent her evenings putting the finishing touches on the hats she would display in the window.

Her legs felt leaden as she walked along the *quai* beside the Seine, the crisp morning air of spring twirling her skirt around her ankles. She longed to pause for a moment on the water's edge and take in the day's beauty, but her head whirled with the list of things she needed to get done before the opening of the store in a mere two days' time. The tips of her fingers tingled just thinking about all she still had to achieve. Her index finger felt stiff and jammed. Hopefully the warmer weather would keep her swollen joints soft and pliable. Delphine blinked as she stood at the entrance to the tunnel leading to Passage Lhomme. A blue-overalled man bent over something laid at the base of the shop window. She hadn't arranged such a tradesman. He stood and ran his arm along the window. What on earth was he doing?

She continued walking towards him, and when she was close enough to see, her mouth dropped open.

Her name, in large, golden, serpentine letters spanned the width of the window.

Hot tears prickled at the back of her eyes, and her nose tingled. She couldn't remember the last time she'd cried. Not when François had accosted her in a dark corner of the factory and given her two options, both untenable: keep her mouth shut and stop encouraging the women of the factory to demand better conditions, or lose her job.

Nor when François had gone to her landlord and accused her of theft, leaving her unemployed and homeless.

But the sight of her name across the window was enough to undo her. She gulped for air, pressing her hand to her pounding heart.

A car horn blasted her from her reverie, and she was unsurprised to see Gabriel crossing the road. A pair of well-dressed young men leant from the car, calling his name.

Delphine rubbed at her eyes quickly and turned a sardonic brow his way.

'Does this happen wherever you go?'

Gabriel turned his head to the car, lifting a hand in farewell as they drove by.

'It tends to,' he said with a little shrug.

A burst of laughter escaped before Delphine could control it.

'It must be hard to go anywhere.'

He smiled back at her and gazed into her eyes. Suddenly the air thickened, became almost soapy, like the hot, stifling summer nights in her airless top-floor apartment.

Gabriel's eyes were the bluest she'd ever seen. Arctic almost. They were almost out of place in his tanned, quick-to-smile face. They weren't cold though. Instead, they were the blue of the innermost part of a flame. Hot enough to melt you if you got too close.

She blinked and the moment was gone. Perhaps she had imagined it. The last thing she needed to be doing right now was thinking about how attractive she found her...what was he? He wasn't exactly her boss, but whatever he was, he was off limits.

As if she could have a chance against Bridgette at any rate. Not that she was interested, because she absolutely wasn't.

'What do you think?' Gabriel asked, gesturing with his head toward the window.

Delphine blinked into the bright spring sunshine. She nodded in what she hoped appeared to be consideration rather than choked silence.

'Honestly, I love it.' Her hand clutched his arm. It was rock hard, all corded muscle through the wool of his jacket, and made Delphine feel utterly strange for a moment.

Gabriel's gaze dropped to her hand and lingered for a moment. Delphine's breath caught in her throat at the look in his eyes as he raised his gaze to meet hers. She released his arm and turned back to the shop, running her palm along the seam of her skirt. It still burned.

'That's not all. Come look.' Gabriel grabbed her hand and pulled her, laughing, past the sign writer and his implements and into the store. They stood in the doorway, waiting for their eyes to adjust to the dim lighting. Linen dolly heads seemed to fill every available shelf space, her designs carefully angled atop them.

This time the tears were unstoppable. They flowed down Delphine's cheeks unchecked. Her name on the window, her designs on the mannequins. Her dreams realized.

Gabriel cleared his throat. 'Er...I hadn't intended to make you cry.'

Delphine shook her head. There was so much she wanted to say but couldn't think where to start. She pulled her gloves off slowly as she gazed about the room. 'Thank you.'

Gabriel dismissed her gratitude with a shrug. 'You don't need to thank me. These are your designs, your ideas. I am just the business man.'

'You're not. You have no idea just how much this means to me. You have changed my life and I will not let you down.'

He smiled as he gazed down into her eyes. 'I know you won't. You couldn't.'

Her hand reached out for him without thought and their fingers intertwined. A jolt of electricity moved up her arm at the press of their flesh.

'I might not know anything about hats but I know about people, and there aren't too many people who would have the courage to get a meeting with me in the way you did. That shows me you are willing to do things that other people might not, and that is important in business.'

'I don't want to be like everyone else.' Her voice wavered and she swallowed to steady herself. Her whole life she had been told her dreams were foolish and that things like this—names on windows, living creatively, financial freedom—were for other people. Never her. Well, she was going to show them all.

Gabriel watched her with a silent gaze, his blue eyes

piercing even in the dim lighting of the shop; as still as the bronze of Michel Ney on his eternal perch in Montparnasse.

'You are definitely not like everyone else.'

She snatched her fingers from his; they burned where they had touched. Nothing was going to stop her dream of making this shop a success. And holding hands with her boss was certain to make a mess of it all. She thought of François and his sticky, alcohol-sweet breath on the back of her neck as she worked. Of his rough hands on her arm, her thighs. A layer of sweat broke out along Delphine's skin and she shivered as the fresh spring air cooled her hot perspiration. Those memories were not welcome here. She shook her head and took a step backward, putting a much-needed distance between her and Gabriel.

The last thing she needed, or wanted, was complication between her and Gabriel. The only thing that mattered was making this store a success.

～

THE TINY BELL, hung on a violet-coloured ribbon, tinkled lightly as the door to the shop opened. Delphine shivered, suddenly cold. Although Paris was slowly thawing out, and the daffodils had begun to push their brave little heads from the frigid ground, sometimes the wind still carried the memories of the bitterly cold winter just past. That must be it. Her shiver had nothing at all to do with the willowy woman who stood in the doorway removing her gloves and peering about the shop as if she had tasted something unpleasant.

'Mademoiselle Vidal. Welcome.' Delphine moved toward the other woman, her hand extended to shake. Bridgette shrugged off her stole, dropping it into Delphine's outstretched hand. How did she make that action look so elegant?

Bridgette's eyebrows replied to Delphine's welcome, and it appeared they were not impressed. So it was going to be like this? Delphine inhaled and got straight to the point. 'I have an idea. Big, fussy hats are on the out. Too matronly. I want to showcase your beautiful cheekbones.' There was a flicker of movement in Bridgette's face at the compliment. 'No brim. Just this stunning Chantilly lace and feather.'

Bridgette's mouth dropped open. 'No brim?'

Delphine smiled. Now she had her attention. She ran her tongue along her suddenly dry lips. A woman as powerful as Bridgette could make or break Delphine's business. Wearing something *outré* to the Paris fashion event of the year would cement Bridgette as a style icon, and hopefully do the same for Delphine's reputation.

'Let me show you.'

Gesturing to the austere wooden chair in front of the large, gilded mirror, Delphine stood behind it and waited for Bridgette to sit.

The hat Delphine had designed was her *pièce de résistance*. The design had come to her in a dream one hot, listless night, when funds were as low as her morale. She had known then that this was the design that was going to be the one that propelled her business. And so she set about making it happen. But she hated that it all depended on this spoilt little show pony.

'Princess Sophia wore a small, brimless hat to the Chantilly races recently, as you probably well know.'

It was apparent by the blank expression on Bridgette's face that she, in fact, did not know. No matter.

'Of course.'

Delphine smiled at the petulant tone of Bridgette's voice.

'My idea is to place the dressing at the back of the head, to allow for your face to be seen from every angle.'

Bridgette lifted her chin, tilting her head this way and that in the light of the overhead bulb.

'Just mine?'

Delphine fought to stop the smile that itched her lips. She had her.

'*Oui*, only your hat. Every other hat I make will be in the current mode.' She wrinkled her nose slightly. 'Just like everyone else's.'

'Show me.'

Delphine all but skipped to the small room at the back of the shop where she had carefully placed the hat, if it could be called that. The current fashion was for wide brims that sheltered the face from the sun and the gazes of any lowly onlookers you wished to ignore. The Grand Prix was renowned for pushing the edge of fashion, and every woman in attendance went to great lengths to outdo the others. Brims had been declining for years now, but Delphine knew that this was her last year to do it before someone else had the idea. It was bold, but that was something Delphine prided herself on being. Her entire future rested on the idea of this hat.

～

THE PARIS GAZETTE, *April 1909*

By now, mes chouchous, I am certain you have all heard the news. The Grand Prix was agog, abuzz, and alight with scandalized whispers.

France's sweetheart Bridgette Vidal has just cemented herself as our fashion queen. Although she was exquisite from head to toe (as always!) in a luscious teal dress, adorned with glass beads that sparkled like the sun, it was her headdress that people were talking about. Now, are you sitting down my lovelies? You'll need to.

The hat, if it could be called that, barely had a brim at all. Instead, the same teal silk that adorned the dress wrapped the base of the hat, bunching outward with a cacophony of peacock feathers at various heights at the back—the back!—of the hat. Which henceforth shall be referred to as the headdress. Apparently there was also a horse race on at the time, but I couldn't tell you who won, and I doubt anyone else could as all we were interested in was trying to catch a glimpse of Bridgette and the headdress.

Personally designed for her by the deliciously mysterious Delphine Altraine, it's safe to say that this headdress has changed what we will be wearing on our heads forevermore.

If you need me, I'll be hovering at the window of a certain hat store on Passage Lhomme, although rumour has it that appointments with the designer are booked out until summer.

CHAPTER 5

Delphine cradled the newspaper to her chest, allowing a bubble of pure joy to move through her. It had worked! All her hard work was coming to fruition.

The hat had looked incredible. The minute Delphine had placed it on Bridgette's head she had known it was going to make a scene. She hadn't attended the races herself. She hadn't the wardrobe, not to mention the lack of a ticket, and had spent the day on tenterhooks. No amount of cleaning or rearranging of the store had calmed her nerves, and she had watched the clock with anxious energy until finally Gabriel had burst into the store at precisely ten past nine in a cloud of wine-fuelled energy.

He had stood in the doorway, staring at her with a sombre expression for the barest of moments before holding his thumbs toward the ceiling, a wide smile splitting his face.

Bridgette had called his name from the roadside and he'd winked once, spinning on his heel and leaving Delphine alone in the quiet shop to quietly sob tears of joy into the fabric of her skirt. A night of fitful sleep had followed and when the first golden rays of morning had appeared, she'd thrown back the covers and dressed for the day, pinning her hair carelessly at the nape. Her heels had tapped a staccato beat as quick as her heart as she made her way out into the quiet streets of Paris in preparation for the newspaper boy.

Who was now staring at her like she had sprouted another head as she stood on the roadside hugging the newspaper. She laughed, and the newspaper boy backed away from her slowly.

'You're quite safe,' she said to the boy's back as he trotted away from her.

She all but skipped down the street toward the shop. Gabriel had promised to return the hat to her first thing this morning, and Delphine had planned an elaborate window display featuring it as well as some of her pre-made and ready-to-wear pieces. Hopefully she could get one or two personalized orders for the upcoming races.

The smell of freshly baked croissants drifted along the street toward her and her stomach growled. The owner of the patisserie was setting out cane furniture on the street side. Her feet slowed and she came to a stop at the doorway.

'*Bonjour.* Coming in?' The owner gestured with his head to the shop.

Delphine had not eaten in a café since before papa had died, the need to save her coins outweighing the temporary pleasure of taking time over a meal someone else had prepared.

But today she felt she owed herself the pleasure. The reward.

'*Oui.* Table for one, please.'

~

THE SUN HAD FINALLY BROKEN free from the shackles of the horizon by the time Delphine finished lingering over her pastry and coffee, and she strode toward the shop with a lightness in her step that had long been missing. A throng of ladies milled about on the footpath on rue de Charonne and Delphine had to push past a group who all seemed to be waiting for something. Out of habit, she studied their hats. Ladies of wealth and style. What were they doing here? Delphine paused as the heel of a ladies maid's shoe met her toe.

'Ouch.' Delphine exclaimed loudly in the woman's ear, to no avail. Resorting to physically removing her by pushing against her shoulders, the woman surprised her by turning on her viciously.

'We were here first. We've been queuing since first light. Get to the back of the line.' She jerked her thumb back the way Delphine had come.

'Queuing? Whatever for?'

The maid lifted her lip but lowered it again as her gaze landed on Delphine's hat. Delphine dipped her chin so the woman could get a better look at the enormous silk bow she had attached to the front of her hat.

'The milliner who made *that* hat at the races.' She informed Delphine as though she were the worst kind of simpleton.

'Milliner?' Delphine was breathless.

The maid, clearly tired of Delphine's ignorance, turned her back to her. Delphine walked in a daze along the block, passing one well-dressed woman after another. There must have been close to a hundred of them standing on the pavement. Her blood pounded in her ears and spots danced at the edge of her vision. It couldn't be. All these women were here, for her?

After what felt like an eternity, she came to the beginning of the line. Women and their maids were pressed against the shop window, hands cupping their faces as they peered into the shop.

'I see something lovely at the back. When the doors open, go straight to it and don't let anyone else get their hands on it.'

'Is that blue? I love the tulle.'

'Mama, I want the feathered one. I must have it.'

Delphine paused at the door and swallowed hard. The sight before her was unbelievable. Truly unbelievable. She had expected one, maybe two women, but this... This was.... Delphine didn't even have the words to describe this.

A head popped out of the doorway, glancing furtively along the queue. Delphine met Gabriel's eyes and he grabbed her hand, yanking her into the dim, cool shop space. He locked the door and leant his back against it. They stared at each other for the barest of moments before bursting into laughter. Gabriel's laugh was loud and fierce and filled Delphine with a fire she didn't quite understand. She bent double, her hands on her knees as her shoulders shook. She heaved a breath to compose herself, wiping at her eyes with the sleeve of her dress.

'What on earth is going on?' She asked once she had composed herself.

Gabriel wrapped his arms around her waist and spun her around, setting her down unsteadily on her feet. His scent surrounded her. It was something dark and mysterious, almost earthy, and Delphine's head spun.

Instead of releasing her, he grasped her hands and twirled her in a *bal-musette*. Delphine tugged and resisted, but he continued to whirl her. She gave herself to the moment and joined him in the dance. He moved with a fluidity and grace that was surprising in a man of his size. She shouldn't be surprised; he was rumoured to spend every night out at the nightclubs. Laughing and out of breath, Delphine matched him move for move, each speeding up until they couldn't keep up the pace. Gabriel held his hands up in surrender and they leaned against each other for a moment, laughing and panting.

'I don't know much about hats, Delphine, but I think the peacock one was a hit.'

Delphine laughed again. Joy burst through her chest, setting every nerve ending on fire. It was. It really was.

'Are they all here for me? Really?'

Gabriel nodded and his smile became gentle. 'Yes *chérie*, for you.'

Tears sprung to her eyes, as unexpected as the dancing had been. She ducked her head and walked to the back of the room, fussing with a collection of hats in varying stages of completion.

'Delphine?'

She clapped her hands together sharply. 'What are we waiting for? Let them in.'

Gabriel stared at her, his gaze sharp and searching. She lifted her chin and met his eyes boldly. Did he doubt she was ready for her moment? It had been the only thing to keep her warm on the too-many-to-count cold nights, when the darkness of her life had felt as if it would never lift.

She had been ready for years.

∼

THE DAY PASSED IN A BLUR. Gabriel had opened the door and allowed in as many people as the shop could fit. All the ready-to-wear hats sold immediately but instead of leaving, as Delphine had feared they would, woman after woman waited patiently for their turn at the seat at the mirrored wall.

Gabriel was a revelation. Jotting down the measurements as Delphine took them, he kept the waiting crowd amused and engaged with light-hearted conversation and well-timed flirting. He had the matrons tittering behind their jewelled hands and the debutantes flushing behind their gloves.

He had noted names and addresses, and carefully written follow-up fitting appointments in the large leather-bound book on the counter. At various times throughout the day, Delphine had looked up to find him watching her with an approving gaze that had made her feel as giddy as a schoolchild.

Her initial desire to impress Gabriel with her efficiency wore off quickly, and they soon fell into an easy rhythm. At sunset Gabriel announced to the waiting crowd that they would require appointments for a later date and dutifully arranged them all before ushering the women from the shop. He leaned against the door in the exact same manner he had that morning, but in a far more dishevelled state. A sprinkling of stubble now shadowed his jawline, and his once perfectly pressed suit was wrinkled.

He rested his head against the door and let out a sigh.

'You must be exhausted,' she said.

He cracked one eye. 'Me? You are the one that did all the work.'

A knock sounded at the door, interrupting her denial. Delphine widened her eyes at him. She hadn't eaten since the pastry this morning, and hadn't had time to take a toilet break since midday. She could not handle another customer, no matter how important.

Gabriel grinned at her whispered curse. He opened the door and the woman from the café they'd visited on their first date appeared. She was holding a box covered with a white linen cloth.

'*Merci*, Suzanne.' He kissed the older woman on both cheeks as he relieved her of the box. The most delicious scent of *moules marinière* wafted into the shop.

'How?'

Gabriel lifted his eyebrows at her. 'I ducked out earlier and ordered. You must be starving.'

Delphine's stomach rumbled right on cue and they laughed. She gestured around the shop 'There is nowhere to eat.'

'No problem. We eat *en paysanne.*'

Unconcerned about his suit, Gabriel sank to the floor and unloaded the box. He laid a crisp, white linen tablecloth on the tiles, followed by silverware, crockery, and finally a steaming pot of mussels.

Delphine huffed in amusement as he pulled a ladle from the box and began to fill her bowl.

'What else is in there? My goodness.'

'Unfortunately, that is it. Perhaps you will allow me to take you for an iced treat after we finish.'

He handed her a spoon, and as their hands brushed against each other, Delphine couldn't hold back the tiny gasp, as soft as a sigh, that escaped her lips. Tingles radiated from where he had touched her, and she was overcome with the urge to reach out and touch him in return. On his hand. Or the patch of skin on his wrist peeking out from under his jacket sleeve. Or perhaps run her fingers along the shadow of stubble on his jaw, to cup his face with her hands. Stroke his cheek with her fingertips.

His eyes darkened and she swallowed.

'Thank you,' she rasped, turning her attention to the food.

The silence between them morphed into something dark and thick. She could feel his eyes on her still, but she stared resolutely into her bowl. He was too close, too big, too manly. Here, in her space, her sanctuary.

She couldn't fall for him. Even if he weren't her business partner, he'd be the last man she would give her heart to. A man whose love life adorned the pages of the society pages, his lengthy evenings at bars seemed to last longer than any relationship he started. She could never get involved with a man like that. Having your heart broken would be a certainty.

Delphine risked a glance at him, and he smiled.

There was a perfect moment of stillness, then the words she had been firmly telling herself grew wings and took flight.

'You do this well.' He gestured around the room. 'Like you've been doing it for years. Like you were born to do it.'

Delphine raised her eyebrows and focused her attention on splitting the mussel shells in her bowl.

'What can I say? I like hats.'

He made a soft, doubtful noise. 'It's more than that.'

'I like taking scraps of fabric and creating something that makes women feel beautiful.'

She risked a glance at him, wondering if she dared share the size of her dreams. She'd stopped saying out loud years ago, afraid that people would laugh at her. A girl from a small town, making hats for Parisian society ladies? Impossible.

'There's more though, isn't there?' he asked, his gaze serious and searching.

She was speaking before she had time to consider her answer. There was something hypnotic about the way he looked at her; he could ask her anything and she'd tell him. She blinked. What black magic did this man possess?

'I like people. I like making people happy.'

He nodded. 'You're good with people.'

Delphine waved a hand at him. 'You're so popular, but I...' She swallowed, 'I don't have anyone.' She thought back to the factory floor. The work had been strenuous, the hours long, the lighting dim, and the chairs hard, but the laughter and camaraderie shared between the women had kept Delphine afloat during her darkest hours. 'It's lovely watching a woman sit at a mirror, watching her face as she sees herself as beautiful. Even if it's just for a moment. You probably think that is silly.'

'I think it is remarkable.'

Her gaze shot up to meet his. His face was earnest and he didn't appear to be teasing her.

'I meet a lot of people and there are a lot of reasons people want to get into business, and mostly it is for reasons that suit them only. But, you, you're different.' His voice was soft, intimate.

The shop was so silent that all Delphine could hear was her own breath as she fought back the prickle of tears that burned behind her eyes. She must be exhausted, overwhelmed from the day's work. Opening up to someone like this was not her style. She preferred to keep people at arm's length. It was easier that way.

'Thank you,' she choked out, busying herself with emptying her mussel shells back into the pot. She reached for the bread at the same time Gabriel did, their hands brushing together. Instead of pulling his hand away, Gabriel covered her hand with his.

His chest rose and fell, more quickly than it had a moment before.

His breath fanned along her face as he leant in close, and she lifted her hand and cupped his face, running her fingers along the stubbled roughness of his jaw and down his neck to the smooth skin at his nape.

His arms closed around her, pressing her close to him.

There were a million reasons she shouldn't be doing this, here, with him, but for the life of her, Delphine couldn't think of a single one.

'Delphine—'

A shudder ran through her at the sound of her name on his lips.

'Please—' was all she managed before his lips were upon hers.

It wasn't that time stopped while they kissed, more that it ceased to exist. There was nothing except his heart beating against her hand as she clutched at his shirt front, and his hands wound through her hair.

'Delphine,' he murmured against her lips.

She kept her eyes tightly shut, fighting the effect his kiss, the feel of his hard body beneath her fingers, was having on her.

She'd just kissed her business partner. The one man that had the power to help her realize her dreams. And she'd just kissed him! Or he had kissed her. She wasn't entirely certain who had started it, only that she had never been kissed with that much hunger. That much passion. What a cruel twist of fate; the first kiss she'd ever experienced, that had made her understand why people did silly things for love, was with someone she could never have. Because she could never have Gabriel. Men like him did not end up with women like her. They might, like tonight, find themselves on the floor kissing them senseless, but men like Gabriel married women like Bridgette. The thought was like a bucket of chilled water had been thrown over her. She scrambled to her feet.

'I'm sorry.' She cringed. What was she apologizing for? 'That was—'

'Incredible.'

'No.' *Yes. God, yes.* Delphine shook her head. 'Inappropriate. Unacceptable. We are business partners. We cannot be,' she waved her hand at the floor, 'doing whatever that was.'

Gabriel froze, a flush appearing on his cheeks. 'You are correct. Please accept my apology. That will never happen again.'

He stood and was packing the dishes back into the box, his face averted. His voice was wooden, the words as stiff as the linen dollies in the window. Her heart sank. He would not be one of those men, would he? Would he punish her for not giving him what he wanted, like François had?

She bustled around the store, mindlessly moving items from one spot to another.

'I—'

'I—'

They laughed, and it dissipated some of the tense energy in the room.

'I'm sorry. That won't happen again. I would never wish to put you in a position you aren't comfortable in.'

He thought she'd ended the kiss because she didn't want it? She had wanted it too much. But she could hardly tell him that. Nor could she make him think it was unwanted.

'It wasn't that I... it... only... this business is the most important thing in my life. I have dreamed of this for years and there is no room to make a mistake that might compromise it.'

He nodded. 'I understand, and I promise from here on, it is strictly business only.'

He held his hand out for her to shake.

It was almost impossible to stop herself crossing the room and launching back into his arms. There was something so utterly charming about his little-boy-chastised demeanour.

She folded her hand into his warm, dry one and, for a moment, the ache in her chest intensified.

'Agreed. Strictly business.'

CHAPTER 6

The season passed in a blur.

The store had become so busy that Delphine had hired two assistants and four milliners which took the bulk of day-to-day work from her shoulders. But she still worked long hours, creating custom pieces for the higher-end customers, as well as designing and completing the final touches on all the ready-to-wear pieces.

As the weather warmed and the days lengthened, Delphine and Gabriel fell into a comfortable routine. They had fallen into a daily routine, nothing they had formally set out but rather, one that had presented itself organically.

Gabriel would appear in the doorway mid-afternoon, with a slice of *galette* and a small glass filled with coffee for Delphine. His appearance in the store always brought a special energy with it. It must have been something to do with the time of day. Just as the light dimmed and everyone began to flag he would appear, a beacon that lifted everyone's spirits. And when Delphine noticed she had begun to watch the clock, fix her hair, and pinch her cheeks to bring a little colour to her face, she told herself it was simply because of the cake and caffeine he brought with him. Nothing more.

And if she noticed they appeared to be attached via an invisible string, well, that was something she kept to herself. She could be labouring over tiny stitches, or in discussion with a client, but if he was in the shop, it was as if only a part of her was performing her tasks. The other part was wherever he was. Her heart picked up speed whenever the sound of his laughter rang through the store, which was often.

They had been true to their word and the kiss they had shared had never been spoken of again. But there were times when Delphine found herself drawn to the spot they had laid together, as if just by standing there she could recreate the feelings that moment had elicited. As for Gabriel, she doubted he ever thought of it again, and although sometimes she would look up to find him watching her with a guarded expression, it would quickly clear.

He wasn't just her landlord; he had become her partner in every sense of the word. His visits had begun as simple check in's, quick conversations about her days, but were now the highlight of her day. They spent most evenings walking along the Seine, basking in the lowering sun, delighting in the fresh, evening air after a day indoors.

Unlike her experience with François, she never resented Gabriel's appearance in the shop. His questions about the business were always insightful and revolved around how he could better support her. He allowed her to speak, listening thoughtfully as she expounded on her ideas for efficiency and improvement, and only ever offered advice when requested.

Delphine pinned the final tiny beaded flower to the current piece she was making for the Comtesse d'Évreux and took a step back to look at it. Gabriel had been the one to suggest using beaded flowers in the hat, after Delphine had despaired about creating a hat that could travel with the Comtesse to the event she was attending in Russia.

He had been right. Not only did the beaded flowers catch the eye, but they would not crush if stored correctly.

She glanced at the clock and stretched her aching back. There was just enough time to fix her hair before Gabriel's arrival, and she couldn't wait to show him the completed version. Although he claimed to know nothing about hats, he had an eye for pleasing design and his feedback was always thoughtful and accurate.

The door opened and he appeared, and a wave of utter happiness washed over Delphine. She couldn't have imagined in any of her outlandish dreams, that she could be this happy.

Life simply didn't get any better than this.

~

THE PARIS GAZETTE, *June 1909*

Well, mes petits choux, you know me, I hate being the bearer of bad news but a gossip columnist bears the weary weight of sharing the dirty as well as the good. An angry little birdy tells me that the milliner you have all been going crazy for has been copying her designs from him. Apparently, this little bird took that little bird under his wing, only to have it bite the hand that was feeding it. I'm mixing my metaphors, but you know what I'm saying.

Alas! My heavy heart aches to inform you this isn't the worst news I will share today. I saw a certain icy silver screen actress with a rather large and rather shiny rock on a particular finger. Although she was dining with a man that was definitely not the delectable Monsieur Lapouge, she was coy when asked about the ring.

'I can't talk about that yet.' She had tittered with a breathless little wink that, I must tell you, I found enormously irritating. Why wear the ring if you aren't going to give me every last, delicious morsel of information to gossip about?

What's that you ask? That, my dear, is the sound of hearts breaking around Paris.

The end of spring brings with it the end of our love affair with both Paris's most eligible bachelor and his milliner. Did any of us ever find out what, exactly, their relationship is? I don't suppose it matters now. No one who matters would be caught dead in a fraudster's headgear, and I don't imagine you would either, would you, my dears?

CHAPTER 7

Delphine slapped the newspaper down on the bench top, so gratified with the sound that resonated through the empty shop that she picked it up and slammed it down again.

The interfering old busybody!

The lying, good for nothing cheat François had to be behind this. She should have known that he would hear about her success and wouldn't let it go. There was no way she had even copied a single one of his out-of-date, for-matrons-only headwear.

Her angry gaze was pulled to the door of the shop, which for weeks had been crowded but was now empty. The *Gazette* gossip column was gospel in Paris, and if she was accused of stealing another's ideas, then she had already been tried and convicted. Hot tears sprung to her eyes and she dashed them away angrily.

'*Madame*, are you alright?'

Tamara, one of the young women Delphine had hired, asked with a concern furrow to her brows.

'Of course, of course,' Delphine said with as much cheer

as she possibly could. 'A misunderstanding. One that will be easy enough to clear up.'

Delphine turned her face from Tamara's doubtful expression.

'It's a beautiful day. Why don't you go and enjoy the weather.'

'Are you sure?'

'Yes, I will fix this and we'll back on track. You'll see.' Delphine was surprised to hear how steady her voice was. It was almost as if she believed it.

Tamara and the other ladies collected their personal belongings and closed the door carefully behind them. Delphine slumped into the chair, gazing around the dim store.

She lifted her chin. This wasn't the first time she'd had something she cared about taken from her, and she knew enough about life to know it wouldn't be the last. This was why she kept people at a distance. Yes, the store was her dream, but it was just things: fabric, straw and stuffing. But people were different. When you lost people you also lost part of yourself. When her mama had died, it was as if a piece of her and papa had died too. The shine had left papa's eyes and never truly returned. Everyone Delphine had ever cared about had left her. She didn't care about François and what he said. She knew what was true and real, and she knew her designs were good enough to withstand any gossip and drama he wanted to create.

The summer tourist season in the south hadn't started yet. She still had time to pack up and start again in Cannes or St Tropez.

Or maybe she should just go somewhere where no one knew anyone from Paris, and adjust her dreams. She had been stupid dreaming so big. A small hat store in a village would serve her just as well. Perhaps the designs would be standard and unexciting, but at least she could do it all on her own and not have to rely on anyone else.

And as for Gabriel. She was certain their kiss had meant more to her than him. He was a renowned womaniser. He wouldn't notice her gone. She would pay him what was owed to him and he'd never think of her again.

She brushed a tear from her cheek. She'd been taking care of herself since childhood; this was no different. Just because she had allowed people in, it didn't mean she couldn't live without them.

Not just people. One person in particular. A tall, flirtatious man with ice blue eyes and hair like brushed silk.

She would arrange to have Tamara pack up the shop and have it sent on to her when she got herself sorted in Cannes. Pulling the door closed behind her, Delphine blinked into the blinding light of the day.

Taking ideas and pieces of silk and wire and creating frothy, beautiful confections wasn't Delphine's only skill. She was a master at rolling her emotions into tiny rosettes and putting them into a box. Any feelings she had for Gabriel would go in that box and into the darkest corner of a shelf. She would never think of him again.

She thought instead of the one person she could take her anger out on. She would find François and she would make him sorry.

∽

DELPHINE STORMED along rue de Charonne, cursing François with every pound of her heels against the cobblestone. The no-good, lying, cheating rat.

For months afterwards, she had lain in bed at night, hot with regret at how she had slunk away quietly in the face of his threats. How terrified she had been the night he had grabbed her in a dark corner of the factory. He hadn't even tried to be subtle about it, so confident of his power over the women in his employ.

'You've been running your mouth and it's going to stop.'

Delphine had fought to keep calm, as his fingers had bitten into her throat. The pressure of his thick, nicotine-stained fingers had increased once, dangerously, and he had released her. Despite promising herself she wouldn't give him the satisfaction, her hand had massaged her throat. She'd felt the crescent-shaped indents his nails had left in the soft skin under her ears.

'You understand, *boudin*? You told that Martinus girl to complain. I had her father in here. I had to pay him off.' He'd taken a step toward her, and to her shame, she had flinched. He'd barked a cruel laugh.

'The way I see it, you owe me for that.' He'd run a filthy nail between his front teeth, gazing at the food he had collected dispassionately before placing it on his tongue. 'Yeah, you owe me. So you've got two choices.'

His gaze had been hot on her chest, and she'd longed to shield herself from his gaze. Instead, she'd squared her shoulders. Let him look. That would be all this scumbag would be getting from her.

'I'm going to dock your pay until you've paid me back, with interest.'

Delphine had swallowed hard. She barely made enough to pay for her room and lodgings. Any leftover she saved. It would take her years to earn the kind of money he was talking about.

François had gazed down at her and sucked his bottom lip. 'Or we can come to an arrangement. You're still young, got a good bouncy bosom. I bet you're a virgin, a sharp-tongued, thick-boned wench like you.'

Delphine had pressed her lips against the bile that had

risen in her throat. François' 'arrangements' were well known in the factory. Often used against women as a way of repairing some minor or imagined infraction of his 'rules'.

When Delphine had encountered the young woman vomiting in the outhouse for the third day in a row, she had encouraged her to report François to the authorities. She'd tried to encourage the other young women who had been rumoured to have been mistreated in this way to get together and report him to the authorities. At least the Martinus girl had received payment. A baby born out of wedlock was a life sentence for a poor woman.

François had taken another step toward Delphine, and she had moved backwards until her lower back had pressed against the fabric cutting station. She had reached behind her, her fingers resting on the cool iron of the razor sharp scissors. She'd pulled them forward and swiftly pressed them against François' groin murmuring, 'I would rather take my chances on the street than let you put one, single, disgusting finger on me.'

If she hadn't been so angry, Delphine would have garnered some pleasure at how François' face had paled. He had raised his hands and taken a step back, but she moved with him.

'And if I hear about you laying one of those fingers on anyone else I will cut your *couilles* off.'

The sewing room, which was usually a cacophony of mechanical noise, had fallen deathly silent. Delphine hadn't dared risking a glance at the women, who she knew would be staring in various states of shock.

She'd moved toward the door, her scissors raised and pointed at François' face.

'You will regret this,' he'd yelled as she had walked from the building.

She should have made good on her threat and cut his

couilles off she thought, as she kicked at a copy of the newspaper cartwheeling along the street. Her steps slowed. Where was she going? Paris was a big city. He could be anywhere. She could try the newspaper office. Perhaps they would know where he was staying. Her steps dwindled to a stop and she leant against a lamppost for support. The anger had drained from her, leaving her exhausted. There was nothing she could do. She couldn't find François and, even if she did, what good would it do? The article had been written, and most of Paris had already read it. She was done for. It was over.

A flurry of movement at the doorway behind her caught her attention. Bridgette stood in the doorway, her face angled just so toward the afternoon sun. A short, thickset man with heavily pomaded hair draped a mink stole over her shoulders, and as she reached up to adjust it, the sun caught the rock on her finger. It sparkled and glittered like the lights had the night of the auction all those weeks ago.

Delphine had fallen from a tree once as a child. She'd landed hard on her back, so hard the air had been forced from her lungs. She had lain there, breathless with shock, stars dancing in her vision. The sight on the enormous diamond on Bridgette's finger had the same effect on her now.

So it was true. They were engaged.

Bridgette glanced up and met Delphine's gaze. She gazed along her nose at Delphine, lifting her lip slightly in disdain. Delphine whirled and shambled off along the street in the direction she had come, listing as she walked, punch-drunk and confused. Her shoes no longer battered out a prestissimo tempo; instead they shuffled sadly. Gab - ri -el. The beat went on and on until she reached the safety of her apartment.

When she reached the top of the dirty stairwell, she clung

to the rail like a lifebuoy, lowering her head until it touched the cool metal.

Echoes of the words she'd fought against her whole life surrounded her.

Dreamer. Fool.

And hadn't she been the worst kind of fool.

The only thing that had mattered to her was making the hat store a success, but somewhere along the line she had gone and fallen in love with Gabriel.

And now, both were lost to her.

CHAPTER 8

With little more than a perfunctory knock, Gabriel appeared in the doorway, panting as if he had run the four flights of stairs to her pathetic apartment.

'Delphine.'

She couldn't bring herself to look up at him. She continued to pack her meagre belongings into her trunk. Luckily, she didn't own much. It made it easy to move on.

'Delphine. The shop. What are you doing? Tamara said you had informed her to close it up and start packing things away this morning.'

Her stomach clenched. She wanted to throw up. The shop she could bear to leave, but Gabriel? She'd never be the same again.

Taking a deep breath to steel herself, she spoke. 'Didn't you see the newspapers? I am ruined. All our orders have been cancelled. It's over.'

'So you're just leaving? Rolling over and allowing lies to chase you away from your dreams?'

She remained silent.

'That is not the Delphine I know.'

Gabriel took a step into the room, and Delphine buried her hands in her suitcase, clenching the fabric of the dress she had worn to that fateful auction in her fists to still the trembling.

'The woman who would spend every cent she has for the chance to make her dream happen would never just give up at the first hurdle. I know they are lies, Delphine, and everyone else will too.'

He was right. She wouldn't have just given up. She would have kept making beautiful hats and found some way to make sure everyone knew François was nothing but a lying cheat, but she could not stand by while he married Bridgette.

'I don't want you to go.'

She chuckled bitterly. It was the perfect thing to say, but of course it was. He wasn't considered France's most eligible bachelor for nothing. She had spent the last twelve weeks watching him charm everyone who crossed his path.

His eyebrows pulled together. 'What do you find funny about that?'

Her mouth was suddenly dry, and even though she swallowed before speaking, her voice still emerged as a croak. 'I'm not sure I find anything funny about that.'

'I mean it. I don't want you to go. I have fallen in love with you, Delphine. I want you to stay, here, with me.'

It took several heartbeats for her to come back to the room, for the words he was saying floated between them. His lips were weaving a magic spell, one that had her feet elevating off the ground.

'Delphine?'

'I'm sorry. I... you what?'

He chuckled and reached for her hand, pulling her to her feet. 'The first time I tell a woman I love her and she isn't even listening to me. I said I love you.'

'You love...me? But Bridgette?'

'Bridgette and I are over. We have been for some time. She is engaged to her latest director and I...Well, the more time I spent with you, the clearer it became that the woman for me has the most amazing green eyes, and a passion for hats that I doubt I'll ever understand, and,' his thumb began to trace tiny circles on her palm and her knees began to shake. 'She is passionate and caring and by far, the bravest person I have ever met.'

He stepped toward her and kissed her forehead tenderly. She wound her arms around his waist and rested her head against his chest.

Her heart beat so hard in her ribs that he must have been able to feel it through his jacket.

Gabriel cleared his throat. 'Should I take that as an indication you might also feel the same about me?'

The hesitation in his voice was the final straw. She burst into tears; joyful, bittersweet, embarrassingly noisy tears. He tightened his hold on her, drawing her close to his body. His embrace was like coming home.

She drew away from him so she could stare up into his eyes. In his gaze she saw his love, his commitment, and in that moment, she knew she could trust him completely. He had given her more than an opportunity to show her skills as a milliner. His unwavering support and belief in her had given her the confidence to extend and challenge herself beyond her wildest dreams. Gabriel was right. François was nothing but a liar and it would soon become apparent when her creations were still cutting edge and his remained nothing but water-coloured versions of other people's designs. She would not run this time. She was going to stand and fight. With Gabriel by her side.

'I absolutely love you, Mr Lapouge. Perhaps even more than I love hats.'

He lifted her off her feet and spun her around. 'More than hats?'

Laughing as he placed her back onto the ground, she lifted a hand to cup his face. 'Unbelievable, but it's true.'

He leaned down and lowered his mouth to hers with infinite tenderness.

'And I,' he murmured against her mouth, 'definitely love you more than hats.'

Their laughter echoed in the room, long after they had made their way into her bedroom.

∾

THE PARIS GAZETTE, *March 1910*

Spring has sprung, dear reader, and you know what that means.

After all these months of fuss and hysteria—and that was just us mere mortals waiting to see if we'd made the invitation list— France's most eligible and no longer quite so elusive bachelor, Gabriel Lapouge and his beautiful, incredibly talented (and wasn't I the first to tell you she was just the thing?) fiancée walked the peony-strewn aisle of Saint-Séverin to join together for eternity in holy matrimony.

Let me tell you, my sad little doves, as you sob into your handkerchiefs wishing you had the connections and money to have made the list, that the bride was simply incandescent. I have had the privilege of attending not one, but two royal weddings, and I can assure you that neither of those brides sparkled in the manner that our exquisitely dressed milliner did today. Her dress was a vision of lace and silk, and her hat was, of course, the most elegant thing Paris, nay France, has ever seen.

But none of it matters a jot. Not a single petal on a single flower was given more than a cursory glance because the bride,

France's milliner princess, glittered, shimmered, and illuminated the church with her celestial beauty.

Like her now-husband, we mere mortals could not take our eyes from her.

And I promise you, dearest ones, that when they kissed, a single beam of sunlight shone through the stained glass, casting them with a rosy glow, as if they had been blessed by Cupid himself.

As for the bouquet, would you believe me if I told you that it just landed in my lap? That I didn't even need to reach out a delicate, gloved hand to catch it? If someone had their foot trodden on, or an elbow was thrown, it certainly wasn't by me, my lovelies, no matter what you might hear.

Now, I don't suppose any of my dear readers know how to get in touch with Gabriel Lapouge's brother?

After all, spring is the season of amour, is it not?

∽

THE END

THE TOYMAKER

By Clare Griffin

CHAPTER 1

PARIS, SUMMER 1924

The heat was intolerable.

Edith wiped her brow with the back of her hand and was rewarded with a slick patch on her skin to match the droplets of sweat beading and trickling down her back. She was ruining the white muslin toile that draped her, but at least it was cooler than the crepe dress she'd walked to the *maison* in earlier that day. The muslin was the coolest thing to wear in this situation apart from the suit she'd been born in. The ornate, silver locket around her neck, smooth and cool on her skin that morning, was now lubricated with sweat. It slid across her décolletage like oil on water, but she wouldn't remove it. She couldn't.

The *premières*, the heads of the workroom, instructed the mannequins and tailors crowding the upstairs suite of 31 Rue Cambon. Edith tried not to pass out. The scent of Chanel No. 5 was heavy in the air, and she had lost count of how many hours she had been in *la pose*. Chanel liked to create her designs on the mannequins themselves, and would cut and pin to make changes after she'd watched them turn and move, to see how the design worked on the body. Sometimes the process took hours. Edith's head began to swim. *Don't you dare pass out*, she scolded herself and straightened her shoulders. 'I'm sorry, Mademoiselle. I am not used to such heat,' she said as Chanel circled around her.

The woman now famously known as Coco Chanel was silent as she looked Edith over. Her lips were the crimson of one of the lipsticks she had just launched, made all the more glamorous by the simple but elegant black dress that skimmed her tiny frame. The understated outfit made the strings of pearls hanging down her chest the true star of her outfit, and, as always, a small pair of scissors hung amongst them.

Her hands glittered with large, coloured, jewelled rings as her fingers busily worked on the design Edith wore. She pursed her lips slightly as she hooked her index finger and thumb around Edith's chin. Her eyes narrowed as she stared at her lips. 'English rose skin such as yours should not be in the sun. Unlike a rose itself, I fear you will not thrive.'

Edith's heart hammered against her ribs, worried the lipstick that Mademoiselle had painstakingly been working on would melt right off her lips. She also wasn't sure if her comments were complimentary or a criticism.

'I think this is my favourite shade. It suits your skin perfectly. I'm happy with my design now. It's working. Get dressed, but try this shade too.' She held up the cream and black lipstick tube as she handed Edith a small, moist towel and directed her to the other side of the show room, close on her heels. In front of a small mirror in the only quiet corner of the salon, Edith began to dab off her lipstick.

'What brings an English rose to Paris?' Edith's heart sped up every time someone asked this question, but she concentrated on parting her lips, her face not giving away the whirlwind that swum inside her. She'd been told by some of the other mannequins that Chanel was quite fond of the women who worked for her, and Edith hoped to become part of the inner circle.

'I needed a change of scenery, although I must admit, I didn't factor in the heat difference.' She turned around, and Mademoiselle gently pressed the bullet shaped lipstick, encased in the cream and black tube, to Edith's mouth and traced her lips.

'I imagine your lips are quite popular with men. You have an equally full top and lower lip. Perfect for advertising my newest venture.' Chanel capped the lid back on and stepped back to appraise Edith. 'It suits your dark hair and blue eyes.'

Edith smiled. 'Thank you, Mademoiselle.'

'It appears these shades both appeal to your tone. A need for a change in scenery is good. You seem very well spoken for a mannequin,' she said in hushed tones should she offend any of the other women. It also helped that the last part was spoken in chopped English.

Edith's pulse quickened, but years of keeping her face impassive during boring dinner parties had her well trained in hiding what she really felt. 'I was lucky enough to grow up on a rather large estate in England. This gave me more opportunities than others.'

Mademoiselle studied her with a keen eye. 'And are you here with family? A lover?'

Edith looked Chanel in the eye, trying to read the situation, but the woman's face was impassive. 'Is my personal status an issue to my working?'

The older woman's face seem to soften somewhat as she tapped the tube on her chin. 'Not at all. I was merely making conversation. We French adore a good love story. It is what our city has been built on.'

'That and croissants,' Edith added, trying to lighten the mood. The sweat was now pooling at the base of her spine and she longed for a breeze. She clasped her hand to the locket around her neck and swung it from side to side on the chain. Chanel's gaze followed the movement like a cat. *'Beau ou belle,'* she said, and before she could stop her, Chanel had taken the locket from Edith's hands and opened it. The item inside, so small, so perfect, fell into Chanel's hands. The breath wheezed out of Edith. Mademoiselle stared at the lock of hair; a perfect, tiny auburn curl, held together by a soft pink ribbon. Wordlessly, she placed the item back in the locket and clasped it shut.

The older woman's eyes moved to Edith's left hand, now clasped around the necklace as if it were the crown jewels. She knew she noted the naked ring finger.

'Go tidy yourself up and meet me upstairs.' With that she moved on to another mannequin and Edith was left standing in the middle of the boutique, tears now ruining her lipstick, a heavy sense of doom in the pit of her stomach.

Edith's cheeks flared. If she lost this job, she wasn't sure she'd be able to buy food by the end of the week, let alone pay rent.

She stepped backwards to press herself against the wall, to disappear from the view of those around her, but her foot connected with another. Trying to correct herself, she over-balanced and careened into the chest of someone else, and the arms connected to the body stopped her from falling. Embarrassed, Edith kept her eyes down and muttered her apologies when a large hand took hers, forcing her to look into sea-foam green eyes.

The man's hair was a rich chocolate brown, slicked back in the fashion, but also unruly at the front and back, as if even the cream couldn't keep the thick locks under control. He was smiling softly, but his brows were steepled with concern. His suit was fine but not new, and his face, unlike Edith's, wasn't glistening with perspiration. It was kind, young, and he had a sense of calm about him. Edith's hand burned where he touched her, her cheeks now flushed with shame.

'Are you alright, mademoiselle?'

'Yes, I'm, I'm terribly sorry for treading on your foot.'

Edith allowed her eyes to flicker to the man's face once more. The man smiled deeply, the movement making his glorious eyes twinkle into creases. 'No harm done I assure you. Now my right foot will be as bad a dancer as my left. My left foot has been jealous for years and will be very happy about this predicament, so really you have done me a huge favour.'

He handed Edith a pale blue handkerchief, cotton, sturdy and reliable, and Edith took it. The initials HB were looped in rich, green embroidery in one corner. 'Are you sure you are alright? I know Coco can be a taskmaster but she is also a genius, I assure you of that.'

Edith nodded her head, unable to meet the man's eyes. Instead, she kept her eyes on the handkerchief. 'Thank you, monsieur, now please excuse me.' She pivoted on her heel and ran for the powder room, fear gripping her that her that Chanel was going to fire her and her one big chance of entering French society and finding security was about to disappear forever.

~

AFTER MAKING herself presentable once more, she slipped into her pale green crepe silk dress and took a few deep breaths. She made her way out of the powder room, through the crowded atelier, and climbed the stairs, watching herself as she ascended the now famous mirrored staircase. Chanel had purposely built the stairs so that she could sit at the top unseen and watch people's reactions to her designs below. Unsure where to go, Edith hovered near the top of the stairs, caught between not wanting to be rude, but also not wanting to appear too familiar.

Her eyes widened as she took in her surroundings. Every inch of the apartment appeared to be covered with art and artefacts. At first glance, the apartment seemed to be all brown, but the further Edith walked in, the more her eyes took in. Ornate carvings, lit by a large chandelier, surrounded a large mirror over the fireplace. Scores of life-sized porcelain deer were scattered throughout the apartment as well as different sized lions. A bust of Venus took pride of place on the mantel, and the furniture appeared to be older than anything Edith had seen before and very expensive. Her fingers couldn't help but stretch out and caress the carvings on the desk.

But it was Mademoiselle's bookcases that took Edith's breath away. Rows and rows of first editions lined the shelves, and Edith felt a sense of calm fall over her as she touched the spines.

'Do you like to read?'

Edith spun around, startled, as she hadn't heard Mademoiselle make her way up the cream-carpeted stairs. She looked tired, but it was gone in a flicker when she looked at Edith.

'I'm sorry, I didn't mean to be nosey...'

Chanel flicked her hand. 'If you weren't interested in my salon, I'd be more worried. It's beautiful, no?' She indicated the apartment and Edith nodded, wanting her dismissal to be over.

'It's beautiful, mademoiselle, but why am I here?'

'You know,' Chanel said, lighting a cigarette, 'your accent is almost good enough to pass as French.' She smiled wickedly. 'Almost. I feel this is not your first time in France.'

'You would be correct. I can also speak Spanish although I have never been there.'

Chanel tilted her head. 'What a life you have already lived, and you're still so young.' She walked across the room and sat on the large cream lounge. 'I owe you an apology for earlier. I was sure I was going to open a picture of your lover. I am very sorry for that intrusion.'

Edith tilted her chin and held Chanel's gaze. 'There is nothing to apologise for.' The two women eyed each other, neither saying anything more, both waiting for the other to react first.

Mademoiselle broke first. 'Even so, I apologise.'

'Apology accepted.'

Chanel smiled and offered Edith a cigarette, which she took and lit. 'Now that we have that out of the way, I wish to invite you to a little soiree I am holding tonight.'

Edith's eyebrows could have vanished through the roof, excitement zapping through her veins. 'Why, that's very kind of you, but I can't see why you would do that.'

Chanel lit another cigarette and waved Edith's words away with her hand, as if the invitation meant nothing. 'Now, now, don't play coy. Think of it as an apology for my lack of tact. So, will you join me?'

Edith's heart thundered. The type of people Chanel would have at this party would be the type of people Edith needed to help her stay on in Paris. Without a rich husband, or at least a wealthy fiancé, on her arm soon, she'd have nowhere to go. Returning home was not an option.

'That's too generous of you, but of course I accept.'

Chanel's eyes lit up, and it appeared as if a weight had been lifted off her shoulders. 'Wonderful! I'm sure we can find something for you to wear.' Her cigarette hand waved towards the wider part of the apartment. 'Go and choose anything from downstairs. The party is at my apartment on rue du Faubourg Saint-Honoré, a short walk from here.'

Edith's gaze roamed around the beautiful apartment with

its decadent wooden decor. It was so beautiful; she couldn't imagine not living here. As if reading her mind, Chanel spoke. 'Do you notice anything missing?'

Edith looked around and finally she clocked the one piece of furniture any human would want. 'I'm guessing you *don't* like to sleep upside down from the roof like a bat?'

Chanel cackled, a deep throaty laugh, and took a long drag. 'Although sleeping upside down would do wonders for the complexion.' She winked. 'Pick something, and then we'll meet downstairs. I have some designs I want to work on. Pick anything. It will all look good on you.' She stood up and crossed to her desk, and Edith walked back down the mirrored stairs into the salon.

There were racks of dresses, coats, hats, shirts, some from last season, all beautiful and elegant but it was the latest designs that drew Edith. Her feet sunk into the plush carpet and she pulled down a gold-cloth embroidered dress. The neckline at the front was square and cut across the top of the breasts, the bodice falling low on the hips where it was gathered slightly, but still hung loose on the body. Below the hips, the gold material blended into embroidered patterns and beads inspired by Russian tapestries.

But it was the back that was the true star. It scooped to mid-way across the torso, the wide straps cinched to reveal the shoulders and bare arms, and two loops of fabric cascaded down the back. One fell straight on the left side and kissed the floor, while the other hung from one shoulder to the other, below the buttocks. The dress ended mid-calf. It was divine.

Satisfied with her choice, she watched her reflection from the corner of her eye as she made her way upstairs. Chanel was busy and only looked up when Edith was directly in front of her. 'Excellent choice. You shall be a wonderful ambassador for me this evening. Follow me.'

They walked down the stairs to the main entrance floor and out of the shop. The mannequins and tailors had finished for the day, and Chanel locked the door and set off, turning right down rue Cambon. The streets were normally quiet this time of year, as anyone who was anyone in Paris normally escaped to the Riveria, but now they were busy thanks to the Olympics. Edith and a few of the other mannequins had been to some of the swimming events where, for the first time, there was a giant fifty-metre pool with marked lanes. Edith had never found watching swimming very exciting, but somehow, when one's national pride was on the line, it was quite thrilling.

After a short walk they reached Chanel's townhouse, a beautiful, cream four storey limestone building, that like so many buildings in Paris, was exquisite. The first-floor balcony was cream stone to match the building's façade, but the level above had a black wrought-iron balcony. Three carved faces sat above the lower level windows. Edith shuddered despite the warm evening air. The faces scared her, and appeared to be unhappy to have found themselves attached to such a beautiful building. Edith took one last look at them and hurried to join Chanel who was at her front door.

As Chanel opened the door, voices could be heard on the other side, and Edith pasted on her best smile. She didn't know where the night would lead, but she knew she would take any opportunity presented to her and run with it. What choice did she have?

CHAPTER 2

*E*dith stepped into the townhouse and shrieked as a blur of two bodies shot past the door. The blur turned out to be two men, white shirts rolled up to the elbows, cigarettes tucked between lips, and holding each other in a headlock while throwing punches to the gut. Edith gasped and looked at Chanel who merely rolled her eyes and walked further into the foyer.

Unsure of what to do, she let the heavy door close behind her and followed. The two men appeared to be arguing over something, but their words were muffled between each other's arms. Both red in the face, from lack of oxygen or liquor she was unsure, but what she was sure of was that one man was Ernest Hemingway.

As if suddenly aware their hostess was among them, the unknown man straightened and bowed towards her. 'Coco!' he exclaimed, while smoothing down his thick, dark hair. Edith was unaware of his identity, but she knew enough about fashion to know that he was wealthy. His hair was cut short, and he had ruddy cheeks and a perfectly trimmed thick moustache above his lip. Hemingway wordlessly made his way over to a small table that held a crystal glass of amber liquid. He threw his head back, swallowed the contents in one gulp and wiped his mouth with the back of his hand. 'Good evening, Coco.'

Chanel ignored both men, barely giving them a nod as she made her way across the room. 'Gentlemen, it is barely evening and yet you both look as if you've been drinking for hours. Not a very good impression for our young guest.' Both men's eyes moved to Edith, and she arranged her red lips in what she hoped was a seductive look.

The unknown Frenchman's eyes widened with interest as he smoothed his hair and made his way towards her. Edith's eyes remained on Hemingway. She had heard a lot about him, most of it not good, but she had to admit he had a presence about him. He was a hulk of a man, broad across the shoulders and with a keen eye. He appeared unmoved by her and moved towards Chanel, or rather, the liquor.

'*Bonjour, mademoiselle.*' The unknown Frenchman stood before her. He lightly took Edith's hand and brought it to his lips. They were wet with drink and saliva as his tongue ran along his lower lip. 'I don't believe we've had the pleasure of meeting. I would have remembered eyes like yours.'

'Stop with the flirting, Mathias, she is far too young for you,' Chanel scolded, but her turned up lips told another story. 'Edith, may I introduce Mathias Rameau. He is in procurement and starts fights with men who could pummel him with one punch.'

'We weren't really fighting,' Hemingway interjected. 'If we were, he'd be out cold right now.'

'Pfft, I would give you more of a fight, if we hadn't been distracted by our lovely host and our friend here, Miss...'

'Carrow. Edith Carrow.'

'Miss Carrow,' Mathias purred, still holding her hand. 'It's a pleasure.'

'I'm sure the pleasure is all mine,' Edith countered, withdrawing her hand. She smiled and tilted her head to take him in. He was not unattractive, but he was not traditionally good looking either. She feared that the ruddiness in his cheeks had more to do with drinking than fighting with Hemingway.

'Come,' Mathias boomed, leading her to the lounge and dining area, 'what can I get you to drink?'

'What's he having?' Edith asked, indicating Hemingway.

'Nothing a woman could drink,' Hemingway said, and as if to prove his point, he threw back his head and downed the rest of the amber liquid in one shot. His gaze held her as if she were one of his hunting prey. If given the chance, he'd probably like to shoot her and mount her on the wall.

Edith walked past Mathias and slunk over to Hemingway, giving both men the opportunity to observe her. She could feel both pairs of eyes on her, one hungry and the other angry. 'Whiskey, is it?' She took Hemingway's glass from his hand and sniffed. 'An old one, too.' Mathias sidled up to her, too close for polite society, but she was playing a game and Mathias was following all her moves.

'No *lady* should know that much about whiskey,' Hemingway drawled.

Edith cocked an eyebrow. 'No man who knew anything about whiskey would waste it by drinking it as a shot, instead of sipping it, savouring the flavour.' Edith walked over to the drinks cabinet where Chanel stood. She paused as if seeking permission, and Chanel gave the barest of nods. Edith picked up the crystal decanter and poured the amber liquid into Hemingway's glass. She replaced the decanter and slowly turned around, bringing the glass to her lips, both men watching her.

'To our host, thank you for having me.' She nodded to Chanel who, eyes alive with curiosity, had accepted her usual flute of champagne. Edith tilted her wrist and allowed the liquid to meet her lips. It burned everything it touched; her lips, tongue, throat, but it also gave her the added courage she needed. Her upbringing in a society family had trained her for this. She'd just never planned on having to use her flirtation skills for survival.

'You do make that drink look very appealing,' Mathias purred beside her. 'May I have some?' Edith turned her head to look at him from beneath hooded eyes and passed the drink to him. He drank in a similar fashion to her, but with bigger gulps. Hemingway harrumphed from across the room and found something else to drink, not hiding the fact he was now very bored.

'How do you know our gracious host?'

'I'm a mannequin for Mademoiselle.'

Mathias, not even trying to hide the movement, now looked her over from head to toe and smiled. 'Well, of course you are. You must be very special to be invited. Coco is very exclusive with these things. How is it I have not seen you before? I surely would remember a face like yours. Such delicate skin.' His finger traced a line on Edith's arm and she smiled, although she felt slightly alarmed. He was very forward. She put it down to the drinks and decided to keep him too distracted to drink more.

'Now, no more of this, mademoiselle. If you are important enough to get invited, then you can start calling her Coco like the rest of us, agreed?' he asked as Chanel came over to talk to Mathias about his business. It seemed Edith had caught the eye of a very rich man indeed. Comforted by the thought, she reminded herself that it was a long way from flirting to security.

More people arrived, and the suite was filled with laughter, the tinkling of glasses, music. Edith sipped her champagne but made sure that her glass lasted, although the bubbles that at first had tickled her nose were now flat.

Mathias tried to supply her with more drinks, but she knew she had to keep her wits about her. But after a while she realised, with the exception of Mathias, most of the guests weren't rich, but artists, painters, writers, and a few male mannequins that Edith had seen around, and she began to relax.

Edith's eyes widened when she noticed Coco speaking quietly to a man in a far corner of the apartment. 'Coco knows the Duke of Westminster?' Edith's pulse quickened.

'Intimately,' Mathias slurred. 'He is done with wife number *deux* and Coco has found herself a new lover. From a Russian duke to an English one.' They watched the couple that appeared to be having a stimulating conversation for a while before another man pulled the Duke was pulled away. Coco's eyes roamed the room and found Edith's.

Coco sidled up next to Edith and Mathias when a familiar voice made Edith turn around. 'I'm sorry I'm late.'

Edith spun towards the deep voice, and her cheeks flushed with heat. The same green eyes that had caught her at a vulnerable moment stared down at her. His hair, slicked back earlier, was now less contained and flopped over his eyes, making them appear even greener. He smiled when her eyes met his. 'Hello again, mademoiselle. I hope all is well?' Edith scrutinized him, trying to assess if he was mocking her, but his brow was furrowed with thought. Before she could answer, Coco noticed his arrival.

'Henri!' Coco cried and rushed into his arms giving him a kiss on each cheek.

'My apologies for my tardiness but there was an emergency at the shop...'

'Pfft, no need to explain. You are here now and that is all that matters. Have you said hello to everyone? It's the same, same people. Come, I'll get you a drink.'

Henri's eyes fell on Edith as Coco began to lead him away,

pulling him through the now crowded suite. He opened his mouth to say something but a woman began to speak and his attention was diverted away.

'I don't know why Coco invites some of these people. Riff raff, right off the street some of them.' Mathias took another gulp of his scotch, his eyes narrowing on the man now known as Henri.

'Then why do you come?'

Mathias grinned, his eyes dark, and Edith had to strain to keep the smile on her face. He leant forward and spoke in her ear, the movement making her shiver but not in a pleasant way. 'Because every now and then I will meet a treasure amongst the rubbish, a diamond in the rough, and it is worth my time.' He tucked her hair behind her ear then placed a kiss on her neck. Edith swatted him away playfully. She would have to make things clearer to him.

'Am I that,' she looked down at her naked ring finger and then back up at him coyly, 'diamond?' Mathias leered at her, and she leant back. 'I'm not that kind of woman,' she said.

He rocked back on his heels and winked. 'You "ladies" never are.' He started to speak again when someone over her shoulder caught his eye. 'Ah, the devil's here. Excuse me, Edith. I need to see a man about some money. Don't move.' He turned around long enough to pick up her hand and kiss it but then pushed through the room. Edith sighed and felt herself relax for the first time all evening. Acting desirable for a man was exhausting.

'Ah ha. Don't move an inch. He means it when he says don't move.' Edith spun around to find Henri next to her, smiling. 'He likes his toys to be right where he left them.'

Edith raised an eyebrow. 'You seem to know a lot about him.'

'Not really, I just know his type.'

'His type?'

'Richer than Croesus and acts like it. He and I have never got along very well. We view the world very differently and can't really move past how the other thinks. Have you known him long?'

'I only met him tonight and he seems perfectly lovely,' she lied.

'Indeed,' Henri said. He looked out across the room and his lips parted as if he was going to say something, but he clamped them shut.

'He seems to know you quite well. What is it about you he doesn't like?'

Henri laughed, and Edith couldn't help but smile at the sound of it. 'I am a dreamer and count my blessings in different currency. Mathias likes to see his belongings multiply and be under his control.' Something flickered over his face. 'It's almost as warm in here as it is outside. Has Coco shown you the top balcony?'

Edith's smile spread across her face. 'No, she has not.'

He took her hand. 'Follow me.' He held her hand as if it were made of glass and could break at any moment as he gently and slowly guided her through the crowd. It was now quite busy and loud, and their clasped hands were unnoticed. She scanned the room for Mathias but he was deep in discussion with... was that F. Scott Fitzgerald? Henri's hands were rough, and Edith wondered what he did for a living. No gentleman would have hands that rough.

They crossed the suite, passed through a closed door, then climbed some stairs and entered a darkened room. It took a while for her eyes to adjust. The room looked as if it was in sepia, all creams and browns, and Edith realised it was Coco's bedroom. 'Henri, I don't think we should be in here...'

'It's okay. Coco and I go way back. Besides, it's not her room we're after, remember?' He paused for dramatic effect beside some curtained double doors. 'Are you ready?'

Edith crossed her arms. 'This had better be worth it.'

With a flourish, he pulled open the doors and the warm night air caressed her face. 'Well?' Henri indicated for Edith to step onto the tiny balcony. 'Come and tell me if it's worth it.' She saw the challenge in his eyes and stepped through the doors, out into the Paris night air. She took in a big, deep breath and smelt the aroma of rich food. She heard singing and raucous laughter. The city was alive. The air was still warm, but up on the balcony, a small breeze cooled her skin. She could see the top of the Eiffel Tower.

They stood in comfortable silence for a while, taking in the sights and sounds of the night.

After a while, Henri cleared his throat. 'You never answered my question.'

'Hmm? What question was that?'

Henri smiled kindly. 'The fact that you can't remember makes me think that you are alright. But I would like confirmation all the same.'

Edith observed the man beside her. He was quiet, but simmered with an intelligence and vibrance she had never come across in a man. He was good looking, yes, but there was something more than just good looks that drew her to him. His clothes were not of the quality of Mathias's, and he didn't have an air of riches about him, and therefore Edith felt she didn't need to put on a front with him. 'I am fine. I think this lovely party more than makes up for my slip of emotions.'

Henri furrowed his brow. 'Crying is not a mere slip of emotions. You were obviously quite upset about something.'

'Not really. Nothing of importance. Just a misunderstanding. I was shocked more than upset.'

Henri chuckled and pulled a cigarette case from his pants pocket. 'Coco can be shocking. I hope she didn't offend your sensitive English sensibilities.'

He offered Edith a cigarette and she took it from him, happy to give her hands something to do. He pulled out his matches and struck a match to his cigarette. The small flame lit up his eyes and once his cigarette was lit, Edith leaned forward and cupped her hands around the flame to help ignite her own. 'And how do you know I am English? Do I not look French?'

She took a drag of her cigarette and stepped back for Henri to look at her dress, which he did with appraising eyes. 'You do look every bit the French woman and your accent is almost perfect, but it is how you carry yourself that gives you away.'

Edith startled. 'And what do you mean by that?'

'French women are at ease with themselves, confident in every meaning of the word. A French woman doesn't need to act a certain way because she just is. What you see is what you get.' He took another drag and blew the smoke out before he continued. 'With you, I think there is more.'

Edith felt her pulse spike. Even though she was standing fully clothed, she felt naked under his gaze. 'I don't know what you mean. It must simply be the fact that I am a mannequin. I am supposed to move and mould to whatever the designer requires of me. Perhaps that is what you mean?'

Henri leaned back on the balcony. 'No, it is not what I mean.' He swiped his hand at his brow. 'Do you mind if I take off my jacket?'

Edith, still musing over his words, merely nodded her head. She watched as he placed his cigarette between full lips, and shrugged off his jacket to reveal a shirt that strained beneath his arms. The jacket had hidden a broad chest and shoulders, and the shirt, cut as of it had been made just for him, fit perfectly.

Forgetting herself, Edith moved forward and ran her fingers down the fabric covering his chest. *'C'est magnifique.'*

'Why, thank you,' Henri teased, and Edith stepped back as if burnt, her cheeks flaming.

'I meant the shirt,' she said.

'Of course you did,' he chuckled quietly. 'It was a gift from Coco. She made it herself. I believe she cut many versions before she was happy with this one.'

Edith grinned. 'That seems about right. She drives her team of seamstresses mad. She never uses patterns, rather cuts each piece out by hand until she is perfectly happy with the result.'

'Ah, that would explain the scissors around her neck. I always wondered why she did that.'

'Have you never seen her work?'

'No, I usually see her socially.'

'You're obviously good friends if she made you a shirt.'

Henri took a drag and turned around and looked out over Paris. 'I was a good friend of Boy's. That is how we met. I was just a sympathetic ear.'

Edith joined him by the balcony railing, unsure what to say. Of course she had heard about Coco and Boy, her lover for many years. She knew his sudden death had hurt Coco deeply. 'Did he love her?' she asked quietly.

'Oh, yes,' Henri said, turning to her. 'Very much. But life gets in the way of even the greatest of love stories. I miss him very much. He was good fun.' Edith glanced sideways at him and noticed a gleam in his eyes that had not been there earlier. She was shocked. She had never seen a man cry before.

'You seem to know a lot of very rich people.'

'Well, they're the ones that throw the best parties.'

Edith threw back her head and hooted. 'Indeed they do, Henri. Indeed they do.'

'Have you been to *Théâtre du Palais-Royal* yet?'

'Not yet. I have been meaning to, but I have been busy

working. By the end of a day standing around getting fitted, I am too tried to take in the sights.'

He gently pulled her by the elbow and moved her until she was standing in front of him. He leaned forward, over her shoulder, their cheeks almost touching. 'See over there?' He pointed to the left.

Edith squinted against the night sky. 'No,' she said.

He leaned further forward until his body was pressed to hers, her whole body tingling, and gently guided her chin in the right direction. She breathed in his scent, something sweet, mixed with soap and tobacco. The door slamming behind them made them both jump.

'What is the meaning of this?'

CHAPTER 3

Edith spun around as Henri stepped away from her. 'Mathias!' Her skin prickled where Henri had touched her, but despite the heat that his body had provided, she was covered in goosebumps. Mathias looked thunderous and Edith tried to act casual, as if the fact he had caught alone with another man was not scandalous. She leant against the balcony smoking, her doll-like façade back in place. 'Henri was just showing me the highlights of Paris.'

Mathias stepped forward; his eyes narrowed. 'I'm sure he was.'

Edith moved towards him and looped her arm through his. 'I've tired of this party though. Do you think you could walk me home?' She pasted what she hoped was a placid, sweet look on her face, and Mathias seemed to cool down under her touch. 'I fear I've had a little too much to drink.' She swayed slightly, as if to prove her point.

'Ernest will be happy. He's drunk half the bottle to make a point to you. He's now three sheets to the wind.'

Edith giggled and leant further into him. 'Well, Ernest is a big man.' Mathias seemed to bristle. 'But not as big as you. You could surely drink him under the table any day.'

'That I could,' Mathias said, patting the hand that was resting on his arm. 'Let me grab my coat and we can go.' He started to walk away and pulled her with him. Edith tried to fight the urge to turn around, but she needed to see him. Must see him.

'Thank you for the cigarette,' she said. His face was unreadable and she was surprised to find herself disappointed he didn't look sad to see her go.

'*Bonsoir*, Edith.'

And as they walked back through Coco's room, Edith couldn't help but feel her heart was about to betray her mind.

∼

THE WALK home was a slow one, Edith having to guide Mathias through the streets more than he of her. The fact that he accidentally on purpose kept grazing her breasts didn't go unnoticed, and she wondered if she had done the right thing. But by the time he dropped her at her door, Mathias did the gentlemanly thing and left her safe and alone.

She slept fitfully, and when she woke the next morning was rewarded with puffy eyes. Lying down with cool teaspoons pressed to her eyelids she let her thoughts wander to the night before. She must have dozed off as a knock on her door woke her with a start. The spoons fell off her eyes, clattering to the floor, and she went downstairs to the front door, clutching her dressing gown to her chest.

She opened the door to find a well-dressed man holding a cream envelope out to her. 'Good afternoon, Miss Carrow. This is from Mr Mathias Rameau. He has instructed me to wait for your reply.' Edith eyed the man warily and took the envelope from him. She slit it and pulled out a heavily embossed cream card.

Dearest Edith,

I would be honoured if you would join me at the opera in my box this evening. The night will not be complete without you on my arm. Please say yes. M x

Edith's smile spread across her face.

'Is that a yes then, mademoiselle?'

'*Oui,*' Edith beamed.

'Very good. I shall be back to pick you up at seven. Please be ready to go as Monsieur does not like to be kept waiting.'

'I understand,' Edith replied, her heart already racing. She turned to go back inside when the chauffeur's voice stopped her.

'Monsieur likes his, ah, ladies to be pretty, but demure. Perhaps wear something that will complement him, but not take the shine away from him, if you follow me?'

Edith held the door slightly ajar, taking in the man's words. '*Merci.* I will see you at seven.' She closed the door and slowly made her way back up the stairs. Who did this man think she was? She stopped in front of the mirror on her dresser and stared at her reflection. *He thinks what you wanted everyone to think. You're a no one from nowhere.* If Edith was to secure her future, she needed to seal the deal, and fast.

∽

EDITH TOOK the warning seriously and was ready to leave by seven. The car, however, didn't arrive till almost eight. By the time she heard the knocker, she was hungry, tired and annoyed. She knew Mathias was playing a game, or perhaps he was just terrible with time. Either way, both were bad habits to have in a potential partner. She opened the door and found him leaning on her door-frame. 'Edith, you look ravishing.' His eyes lingered over her simple black dress and she smiled.

'Thank you, you look rather dashing yourself.'

She started to move out the door but he didn't move. 'Perhaps,' he said, running a finger down her arm, 'you could invite me inside for a drink first?'

Edith smiled. 'I could do that, but this wonderful man has invited me to an opera, in a box, and I so very much wish to show him off to all of Paris.' She held her breath, waiting to see if her tactic would work. She had already gleaned that he was a proud man and one whose ego liked to be stroked. A lot.

He sighed, but he was smiling. 'Very well. Let us show me off to Paris.' As the car wound through the streets on the way to the theatre, they made small talk, mostly Mathias talking about himself. Edith just smiled and listened. If her plan worked, she would have to get used to pretending to listen to him.

They made their way inside and through the crowded foyer, Mathias greeting and being greeted by many. Eyes locked on her, wondering who was the mystery woman on his arm. Edith's skin prickled and, for a moment, she thought someone from her past was nearby, but instead she turned to be greeted by two green eyes focussed on her as Henri made his towards her. Edith's stomach fluttered but the butterflies were squashed when she realised there was a beautiful, exotic woman on his arm.

'*Bonsoir*, Edith.'

Her skin bubbled. '*Bonsoir*, Henri.'

'May I introduce you to Camille?'

'*Bonsoir*, Camille.' The woman was stunning. With beautiful brown eyes, caramel skin and pouty lips, even Edith couldn't keep her eyes off her. A fire flickered in her chest and she was confused. Mathias turned back to Edith and reached for Camille's hand.

'And who may this be?' He pressed her sun-kissed skin to

his mouth and Camille smiled politely, obviously not feeling anything towards him, and why would she? Henri looked handsome in his dark double-breasted suit.

'Mathias, may I introduce you to Camille? She is a singer for the stage.'

'Oh, an actress. How very bohemian. Have I seen you in anything?' Edith was taken aback by his attitude towards her now that he knew she was an actress. She knew from her own upbringing that actresses, while enjoyed by many of the men in her circle, rarely became wives. Edith's cheeks burned. A mannequin was not much better. But Camille only stood taller and answered him politely.

'Are you looking forward to the opera?' Henri asked Edith, allowing her to pull her eyes off Camille.

'I am, yes. I have never been here before.'

'Ahh, then you are in for a treat. Mathias has chosen well.'

Edith looked back over her shoulder at her date. 'Yes, he appears to be very cultured in these matters.' She was lying, and the amused smile Henri gave her in response, a slight tug at the corner of his lips, made her think he knew she was lying too.

'Yes, Mathias is a great supporter of the arts.'

'Have you and Camille been together long?' The foyer lights flickered indicating the show was about to start, and Edith felt her arm being tugged away. Not waiting to hear Henri's response she looked at Camille and nodded. 'Lovely to meet you, Camille. I hope to see you perform soon.' She smiled although it hurt her to do so.

'*Merci*, Edith, lovely to meet you too. Enjoy the view from your box.' The couples were pulled apart by the crowd making their way to their seats. Once they reached the box, she realised she had a perfect view of the theatre and tried to concentrate on the stage, but her eyes began to seek out Henri. The lights went down. The moment the theatre went dark, Mathias pulled her towards him, his hand squeezing her arm, his hot lips on her neck.

'We'll be seen,' Edith whispered, his hands now roaming all over.

'No one is watching.'

Edith knew otherwise. The orchestra began, and the stage lights lit up the audience. The singer walked out on stage and began her aria. As Mathias pawed at Edith, she looked out into the crowd below. That is when she saw them: two green eyes, watching her. His face seemed pained, and Edith's heart rate spiked. As if held under a spell, she couldn't break eye contact with him, imagining that it was Henri at her side and not Mathias. The song ended and the applause broke the spell.

She dragged her eyes away from him and pulled herself from under Mathias and grabbed his face with both hands. 'Only my husband will get more from me and in the privacy of my own home.' She pressed her lips to his mouth, but felt nothing. Two green eyes appeared behind her lids. Mathias sighed and pulled away.

'I am not one of your ladies.'

'I see that,' he grunted, adjusting himself in his seat. Fear rose as she felt she was losing him. She placed her hand on his thigh as the next song began.

'But I'm happy to partake in acts not seen by others.' Mathias turned to her grinning and took her hand in his, squeezing it.

'Like I said, I can see you're not like the others.' Edith suspected that from that night on, she would never listen to that opera with pleasure again.

CHAPTER 4

On a rare day off, Edith decided to take advantage of everyone being occupied with the Olympics and go to the most photographed place in Paris; the Eiffel Tower. As a last-minute thought, she grabbed her camera, pushed her straw hat on her head and made her way out the door. Mathias was occupied with business, and Edith had missed the freedom her anonymity had brought her. When you live in a city where no one knows you, you can move and go wherever you like, but Edith felt those days were disappearing.

She decided to stroll by the water and headed towards the Seine, taking in the city in all its glorious summer wonder. It was still early in the morning, the sky a pale baby blue, but the city was already bustling with tourists and locals enjoying the light morning air before the heat of day struck. The smell of coffee and pastries wafted past, mingling with the sounds of hurried conversations. She crossed the Seine and walked past St Francis Xavier church then on towards the iron structure.

She wasn't sure what it was about the tower that made her feel calm. Perhaps it was the size. Or perhaps its solid structure, despite the fact the tip would move in a strong wind. Or maybe it was what it stood for: freedom. Edith had felt out of control of her own life for so long, she relished what Paris had to offer her. She tilted her hat back and brought her Leica to her eye. Using the lens to focus, she tried to fit the complete structure in the frame.

She stepped backwards and fell against a solid mass. Jumping with surprise, she turned around to a familiar face. 'Henri! I'm so sorry! I fear I have now offended your good dancing foot.'

'It's okay. If anything, you have made it happy. It was feeling a little left out.' He smiled and his eyes twinkled with mischief. 'That's a beautiful camera. May I?' He held his hands out and Edith passed it to him. 'How long have you been into photography?'

Edith shrugged. 'For as long as I can remember. My brothers...' Edith caught herself, her cheeks flushing as she reached for the camera.

'You were saying?' Henri asked.

Edith fiddled with the camera lens, keeping her face lowered. 'Friends of mine, their brothers were interested, that's what I meant to say. I am fascinated that a moment in time, light, dark, shadows, can be captured forever in a single frame. It's almost like being a time keeper, I suppose.'

Henri smiled. 'That's a beautiful way to look at it. Is Coco aware of your skills?'

'I'm not sure I would really call them skills; it's more of a pastime. Besides, I've never tried to photograph people, just landscapes.'

Henri leant back and spread out his arms. 'Now, I am no professional like yourself, but allow me to be your first subject.' Edith laughed as Henri struck a range of poses, each more ridiculous than the one before. She moved him in front of the Eiffel Tower and snapped away, only stopping when she had to wipe away the tears of laughter.

'No more, I can't!' Edith said, clutching her stomach. 'And I'm out of film.' She sat down on the grass and tucked her knees underneath her, her white and blue dress fanning out over them. Henri joined her, picking up a blade of grass and twisting it between his fingers.

'It's a shame that film is only black and white. I will have to remember the colours in my mind,' she said, placing the camera down on the grass.

'No photograph could do the blue of your eyes justice anyway,' Henri said. 'A painting would be more expressive.' Edith's stomach fluttered but, Camille's beautiful face coming to mind, she ignored his compliment.

'Where is Camille today?' she asked politely.

Henri shrugged. 'With her lover, I suppose.'

Edith gasped. 'Do you...rather...do you have an arrangement?'

Henri's thick eyebrows drew together. 'An arrangement?'

Edith's cheeks flushed. This was all too Continental for her. 'Do you take on other lovers?' she asked. Henri's mouth twitched and he threw the blade of grass away.

'As far as I know she has only one lover. We are just friends. Her lover is not a fan of the opera so we often go together. That, and her lover is a married man.'

Edith's shoulders released the tension she hadn't realised was there. 'I see. Well, I'm glad she has an opera friend.' She smiled, and when he grinned it was as if the sun itself couldn't compete with his rays. 'So, tell me, Henri. Do you like ice cream?'

'Why, yes I do.'

'I happen to know of a little café at the foot of the tower that does the best ice cream in Paris.' She stood up and tucked her camera under her arm. 'Last one there buys!' She sprinted off on her toes and swung her arms as she raced across the grass. Henri had not been expecting the race and she was in front. They dodged and weaved around people sitting or strolling, and Henri eventually pulled up next to her. As they approached the tiny café, Henri fell behind and a victorious Edith grinned back at him.

'I'll have two scoops please.' Henri, barely panting, bowed graciously in defeat. As he went to place their orders, Edith smiled to herself as she pondered how nice it was to be herself for once, and not the perfect wife-to-be she felt she needed to portray. It was also nice, for a change, to be around a man who let her win.

∽

For the next few weeks Mathias wined and dined her, Edith becoming his latest obsession. He brought her flowers and took her out for dinner and more shows in his box. It appeared he was now a big fan of the opera. They attended parties and soirees for the crème de la crème of Paris society. He bought her dresses and lingerie he never got to see, but hoped one day soon that he would. But she hadn't seen a pair of green eyes since that day at the Eiffel Tower.

Even Coco was surprised at his interest in Edith. They were smoking in her suite upstairs, after Coco had offered her something to eat. 'You're fading away,' she had said and now, after their meal, both women were reclining on the couch. 'He has become very fond of you,' Coco said while looking at her sideways. 'Fonder than anyone I have known.'

'Perhaps he is just ready to settle down?'

Coco tutted as she blew a long plume of smoke. 'Knock that notion out of your pretty little head, my dear. He will never marry.'

Edith's chest seized.

'Men like Mathias do not settle unless they have to, and he doesn't have to yet. Once he feels his legacy must be established, he may find a young woman who will pop out multiple children without question.'

Edith coughed on her cigarette and tapped it out into the ashtray.

Coco did the same. 'I don't say this to hurt you, rather to prepare you for the inevitable. You're too much of a firecracker for him. I'm surprised you're not bored already. I can see what he gets out if it, a pretty girl on his arm, but what do you get out of it?'

'He has introduced me to some wonderful people and places.'

'Yes, but there are only two people in a marriage. Other people and places won't cuddle you in the middle of the night. Is it marriage you're after?'

Edith sat up. 'Are you asking, or are you asking on his behalf?'

Coco shrugged. 'Purely making conversation. I am not his guardian, nor his spy. I've grown fond of you, but you seem to want more. Perhaps something more than just marriage and babies?'

Edith's hand clasped around her locket and she kept her eyes on her lap. 'He would mean security and stability.'

Coco sat forward, an intense look in her eyes. 'No woman should be at the mercy of a man. She should never have to depend on one. A woman should make her own way in the world.'

Edith's pulse spiked. 'With all due respect, not all women have that choice.'

'You have that choice.'

Edith looked up, eyes blazing. 'I wouldn't expect a woman who has all of this to understand. Some of us have lost everything and have had to start again.'

Coco leaned forward. 'And you have started again. You came to Paris in a cocoon and blossomed into a butterfly. Be the butterfly that flies in the open meadow, not the butterfly that gets pinned to a board under glass forever.'

Edith leant back against her seat.

'I just want to make sure you are happy to be with Mathias for the right reasons.'

Edith suddenly felt itchy. She stood up and walked to the drinks cart, poured herself a drink and cradled the crystal tumbler in her hands. 'I do love him, very much,' she heard herself say and almost believed it.

'Then I guess you have your answer,' Coco replied. 'Have you got plans for this afternoon?'

Edith shook her head.

'Then would you mind running an errand for me?'

'Of course not. The weather is beautiful outside.'

Coco got up and walked across to a cupboard and pulled out a small felt bag. 'Could you please take this to a shop on rue de Charonne? It is a little bit of a walk, but like you said, the weather is spectacular.' She walked over to a small desk and wrote the address down on some stationary, handing both to Edith. '*Merci*, Edith.'

Edith nodded, finished her drink and began to make her way to the mirrored stairs.

'Oh, one more thing. I almost forgot. Mathias left word he would be away for business, but he'll be back by tomorrow afternoon.'

Edith was surprised, as she had seen Mathias the night before, and he hadn't said anything.

'Oh, he didn't say.'

'Business. These things crop up from time to time. Enjoy your walk.'

Edith waved her goodbye and then walked down the stairs, her mind racing. She couldn't help but feel that Coco

A SEASON IN PARIS

and Mathias spoke a lot more than she let on, and perhaps knew more about their relationship than Edith did. She also felt as if she'd just partaken in a test, but she wasn't sure if she'd passed or failed.

~

EDITH STEPPED onto rue Cambon and smiled into the warm air, her nerves easing once she was in the sunshine. Placing her simple straw hat on her head, she looked at the address and turned left from the shop and made her way down the street. The streets were full of different accents and languages. The city was buzzing with all the extra people for the Olympics, and the air felt electric. The sun warmed her skin, and Edith enjoyed the solitary walk.

She entered rue de Charonne and pulled out the address. She looked up at the store in front of her and back down at the paper. *La boîte Magique*. Where had Coco sent her? The small storefront had a wooden façade, the ivy hanging like tendrils around the edge of the square wooden windows. She stepped towards the window and looked in. 'A toy store?' She stepped back to check the numbers again. She entered, and a bell tinkled above her head.

Toys of all shapes, sizes and colours such as she'd never seen before packed the store. She sniffed the air. Wood and sugar tickled her nose, and she didn't think she'd ever smelt anything as good. Bubbles floated across her face and Edith turned to discover the source. She gasped. 'Henri?'

The corner of his green eyes crinkled into a grin. '*Bonjour*, Edith. I was wondering when I would see you in my shop.' Never had two words elicited excitement in her, and she shivered.

Edith looked around, amazed. 'This is *your* shop?' A whispered conversation in the back of her mind from the first night at Coco's came to the fore. 'Your shop... you were late to Coco's party because of something happening in your shop.'

'That is right. You have an excellent memory. Would you like me to show you around?' He took her through the shop, showing her the beautiful toys and trinkets on the shelves, then led her through a curtained doorway and Edith gasped. The room was floor to ceiling full of shelves of wooden toys in different states of creation. Some were still chunks of wood with a label of what they were to become, while others had already begun to be whittled away.

'Who is making these?' She pulled out a half-carved ballet dancer and held it between her hands. The detail took her breath away. The legs were in an arabesque position, with the foot of the supporting leg in a perfect arch, and the other leg, carved with muscle, pointing straight out behind. The back was delicately arched. 'This is beautiful.'

'You like it?'

'Yes, it's so... life like. It's beautiful. The detail is exquisite. Who makes these?'

She noticed his cheeks turn slightly pink, and he ran his hand through his hair, not making eye contact with her. 'You do?' She thought back to the night he'd taken her hand, struck by how large and rough they were. 'Henri, you're very talented.'

'Not really. Just something to do to pass the days when the shop is quiet.

Edith looked around her and laughed. 'Then you must not have many customers.'

He started to speak but the bell above the door tinkled and they both chuckled. 'Go and see your customer,' she said. 'Can I keep looking?'

'Of course, take your time.' He walked back into the shop, and she kept browsing. Her eyes couldn't believe the things she saw, like nothing she'd ever seen. She heard Henri's friendly voice serving the customer, then pulled up short. Her gaze was drawn to a black cloth hung over something in a back corner. She went to move past it, but she found herself drawn to it, this mystery item that for some reason needed to be shrouded from sight. She reached her hand out, but then brought it back to her chest. Henri's voice sounded closer.

She quickly skirted away from the hidden item and pretended to look at something else when Henri walked back in.

'Sorry about that.'

'Never apologise about a customer.'

'What brings you all the way over here? It's not exactly close to Coco or your home.'

'Oh!' Edith suddenly remembered the bag Coco had given her. 'I almost forgot. Coco asked me to give you this.' She unwrapped the small velvet drawstring bag from her wrist and held it out for Henri. His fingers brushed hers, and it was as if she had lightning struck her. The hairs on her neck and arms rose and as if it had set every nerve ending alight. He gently pulled the bag open, and a wide grin spread across his face.

'I had forgotten she had this.' He pulled out a tiny wooden box. 'Open it.'

He held his hand out and Edith picked it up, trying to avoid his fingers this time. Henri had constructed the box from various kinds of the wood, the different shades making a parquetry effect. She turned the box over and looked for a button or latch. She turned it right side up, spun it around, but could not find any means of opening the box. Chuckling, Henri leaned towards her and closed his hands around hers. She felt as if she was on fire.

He placed his thumb over hers and gently pushed her

thumb along the side of the box. With a small flip, the lid sprung open and broke off in his hands. 'Ah, I'm guessing that's why she got you to bring it to me. It shouldn't do that. Follow me.' He crossed to the wall that held the mystery object and pulled out a larger box. This one fitted inside her palm. 'try to open this one.'

Running her thumb down the side of the box again, she felt a slight, almost missable ridge. She pressed her thumb against the side and the catch released. She ran her finger along the edge and carefully opened it. The box smelt like winters past, the earthy scent making her smile. 'It's beautiful, Henri.'

'*Merci*. It has become a big seller amongst lovers.'

Edith's cheeks flushed slightly, but she asked anyway. 'Lovers? I don't understand.'

'Well, what better way to hide your love letters than in a box that does not open? Each box is different and opens a different way. It has become my best seller.'

'Even more than all these toys?'

'By far.' A cuckoo clock chimed two in the afternoon, and he looked at her. 'Have you eaten?' Her stomach grumbled, betraying her. Henri grinned. 'Come, then. Let me close up the shop and I will find us some food.' He ducked out into the shop and Edith's fingers itched to pull down the black material. It was calling to her. Taking a deep breath, she tiptoed to the shelf. She didn't know what she was scared of. It was just a toy… wasn't it? She was reaching into the shelf when Henri walked back into the room. She hit her hand on the shelf above and swore.

'I'm afraid I'm no Maxim's, but I have some onion soup and freshly baked bread.'

Edith hid her throbbing hand behind her back and nodded. 'Sounds delicious.' She followed him further into the toy shop and through a black curtain that hid a staircase. He led her up and into a small, sunlit apartment above the shop. It was tiny, but functional. A small green table sat in the centre of a compact kitchenette.

Edith walked over to the windows and looked out into the street as Henri heated the soup. Streaks of afternoon sun accompanied by a breeze came through the open windows. She kicked off her shoes and walked over to his bookcase. She felt at ease for the first time in days and revelled in it. She didn't feel as if she had to impress Henri or pretend to be someone else. She pulled out a tattered copy of *The Picture of Dorian Gray*. Surprised, she sat on an armchair and tucked her feet beneath her. 'You're a fan of Oscar Wilde's?'

'Oh, yes,' Henri said as he stirred the pot of soup on the stove. 'He is one of my favourite writers. Very humorous.'

'I'm surprised he is to your taste.'

'Why? Because I am not English? Humour does not have borders. It can travel across seas. Just because I am French does not mean I don't find him funny.'

Edith didn't answer as she started reading the book. There was a quiet ease between them. When Henri placed the bowls and bread on the table she got up without a word and they ate. She enjoyed the food, the soup filling her stomach, and a heat passed through her she assumed resulted from the hot food and the warmth of the apartment.

'Your shop is very beautiful,' Edith said.

'*Merci*. It was a hat shop before I rented it. A very successful one. You may have heard of her? Delphine Lapouge? So successful she's moved on to bigger and better things, but the shop is perfect for me.'

'I've heard of her. Coco despises her.'

Henri laughed, and Edith thought it was a laugh she would never tire of. 'Coco would.'

Edith ripped a chunk of bread and dipped it in her soup.

'Do you approve of Coco's latest lover?' she asked, as she nibbled on her bread.

'It's not really mine to have an opinion about, is it?'

'I mean as a friend of Boy's.'

Henri took a spoonful of soup before he spoke again. 'Coco can look after herself.'

'I heard Mathias refer to him as Bendor. That seems such an odd name for a duke.'

Henri chuckled and leant back in his chair. 'There are two theories, but I prefer to believe this one. He got the nickname after a prize thoroughbred of his grandfather's, Bendor.'

Edith stared at him to assess if he was telling the truth and then burst out laughing. 'Is that true?'

'So I've been told.'

'Only the noble,' she said, more to herself than Henri.

'What brings you to Paris?' Henri asked as they sat back on their chairs, red wine glasses in hand. 'Adventure? Love or a lover?'

Edith grinned, the red wine coursing through her veins. 'Why do you French always assume it has something to do with love or a lover?'

Henri smiled, and her stomach fluttered. 'Because what is better than love or a lover?'

Edith tilted her head back. 'Food. Wine. Family.'

'And where is your family?'

Edith froze. She put her wine glass down on the table a little too hard, the liquid almost splashing out of the glass. She had let her guard down. Foolish woman.

'I don't have any.'

'You must have, everyone has some family.'

Edith gritted her teeth to keep the tears at bay. 'Well then, meet the first person with none.'

'Are they dead, or did you leave them?' His tone had changed, and she looked at him. His face was unreadable.

Something cold had replaced the jovial glint in his eyes from moments before.

'What does it matter? When you have no one, you have no one.'

Henri's eyes narrowed somewhat, a muscle ticking in his jaw. 'There is a big difference between choosing to have no one and losing everyone. Why would anyone choose to be alone?'

Edith glanced around the apartment, noticing that no photographs adorned any of the surfaces. 'And where are your family, then? You can't lecture me and then have no evidence of one of your own.'

Henri stood up, his fingers resting on the table, his knuckles white and shoulders hunched. 'I didn't choose to lose mine. The Germans made that decision for me, along with destroying any evidence they'd ever lived.'

Edith sank back in her chair, all the fight gone out of her.

'I need to return to my shop. Thank you for joining me for lunch.'

Edith's mouth sprang open. She started to say something, but the blaze in his eyes stopped her. 'I will fix Coco's box and send it back to her.'

Edith stood up, the chair scratching across the wooden floor. She walked back over to her shoes discarded by the window and turned around to find Henri by the door. She slunk across the room.

'Henri... I'm so sorry.'

He turned and looked her in the eye. 'So am I.'

Clutching her shoes, she moved past him and slowly walked down the stairs. She stopped at the bottom, half-expecting him to follow her but instead the apartment door closed and she heard the key turn in the lock.

CHAPTER 5

Edith arrived back at Coco's shop to discover that Mathias had left another message for her. She was to stay at the Ritz until his return. Apparently, worried about how many people were in the city because of the Olympics, he wanted her close to Coco. At first flattered and amazed by her suite, she quickly realised she was now a kept woman. What did he expect from her on his return?

She took a long bath with the windows to her room open as the sounds and scents of the early Paris evening drifted through the curtains. Although she tried to block him out, her thoughts kept returning to Henri and how she had upset him. Guilt weighed heavily on her stomach. When she got out of the bath, she walked to the wardrobe to find it stocked with the latest fashions. A red silk dress drew her eyes. It was loose on top, but cinched low over the hips with a silk rose on the left hip where the fabric draped lower than the hem. The back was cut lower than any dress she'd seen, and she gasped when she realised it was a Michelet. The fabric slipped through her fingers as she held it against her hand. It was cool against her humid skin, and she gently placed it on the bed. This would be the dress for Coco's soiree.

The party was small, just a few of Coco's closest, which, now that she was linked to Mathias, meant Edith too. Every time the door opened, she hoped for green eyes, but it disappointed her every time. After a few hours, she was tired and bored with the same mindless chatter until her ears pricked up on hearing Henri mentioned. 'He was supposed to be here tonight, but cancelled at the last moment. So very rude.'

'That's not like Henri,' one of Picasso's latest obsessions said. 'Is everything alright?' Coco waved her hand to indicate there was nothing to worry about. After another drink, Edith made her excuses and went back to the Ritz. She lay on her bed, still clad in the dress, unwilling to take off the beautiful haute couture. She had begun to drift off to sleep when there was a knock on her door. She thought she had mistaken it until she heard footsteps.

Confused, she got up and opened the door to find no one there. She looked both ways along the hallway but it was empty. She started to close the door when something on the floor caught her eye. There, in the middle of her doorstep, was a wooden box. The same wooden box that she had held earlier that day. She knelt down and picked it up, the beautiful box smooth in her hands. She pressed her thumb against the panel and the top popped open. Inside was a small, folded piece of paper.

Please take this box as a token of my apology. Family is very important to me, in fact it is everything to me and I could never walk away. However, I understand that not everyone had a family like mine, and you must have had a good reason to leave yours. I am sorry. Henri.

Her heart fluttered, and she stepped back inside her room. She folded the paper back inside the box and closed it, hugging it to her chest. She hadn't realised how much she wanted things to be okay with Henri. She lay back on her bed, her heart thundering. Her heart could not betray her when she was so close to redemption.

~

SHE AWOKE to a smell she was unsure of and something on her face. Her chest was tight, and she felt stuck. Alarmed, her eyes sprang open. Mathias was on top of her. 'What are you doing?' she shrieked, trying to push him off her.

'*Ma Chérie, ma Chérie...*' he murmured, kissing her before rolling off. He started laughing, and Edith scooted backwards. 'I knew you would look beautiful in the red dress. How was Coco's party?' He took a swig from a champagne bottle as he waited for her answer.

'What are you doing here?'

'It's my room. Or should I say, *our* room.'

Edith scooted back a little further. 'You know I am not that kind of woman.'

A look crossed his face, but she was unsure of what it meant. 'Then why did you say yes to the room?'

Her heart rate returned to normal once more as she weighed up her answer.

'Because I love you,' she heard herself saying, the lie hurting like the deepest cut.

Mathias smiled as if this was the only and correct answer, and he reached inside his shirt pocket. 'You are an angel from heaven, *ma chérie*. Marry me.'

It wasn't a question. It was a statement, as if a question wasn't warranted. Of course she would marry him. Her heart skipped off kilter. She had done it. She'd found a man who could look after her. Money would never be a problem again. No one would care about her past once her future was secure.

'Yes,' she said. 'Of course.' He pounced on her, smashed his mouth against hers and pinned her against the bed. As his kisses ran down her face and neck, one face came to her, one pair of green eyes, and they were disappointed in her.

CHAPTER 6

*E*dith stood outside the toy shop, unsure why she was there. Her new Cartier engagement ring sparkled in the summer sun, and people smiled at her, as if they could recognise the happiness of a newly engaged woman. Never had she been surrounded by so many people obsessed with love. Taking a deep breath, she stepped into the shop, the little bell advising her arrival.

'*Bonjour*, Edith,' his deep voice said, and she realised he already knew. Of course he knew. Coco had been one of the first people to find out about the engagement. 'Tell me, do English women normally marry people they don't love?'

'If it means security, yes,' she snapped back, her chin held high. 'Do not judge me.'

'I will judge you.'

'Why?'

'Because you deserve to be happy.'

'And I won't be happy with Mathias?'

'No, you won't.' The words were like a slap in the face and she pursed her lips, trying to control her emotions. Normally she was so well controlled. Normally she could hide what she felt, but when she was around Henri, she had no control.

'You can't say that to me.'

'I just did. I am sorry this is your fate.'

'My fate? My *fate*? You make it sound as if it's a death sentence.' He walked towards her and took her hands. Trembling, she let him take them. The electric shock of his touch spread through her.

'Please don't marry him,' he said softly, so much so that she leant towards him in order to hear. They were alone in the shop, but she felt as if all the eyes of the world were upon them. 'I… I thought I would have more time. It is a very quick engagement, *non*?'

Edith's trembling turned to shaking. 'We hope to be married by the end of the Olympics.'

'Why so quick?'

'Mathias would like to start a family.'

Henri swore and ripped his hands out of Edith's, one hand running through his hair. 'Of course he would, and tell me, has he tried?'

Edith's cheeks flushed. 'I am not that kind of woman.'

He turned his eyes, deep with pain, to her. 'Forgive me, this is not a question of your virtue, rather his. He… he not a man who likes to hear the word no. I blame his parents.'

Edith snickered, her blood bubbling. 'We're all products of our parents' mistakes by your telling. It was a mistake coming here.'

She turned to leave, but he grabbed her hand once more. 'Why did you come here?'

Edith tried to wrench her hand out of his, but he held tight.

'I don't know.'

'I think you do.' He pulled her towards him, and she thought her heart was going to beat right out of her chest. Those electrical sparks were now full-blown fireworks and there was no going back. He pulled her against him, and his arms circled around her waist, her neck arching back so she could look at him. His eyes searched her face as if seeking permission, and then he pressed his lips to hers.

She had never been kissed like this. He kissed her softly, slowly, as if they had all the time in the world, and her head swam from the passion of it all. Their lips moved together as if they had been doing it all their lives. One rough hand cupped her face while the other pressed against her back, the only thing holding her upright.

They came up for air when the bell above the door sounded, and they ripped apart, both breathing heavily, both unfinished. She spun on her heel and ran into the back room, not looking back. Still breathless, she rested against a shelf, her fingers pressed to her lips. She felt as if she was on fire. Her gaze travelled until the mysterious dark-draped object she'd previously seen caught her eye amongst all the colour of the toys. She looked over her shoulder. Henri, sounding flustered but friendly, was helping whoever had come inside the store. Now was her chance.

She stepped towards the shelf, her right hand reaching forward. She didn't hesitate this time; instead, she gently pulled the material down and gasped. She was looking at herself.

CHAPTER 7

It was like looking in a mirror. The carving was a miniature version of her, every hair painstakingly carved and curled around her face just as hers did. Her eyebrows, the curve of her lips, her cheekbones, all carved to look lifelike. But it was her eyes that had her. They looked back with an expression they had not had for years. A twinkle. Light. Love. Happy eyes.

She picked the carving up with her hands and touched her fingers to the eyes. They were her eyes. She didn't realise she was crying until the tears splashed onto the shiny wood.

'Do you like it?' She jumped, almost dropping the carving, but held it against her chest, cradling it.

She could not speak. Her tears turned to sobs, and her shoulders shook. She gripped the wood and her knuckles turned white. 'Why?' is all she could muster.

'Isn't it obvious?' He stepped forward. 'I love you.'

Sadly, she shook her head, and Henri wiped the tears from her face. 'I can see I have shocked you. Please, let me make you a cup of tea.' She let him guide her up the stairs and all the while she clung to the miniature in her hands. Henri added some wood to the stove to boil the kettle.

She sat on the couch. 'The eyes, they're not mine.'

Henri came and sat opposite her in the armchair, his brows drawn together. 'What do you mean? It is you.'

'No, they... they don't sparkle like this anymore. They did once, but these eyes belong to someone else.'

Henri smiled. 'I assure you; they are your eyes. It is what I see every time I look at you.'

Her heart pained. She shook her head. 'No, you don't understand.' Her hand went to her locket and froze. If she told him, there would be no going back. He would want nothing to do with her.

He came to kneel at her feet, his hands enclosing hers around the locket. 'I love you, Edith. There is nothing you can tell me that will change that.'

'You say that, but you don't know the truth.'

'I have spent weeks making a carving of your face. Is that not a proof of my love for you?'

She laughed softly. 'I think it shows you are mad.'

'Mad for you, Edith my love. Tell me, or don't tell me. I will love you either way. I learnt a long time ago that a woman's heart has many layers. Many that we, as men, can never understand.' He took the carving out of her hands and placed it on the small table behind him, and took her empty hands. 'Let me make us some tea. Isn't that what you English love? What's the saying? Anything can be sorted out by a cup of tea?'

She smiled and wiped her eyes with the back of her hands. 'That's right.'

'Right then.' He gently kissed her on the forehead and walked away to make the tea. She sat back on the green couch amongst the mismatched cushions and sighed. She had seconds to decide and test if what he said was true. Henri came back with the teacups, a jug of milk and a bowl of sugar. They took a few sips before she spoke.

'I have a daughter.'

Henri paused, the cup to his lips, as his eyes widened. 'I had no idea.'

'I… I was in love. Not, I thought I was in love, but I knew I was in love. It… wasn't a match either of our families was happy with. My parents had a few beaus selected for me, and none of them included second sons.'

'I can see you're confused. I'm not quite who I say I am. I am the only daughter of Lord and Lady Henchley. They brought me up as a lady, taught how to ensnare a man of good background and fortune, and not let him go until we were husband and wife. I was also taught practical skills suitable for a lady, like music and embroidery, but not encouraged to read. My prime purpose in life was to get a husband.'

'I am so sorry.'

'I am no longer rich or even connected to my family anymore. You once wondered how I could walk away from a family. Well, this is how.'

'I think I might need more tea,' Henri joked.

'You very well may, and you might burn that doll to make it.' She took another sip of tea and continued.

'James and I loved each other very much. He wasn't like his older brother Thomas, and I only ever agreed to go to their estate in the hopes I would see James. Thomas and James couldn't be more different. Thomas, raised as the next Lord Costling, had all the entitlement and arrogance expected in a man of his ilk. He was a terrible gambler, womaniser, and a drunk. He had already fathered several bastards. James, being brought up as the spare to the heir, had a lot more freedom and was interested in everything his older brother wasn't; art, books, music, photography. He detested hunting and gambling and, thankfully, was not a womaniser.'

Henri leaned back in his chair.

'It happened gradually, but James and I became close. Closer than two people who are not married should be. He was going to ask my father for my hand, when his brother somehow got wind of it and cut him off at the pass. Thomas didn't love me; he just didn't want to lose.'

She took another sip of tea. When she had finished, Henri took the cup from her hands and poured her another one, exactly as she had just made it. 'My father of course said yes, and I said no. When I told them I was in love with James, they all laughed. No daughter of my father would marry a man with no title, so he informed me I had to marry Thomas. Especially as I had started to show. I had known for a while that I was pregnant but was too scared to tell anyone. I think I really thought I could make it work.'

'We're all fools when it comes to love.'

'I was a fool to think they'd allow us to marry. They sent James away, and Thomas was at our house more and more often. The longer he stayed, the more he drank. One night he found me alone in the library and forced himself upon me. He only stopped when his hands found my swollen belly. Disgusted, he spat at me, and told me the engagement was off. He wouldn't marry damaged goods. I informed him that neither would I.'

'Oh, I bet he didn't like that.'

'No, he didn't, but he disliked that the baby was his brother's even more. Somehow, in his mind, he saw his brother had won; that James had beaten him to something when he was used to the opposite. Thomas thought only of my maidenhood. I thought of love.'

'Where was James through all of this?'

'He was away doing some business for his father, which he did whenever his brother was too drunk. It was becoming more frequent. Thomas informed my father that he would not marry a whore and the engagement was off. At last I could breath, and James and I could marry.' Tears ran down her cheeks. A few splashed into her tea.

'It was Thomas who informed me of James' death. He was... triumphant. His parting gift to me was informing me that my child was not only a bastard, but they would raise the child in their family and away from me. Thomas had a new fiancée, and they wanted to raise James' bastard as one of their own. I would have none of it. I went to his father and told him my child was James' and I'd raise the child, and not by someone as disgusting as Thomas.'

Henri put his teacup down and kneeled in front of her once more. His finger caught the tears on her cheeks. 'You are so strong, *ma chérie*. I am so sorry you had to live through this. When... when I judged you for leaving your family, I had no idea of from where and whom you had come. Still, it sounds like your family supported you?'

Edith snorted. 'Once the engagement was off, they knew it was only a matter of time before everyone found out why. I was sent away to a house for the rest of my confinement and was to return as if nothing had happened and secure another wealthy husband. I had a few months to plot my escape. I was not giving up my baby, and I was not staying around at the house.

'I was lucky that my aunt, my father's sister, who the family considered the black sheep, found me and took me away for the rest of my pregnancy. Turns out it wasn't hard to find me, as the women in my family had been going there for generations.'

'Some people have a holiday house, others a baby farm.'

'Exactly.' She smiled weakly. 'Rose was born perfect. She has lots of curly hair like her father but my eyes. She is the perfect combination of us both.' Henri was now sitting next to her, his arm around her shoulders. 'For months I was so happy. My heart ached for James but having Rose made me feel as if I still had a part of him with me.' She opened the locket and the curl of hair fell into her hands.

'My aunt has looked after her for as long as she can, but she is leaving for America soon and so, together, we came up with a plan.'

'Operation find a rich husband. But does Mathias know?'

'No. Please don't judge me. The plan was always that I would tell him once we were married and, hopefully, once he had his own child on the way. That way, he wouldn't be so quick to get rid of me. I would do anything for my daughter. Anything.'

Henri cupped her face with both his hands. 'You are even stronger than I thought, Edith Henchley, even more beautiful in my eyes. How did James die?'

Edith looked up to the ceiling, hoping to stem her tears. 'A broken heart, Thomas said.'

'What a strange thing to say.'

'Thomas is a strange man.'

'I would never normally say this, but I think you are better off without them. You are such a strong woman, Edith.'

He handed her a handkerchief and she blew her nose. 'You don't think less of me?'

'Less... how could I think less of you? You have endured the worst treatment a woman could endure, and you are still standing. Smiling and thriving. I assure you Rose's eyes are yours.'

He kissed the top of her head. Exhausted, she collapsed against him. She felt as if someone had lifted a weight off her and for the first time in a long time—she felt safe. 'Thank you for saying that.'

She lay in his arms for a while and must have drifted off

to sleep. When she awoke, she was still on Henri's chest and his arms were still around her, but the sky had turned to a pink and mauve hue of evening. 'I'm so sorry,' she said, pushing off him, but his arms remained around her.

'Never apologise to me, Edith. You have nothing to apologise for.'

'Your shop...'

'I closed it before we came up here. You are more important.'

'And that is why you will never be a rich man,' she teased, rubbing her eyes.

'After everything you have told me, I have wondered why you would want to put yourself back into that world of titles and money. It sounds like you escaped and now you want to go back?'

Edith nodded, not able to meet his eyes. 'It's the only thing I know, and the only way for me to survive. I have few skills, and they are to look pretty and find a husband.'

'They are not your only skills, Edith.'

Edith stood up, her cheeks flaming. 'Thank you for your hospitality, and for listening. I'd appreciate it if you didn't repeat it. I have clean slate in Paris and I would like it to remain that way.' She smoothed her hair, which had become messy after lying against Henri.

'You're going back to him?'

'Have you not been listening? He is my future. Rose and I need him.'

'He doesn't love you.'

She held up her left hand. 'I beg to differ.'

'He loves the idea of you. He doesn't see you. I will support you and baby Rose.'

'Henri, please...' She made her way across the room, but he stopped her at the door, pinning her against it, and her heart raced.

'I love you and only love you even more after what you just told me. I will protect and love you and Rose. I want us to be a family. Will you marry me?' He kissed her and while her head said no, her heart and body said yes. She gave in to them and the room spun.

CHAPTER 8

When she awoke, Edith was confused. The night sky was above her and a man's limbs entwined with hers. Henri's even breathing made her smile. Her stomach grumbled, and she wriggled her way from underneath him. Her clothes were strewn across the floor and she crept around on tiptoes picking them up. Her diamond ring caught the glint of the moon and she shivered. She couldn't wipe the smile off her face. She would end her engagement with Mathias and come back to Henri before he even woke up.

She quietly got dressed and found a notebook on Henri's table and scribbled him a note.

There is something I must do.

Lovingly yours, E

She took one last look at Henri's sleeping form and walked out of the apartment.

During the walk back to the Ritz, she felt light, as if she was walking on bubbles. She lifted her head to the night sky and smiled. She felt as if her confession had restored a part of her. There was no way she could continue with Mathias. The ring that she had been so happy about only that morning now felt like an anchor, pulling her down to the depths of the ocean, to the parts no light reaches. Mathias was her past. Henri was her future.

She stepped into the foyer, and her faith that everything was going to be alright waned. Mathias was by the desk, yelling at someone, and suddenly she wasn't so brave anymore. He caught sight of her, and his expression changed to relief. 'Edith, where on earth have you been?' He enveloped her in a hug and crushed her lungs as he pressed her under his large frame. 'I was so worried.'

'I don't see why,' she squeaked.

'Why? Why? I've told you why. The streets are filled with people from all over the world... from god knows where, these athletes... and you are walking around with a giant emerald and diamond ring.'

'So you are more concerned about the ring than the woman wearing it?'

He pulled her to arm's length. 'The woman wearing the ring is also important. Come now, let's have some supper. You look exhausted. What have you been doing all day?' Henri's naked torso flashed into her mind and she blushed.

'Just a bit of exercise. Walking around.'

'Well, from now on, you will have someone with you. I don't like the idea of you being alone.' They made their way to the elevator.

'Mathias, we need to talk.'

'Yes, we will, after you've had a bath.'

'It's rather urgent...'

'What's more urgent than getting the stink of the city off you? Some Chanel perfume will help too.' He held her hand in a vice-like grip, the diamond cutting into her fingers as they exited the lift.

'Really Mathias, I don't think...'

He yanked her closer to him and pushed her up against

the hallway wall, her head bouncing off the wallpaper. 'I can smell him on you.' Laughter travelled towards them, and he smashed his mouth against hers to make it appear as if they were lovers who couldn't wait to get to their room. Edith felt sick. When the people moved past them, he grabbed her hand once more and dragged her to their suite.

When they were inside, he threw her across the room. Edith stumbled and fell to the floor. 'From now on, you stay in here. No more working for Coco. No more walking the streets like a whore. You are my fiancée and you will act accordingly.'

Edith, heart pounding, pulled off the ring and held it up. 'I am no longer your fiancée. Consider this your notice.' She threw the ring at him, but it fell short and landed on the ground between them. She stood up. 'I am not something to be locked away, like a specimen under glass. You can't tell me what to do.'

He was upon her before she could react. The slap made her vison blur. A ringing began in her ear. She tried to step around him, but he blocked her way. He slapped her again, and she stumbled backwards into a table. Her cheeks stung. The next blow had her on the floor. He loomed over her, his gigantic frame menacing. 'You will be mine,' he hissed in her ear and, pulling her to her feet, yanked her across the room before throwing her once again to the floor. Her heart rate was going so fast now that she could barely breathe.

'You will be my wife.'

The last thing she remembered was another backhand to her face. And then the world went black.

∽

EDITH OPENED HER EYES. The room was dark. She moved her head and the room spun as the light started a hammer in her head. Every muscle ached. She felt as if she were made of stone. Covering her eyes, she tried to sit up, but her head still swam. What was wrong with her? Flashes of the day before came back to her. Then, like a film she no longer wanted to watch, she couldn't stop the images that came.

Her senses suddenly heightened. Where was he? She looked around the room then scrambled over to her bedside table, her hand pulling open the drawer and scurrying through it looking for a weapon. Her fingers brushed the nail file and she gripped it in her hand. Standing up, she began looking around the suite. She let her ears do the work her eyes were not up to, but she couldn't hear anything but the muffled noise from outside. She was alone.

She made her way to the bathroom and ran the bath. Avoiding the mirror, she focused on the water filling the bath. Sinking into the scorching water, she scrubbed until her skin was raw. As she cleaned, she came up with a plan. She would pack quickly and disappear. She didn't need much. Her hand moved to her locket, but it wasn't there. Suddenly panicked, she looked down to find the engagement ring around her neck on the chain where her locket should have been. 'Bastard!'

Edith slowly pulled herself out of the bath and ripped the chain from her neck. She felt the cut to her skin, but didn't care. It proved to her she was still alive. She dressed hurriedly and threw a few clothes into a small case. She turned the room upside down but couldn't find the locket. Realising she didn't know how long she had until Mathias returned, she picked up her suitcase and ran to the door. But the handle wouldn't turn.

Edith yanked on the door again, but it wouldn't give. She went to the side door to the adjoining suite, but it too was locked. Moving to the French windows, she found them also locked. Every door. Locked. She ran to the small table where the phone normally sat, but the phone was gone. Edith glanced at the balcony door. She walked towards it and paused. Her hand moved to the golden handle and she pressed her fingers down. It gave way. She swung the door open and the heat of the day hit her.

She stepped onto the small balcony and looked down. She was trapped, and the only way out was three storeys above the ground.

CHAPTER 9

Mathias returned some time later to find her smoking on the balcony. '*Bonjour*, Edith. I hope you enjoyed your sleep-in. I have brought you some food. I thought you might be hungry.'

Edith kept her eyes on the city. 'Where is it?'

'Where is what?' Mathias asked unconvincingly.

'I won't play your game.' She turned her eyes to look at her attacker. 'So I will ask again. Where is it?'

'You've become such a bore, Edith.'

Edith flung herself across the room and knocked him out of his chair. She had the element of surprise, and she dug her nails into his flesh and eyes as he cried out. 'Where is it?' she screamed. She pressed the nail file to his neck and sunk it into his skin, piercing the layer and drawing blood. 'Tell me!' Edith was shocked at how easily he overpowered her once more as he slammed her to the floor. A swift blow to her head silenced her screams, and then darkness.

This time, she didn't bother to open her eyes. She knew where she was and that she couldn't escape. Her heart hurt more than her body, and she just lay there. Mathias came and went, but no one else entered the suite. He informed her he had told Coco she had gone away for a while to find the perfect wedding dress, and that she would no longer be working for her. 'And I wouldn't even think of your lover. He has also given up on you. Coco has also informed him you have gone away. No one is looking for you, my little *prostituée*.'

Edith had no idea how long she laid on that bed. She didn't have the energy to move. She regretted how vague she had been in her note to Henri. If she had said she was returning, then he would have come looking for her. She squeezed the tears from her eyes. But her note was non-committal. He probably thought she'd decided that she'd made a mistake with him. Oh, how she was a fool!

Mathias only checked on her to make sure she was still alive. 'You must eat something, Edith. I don't want you losing those lovely curves of yours. I want you to look beautiful on our wedding day.' He pressed his lips to her forehead, and she curled up under his touch. 'You will love me, Edith; it's the only way you will get out of this room. That reminds me. The priest will marry us tomorrow, so be a good girl and eat your food.'

She rolled over. 'You can't be serious,' she hissed.

'As serious as a guillotine. We are to be married tomorrow.'

'I won't do it.'

Mathias sat down and pouted his lips as if he were speaking to a child. 'You will do it. If you ever want your precious locket back, that is. I've been doing some digging into your past, my dear, and what I found was nothing short of scandalous. At least I know you can produce children, *Lady* Edith. Even if they don't last long enough to name them.' So he didn't know everything. 'Tomorrow, Edith. I have a dress hanging on the back of the door. Once and only once you are my wife in the eyes of God will you leave this room.'

He stood up. 'You have no choice. We'll be happy. You'll see.' He patted down his sweaty forehead with a handkerchief and made to leave. 'Until tomorrow, then.' He bowed to her and walked out of the room. Edith sunk against the pillow, her mind racing. She knew he wasn't joking and would somehow have the power and money to coerce a priest into marrying them, even if she protested. But if she got out, then she could run. Call out to people. Get someone to help her.

A voice out in the street caught her ears, and she stepped towards the balcony. Looking down amongst the crowd, it took her awhile to find the voice but when she did, a smile spread across her face. She began to plan her escape.

∼

MATHIAS FOUND her in her wedding dress, looking every bit the radiant, albeit slightly starved, bride. His smile almost looked authentic. 'I knew you would come to your senses.'

'There is one thing I want from you.'

'Only one?'

'I want to wear my locket.'

'After we are married.'

'No, I want it now.'

'No.'

'Then no wedding.'

Mathias smirked. 'I like how you seem to think that you are in charge here. The priest will be here at any moment. With photographers from several prominent newspapers to capture the moment forever.'

Edith's heart raced. 'We're not going to a church?'

'God is all around us, my love. The priest has seen to that.

Well, the substantial donation to his church has seen to that. You didn't think I'd let you out of here before you're my wife, did you? So you could run to him? Edith, I haven't gotten to where I am today without being several steps ahead. Which, by the way, would not work anyway. Terrible tragedy, really.' His eyes flickered to hers, excited.

She turned her back on him. 'You seem to think me a fool too.'

'Here,' he said, flicking a newspaper to her. 'Read this. Tragic really.' The newspaper fell at her feet.

Magasin de jouets perdu au feu.

'It happened last night. They believe the owner was somewhere in the building when it burnt down. They pulled the charred body out this morning. Terrible ending.'

Her tears blurred the headline.

'I hear burning to death is one of the worst ways to go.'

There was a knock on the door. 'That will be our witness.'

Edith didn't turn around but knelt down and picked up the newspaper, her hands trembling. This was her fault. She had done this. She heard Mathias happily greet someone and the door clicked behind them. It wasn't until she heard the thud that she turned around.

Coco stood over Mathias' body, a heavy wooden lamp in her hands. She glanced at Edith and clucked her tongue. 'You should be in one of my creations, not a Michelet.'

Edith ran to her. 'Is he...?'

'No, just knocked out, but we don't have long. Follow me.'

'Wait!' Edith leant over his body and rolled him over, her fingers rummaging through his pockets. She only released her breath when she felt it, that and the broken chain with the ring that Mathias must have recovered from the bathroom floor. She clutched the locket to her chest then slipped the ring off the necklace to place back in his pocket, but Coco stopped her.

'Keep it. You may need it for money one day.'

'I don't want any part of him with me.'

Coco took it off her. 'Then I will keep it in case you ever need it. Now let's go.' They locked the door behind them and ran down the hallway. They must have looked a sight— Mademoiselle Chanel and a woman in a wedding gown running out of the Ritz and into the busy streets of Paris. They piled into a waiting car waiting and sped away.

'I have so many questions… I…'

'Here, he wanted me to give you this. It's the last time I am playing match maker or messenger.' Coco handed her the wooden box. The same wooden box she'd last seen in Henri's apartment. She pressed her thumb into the trigger and the box sprang open. Her carving was inside, together with a note. With trembling fingers she unfurled the note.

Until we meet again, my dear Edith, I wait for you. Until then, keep us together. Yours eternally, Henri xxx

Confused, Edith looked down into the box and found a second carving; this one was a man with the greenest eyes she had ever seen. She clutched it to her chest and cried. 'Until we meet again,' she whispered to herself and wondered how much the heart can take before it breaks for good.

CHAPTER 10

Coco took her to a place in the country, far away from Paris. She was very quiet on the drive there and left Edith to her thoughts. When they reached the estate, Coco put her hand on hers. 'I am leaving you here. He can't get you; you are safe. Mathias won't be bothering anyone anymore.' She looked out the window on her side of the car. 'I have said sorry to you once before and I'm going to say sorry one last time. I shouldn't have encouraged your union with Mathias. I had heard murmurings, but one always thinks these are an exaggeration of the truth. We are French; it is what we do. But I never thought him capable of... this.' She turned back to look Edith in the eye.

'There are plenty of servants around if you need anything and lots of clothes, even some of the Michelet's that you seem to like so much. When you are ready, you may leave and go where you like. I will organise for someone to pawn this ring and get the funds to you. Start afresh. Bloom somewhere away from Paris.'

'But Mathias...'

'Will serve some time at the president's pleasure. His past

has collided with his future. When they release him, he will be too old to harm you. I hope by then you are a fat and happy housewife and mother.'

'Thank you, but I've lost everything. I have nothing to live for.'

Coco watched her with discerning eyes. 'When I met you, I was at first struck by your beauty, but also by your resolve. I saw a part of me in you. You were the narrator of your life, and no one else. You told people only what you wanted them to know and I respected that. But you have an inner fire that burns so fierce, so strong. You are stronger than you think. You do it for love.'

'But love has done nothing but destroy me.'

'How very French of you. We believe the highest power is love, and you must do anything for love, *non?*'

She squeezed Edith's hand. 'You have been given a second chance. Don't waste it on self-pity.' She took her hand back and nodded towards the house. 'Good luck, Edith.'

Edith took one last look at the woman who was Coco Chanel, no less an enigma than the first day she'd met her. She nodded, taking her cue, and got out of the car. She watched the car drive away until it was a speck in the distance. Dress and shoes dragging on the stone driveway, she made her way into the house and into an uncertain future.

⁓

OVER THE NEXT FEW DAYS, she slept, ate, and regained her strength. The servants left her alone, and she soon realised that the house was where Coco and Boy had their past rendezvous. She cried herself to sleep, and when she awoke, she cried again. She kept the carvings next to her on the bedside table, the one of Henri watching over her like a talisman. She forced herself out for walks. She could not concentrate on reading, the words jumbling together and not making any sense.

Over the weeks she healed physically, the scars on her heart and mind not visible. She found herself drawn to a huge oak tree in the middle of some fields and often sat beneath its shade in the heat of the middle of the day.

This day, she felt her lids getting heavy, her stomach full after a lunch of brie and bread. She awoke when the sun peeking through the leaves had disappeared and a shadow fell over her. She looked up at the shadow through her fingers and her heart stopped.

'*Bonjour*, Edith.'

She sat up straight, her heart surely about to burst. 'Have I died?'

The face smiled. 'I hope not, because that would make what I'm about to do very awkward.' He knelt down so that he was at her height and smiled. 'I have missed you.'

Edith's vison blurred. 'I thought you were dead. No one said... Coco...'

'Coco didn't tell you where I was? It was she that brought me here.'

Edith's cheek flared with anger. 'She told me nothing. She just gave me the box with our carvings and your note, which I took to be written before you'd died in the store fire!'

'Oh, my Edith.' He laughed and Edith hit him.

'This is not funny!'

'I'm sorry. You are right, it's not, but Coco probably assumed I'd explained myself in my note. She doesn't like to get too involved with these things.'

'But she was friends with Mathias...'

'She has been my friend for longer. She gave you what she

thought you wanted. She didn't know we were something more.' He placed his hand to her face, and she gasped.

'Your hands!' They were covered in bandages that wound along his wrists and under the sleeves of his shirt.

'The reason for my delay, I'm afraid. The fire took more than just my shop and apartment.'

'Will you be okay?'

'They will heal. I may not be able to carve for a while, but it could have been much worse.'

She took his hands, and raising them to her lips, gently kissed them.

'But the body...'

'The reason for my injuries. The setter of the fire got stuck and I tried to save him, but the roof collapsed and cut him off from escape. A horrible way to go for someone who was just trying to make some money.'

'That's a very kind way to look at the person that tried to kill you.'

'He wasn't trying to kill me. He made sure I was out before he set fire to the building. His conscience allowed arson but not murder, it seemed.'

Edith snuggled into his arms. 'I can't believe you are really here.'

'I am so sorry I couldn't protect you. I am so sorry he hurt you. If I could get my hands on him...'

'Coco said he is going to prison.'

Henri pulled back from her. 'So you haven't heard? No, I suppose you haven't. Mathias is dead.'

'What?'

'Found face down in the Seine. The coroner ruled it accidental drowning, but rumours say he was helped into the water.'

Edith shook her head. 'It is all too awful to think about.' She pulled his arms around her. 'I am just glad you're here.'

They sat quietly under the tree in each other's arms, planning their future with Rose until the sun disappeared behind the hill, and then they lay in each other's arms under the stars. The future was before them, exciting and new.

~

THE END

THE SECRET ARTIST OF PARIS

By Sarah Fiddelaers

CHAPTER 1

GIVERNY, AUTUMN 1935

She could see five of them from her vantage spot hidden up amongst the oak and chestnut trees on the hillside. A family on the river bank messing about with a little red boat. The two brothers were taking it in turns to row their small sister along the bank. An imperious little lady, her white-blonde hair caught the rays of sun as it headed into the golden hour, her hands never still as she directed her brothers from the front of the boat. The father stood on the bank in his shirtsleeves, legs astride and hands on hips, bellowing instructions at the children in the boat, and laughing noisily at their antics. They didn't pay him much attention, no more did his glamorous, languorous wife, golden-haired like her daughter and lying stretched out on a picnic rug in the sun. She wore a low-backed, skirted red maillot, her already brown limbs bronzing further. Her attention seemed caught up in the thick book laid out before her.

The little boat came back to shore and the father pulled it in, and then fell to talking with his sons, with a lot of energetic arm movements that looked as though he were rowing for his life.

Genevieve looked down at her painting, to the scene she'd tried to capture half an hour ago from her secret hide in the autumn leaves. It had just been the two younger children in the boat then; the oldest son had been on the bank next to his father, and it was the way he watched his father that had caught Genevieve's attention.

She knew this family, although they did not know her. They were staying at the same hotel as Genevieve and her mother. They were extremely wealthy, everybody else in the hotel knew that about them before they even knew their names, and they were German. Perhaps had they not been so very wealthy, they would not have been tolerated. Genevieve had suspected, when she first came to hear of them, that the von Mylius family were the reason for their own sudden departure from Paris, and arrival in the russet-coloured countryside of Normandy. Amelia, her mother, had a knack for knowing where to find wealthy, middle-aged men needing affirmation of their masculinity.

Genevieve had noticed them in the dining room the night before. The Baroness, who was truly beautiful, had received many glances from around the room, and the eldest son, Sebastian, had come in for his fair share of admiration too. He was very handsome; everything their new chancellor was trying to sell as the new German man, to be on display at the Olympics next year.

He was tall, his shoulders were broad, and he had an open face, as though he had no secrets at all. His hair was light brown, streaked through with gold from the sun.

Genevieve scratched her stiff-bristled brush on her palette and lightened the side of Sebastian's face on her canvas. She knew his name because the family constantly called on him. His mother got him to organise a hundred little tasks for her every day, the sort of things her husband ought to have seen to. The younger boy was forever seeking his approval and desperately hiding his need, and the little girl seemed to look on him as a sort of demigod sent for her entertainment. The Baron just existed in their midst, like a tree in a landscape. Necessary to give the picture form and depth, but not particularly interesting.

Only Sebastian noticed his father.

Genevieve, whose glance had wandered back down to the beautiful family by the river, pulled her knee up to her chin and frowned down at her canvas again. It was no good looking at them now; she wanted the moment from before.

Something moved in the leaf mould behind her, and she turned to see what sort of animal had braved her presence to come so close. It wasn't an animal; it was the little yellow-haired girl from the family below.

'*Bonjour,*' said the girl in harshly accented French.

Genevieve stared at her. Her hair was perfectly neat in two straight plaits down her back, despite a whole afternoon on the river and a rummage up the hillside. Her pinafore dress was damp around the hem, but the white shirt underneath was still pristine. She was like a well-made doll, untouched by exertion.

Genevieve, pushing her unruly blonde curls off her forehead, nodded at her.

'What are you doing? Are you hiding from someone?'

'No.'

'You're from the hotel, aren't you? I saw you at dinner last night. You were with the woman with the funny hands.'

Genevieve smiled to hear Amelia so described. Oh, how she would hate that.

'My mother,' she said.

'Oh. I thought perhaps you were her companion,' the little girl tilted her head to the side, considering Genevieve. 'Well,

I'm Tabitha. That's my family down there. Golly, I wish I could wear trousers,' she said, eyeing Genevieve's navy cotton sailor pants and white knit sweater-blouse. 'Mutti won't let me. She says trousers are for boys, and I have to learn to be a lady. What are you doing? Are you an artist? That's very good.' She hesitated, coming cautiously closer to the painting and peering at it. 'Why, it's us!'

'Yes,' said Genevieve, because silence didn't seem to be an option with this child. Her curls fell forward again and as she pushed them back with her free hand, her fingers twitched on her brush.

'That's me and Max in the boat, and Mutti on the rug, and Vati and Sebastian being old men together.' She continued to stare at the painting, and then laughed.

'Sebastian does do that thing with his head, you know. All the time, tips it forward as though he is thinking very heavy thoughts, so you think you ought not interrupt, but I always do anyway and he never is cross with me. Are you in love with him? Is that why you painted him?'

'I painted all of you,' said Genevieve, not meeting the candid, curious eyes of the child, but mixing up some blue paint on her pallet to distract herself.

'Yes, but girls are always falling in love with Sebastian. He is very handsome.'

Genevieve didn't answer, but slowly, and very carefully because her brush was all wrong for the task, with too many bristles going in their own direction, she added some blue to the shimmer of colours in the river on her canvas.

'Don't you think he is very handsome?'

'Yes, very,' she said dispassionately, and then added for good measure, 'his eyes are rather far apart.'

'They are not!'

Genevieve shrugged. The sound of someone climbing the hill behind Tabitha could be heard and the child sighed.

'They've come looking for me. Shame, I wanted to stay and watch you paint. Can I come with you another time?'

'No.'

Tabitha pouted, and the footfalls grew louder as the tall form of Sebastian could be seen striding towards them.

He called out to his sister in German, and she giggled and answered back.

'I beg your pardon, mademoiselle,' said Sebastian, stooping under the low branches Genevieve had secreted herself beneath. 'I hope she has not been annoying you.'

He leaned on a low branch to support his stooped frame as he looked directly at her with light blue eyes. Genevieve smiled at him. His eyes *were* rather far apart, but had she not been in the habit of studying people so much, she wouldn't have noticed. It made him appear like a child in wonder. Perhaps he was.

'We were arguing over the aesthetics of your face,' she said, because she wanted to make him blush. He laughed out loud, and she could see that she'd surprised him.

'I only wanted to know if she thought you handsome. She painted you, see?'

'I painted all of you,' Genevieve repeated. 'Perhaps I think your father handsome.'

Sebastian chuckled but Tabitha screwed up her nose.

'Vati? No, you couldn't.'

'Tabitha, that's enough,' said Sebastian, still smiling, but with a note of authority in his voice. 'May I see the painting, mademoiselle?'

His French was very good, and his manner was— Genevieve couldn't put her finger on it. It wasn't charm. She was used to men who deployed charm to get smiles and favours, and he wasn't flirting with her. He was simply being friendly, but for some reason he was very compelling. She hesitated.

'Only if you wish to show it, of course,' he added.

Genevieve saw then that he understood, and that made it easy to show him.

'It's not finished; it's not even very good. The light is tricky.' She pushed her curls back again and looked at him fully.

Sebastian was gazing at her painting, his eyes roving over the details. He fixed on the little group in the centre of the picture, on the bank of the Seine, and his lips pressed together and he looked— sad.

'You do not like it, monsieur?'

He looked up, and there was no artifice or embarrassment in his gaze.

'On the contrary, mademoiselle. You have captured elements of our family that I do not think many people see.' He glanced back at the painting and his look grew more serious. 'And, to repay your openness in kind, I should tell you that it is that skill, bringing to light the things I would rather not be a part of our family life, that makes me sad.'

Tabitha rolled her eyes and said something to her brother in German. He smiled down at her.

'Tabitha tells me I should stop philosophising and ask you to join us for our picnic.'

'I didn't know how to say it in French,' Tabitha explained.

Genevieve smiled, touched by the unexpected courtesy of this explanation.

'I need to finish painting before the sun goes down,' she said.

'In which case we ought to get into position, hey, little scamp?' The seriousness fell away from Sebastian and he looked younger, more like a brother than an uncle. Tabitha's smile grew, and the little pucker that had been pinching her brow disappeared.

'Yay! I'll make Max take me out again, and you and Vati

can bore on together again. *Au revoir.*' She waved energetically at Genevieve. 'See you at dinner tonight.' She disappeared noisily through the undergrowth and Sebastian smiled after her, but the gravity had returned to him.

'May I ask your name, mademoiselle?'

'Genevieve Dupuis.'

'Mademoiselle Dupuis.' Sebastian nodded at her, and even though he was leaning down over a tree branch, the gesture was very formal. 'I am Sebastian von Mylius. Thank you for sharing your painting with me.' He straightened, untangling himself from the branches, and hesitated before he followed his sister.

'We are a family on the brink of something, don't you think, mademoiselle?'

'I am not sure, monsieur.'

Sebastian looked at her carefully, reading her before she could hide her thoughts.

'You think we are already past that, and things can no longer be altered?'

'I would not presume to say, monsieur.'

'No.' He glanced back at her canvas. 'Only to paint.' He looked steadily at the painting one last time, and then glanced behind him through the leaves at the family group by the river.

'I hold more hope than you, mademoiselle. I do not think things are at a point where they cannot be improved.'

Genevieve did not know what to say. There was such sadness in his blue eyes, although his face remained calm and he even smiled a little as he spoke.

'Please, monsieur, it is just a painting, and not even a very good one.'

'You are wrong; it is very fine. I do not say that as any mere pleasantry.'

Tabitha's voice could be heard calling out to her brother from further down the hillside.

'I'll return to my place before the light eludes you. Mademoiselle, it has been a pleasure to meet you.' He gave another funny little nod, and then strode out of the trees and down the grassy hillside, back to the river.

CHAPTER 2

'Where have you been?' Amelia snapped when Genevieve walked back into their small, pale-green room at the large guesthouse in the small village of Giverny, on the Seine.

'Walking,' she replied. The light, airy feeling that had filled her chest during the course of the afternoon in the woods darkened and deflated. She'd wrapped up her painting things in an old scarf, and given them to the hotel clerk to keep safe and secret for her in one of the private lockers.

'What is that?' Amelia asked, grabbing Genevieve's wrist and staring at a streak of white paint Genevieve had missed when she was cleaning up. 'Have you been painting?' Her mother's dark, fierce eyes bored into her, and Genevieve stared back at her.

'Not exactly. There was an old fisherman down by the river repainting his boat. He asked me to help him turn it so he could paint the hull.'

Amelia's sour mouth puckered in suspicion as she looked at her daughter, eyeing the stained blouse and wide pants on her narrow hips.

Amelia was dressed in an olive-green, slim-waisted

cotton dress with a pointed collar and capelet sleeves. She wore her long, black and silver curls loose down her back, and her skin had turned sallow because she avoided the outdoors. She was a tall, thin, angry woman who, when she'd been younger and still painting, had been called fascinating. Genevieve knew this because she'd read it in an article about her mother once. Amelia still had enough of her natural charisma to make herself rather compelling, so that she drew people in, like a spider to her web.

'John arrived last night,' Amelia said, draping herself along a spindle-legged settee. She picked up her drink and leaned back on the cushions, her long legs stretched out along the sofa, and both her claw-like hands holding the stem of her cocktail glass with difficulty. She often reminded Genevieve of the puppets they worked on in the doll hospital back in Paris, with their over-animated faces and their tenuous grip on anything they tried to pick up.

Genevieve took a cigarette from the box on the coffee table by the sofa, brushing the tip of it across the palm of her hand as she released her breath. So that was the reason for the sudden flight from Paris. Her father was about again. Genevieve lit the cigarette and leaned back against the door-frame, wondering how many cocktails Amelia would need before she would countenance any questions about the man they called John.

'His wife's gone off on a painting trip he tells me.' Amelia snorted. 'I don't know why she bothers. Sunday's banal flower pictures are not worth anyone's money. She got a write up in a paper no one reads, and she's infected with misguided self-belief.' The cocktail glass wobbled in her clenched hands. 'None of them were getting any notice by the critics when I was painting,' said Amelia, not looking at Genevieve, but glaring at her useless hands. 'It was only when this blasted disease took me that the critics needed them. They were looking for a trace of the excitement I gave them. They didn't find it, of course, and they forgot everything I'd taught them.' She broke off, her mouth working like the flapping of a bellows. Downstairs, the grandfather clock chimed the quarter hour.

Amelia looked up at Genevieve with loathing in her eyes, and the room darkened as the sun dipped below the horizon.

'What are you doing?' her mother snapped. 'Go and get dressed. I want you to wear your yellow frock, something that says daddy's little girl. Leave your hair down.'

So that was why she'd been brought along. It wasn't just a lovers' reunion. They were to touch Amelia's old lover for some funds in the name of supporting his long-lost daughter. Genevieve sighed, stuck the cigarette into her mouth and shuffled off to her room to get dressed.

∽

THE NEXT DAY, thanks to the distraction John provided, Genevieve was left in peace. With Amelia gone for the day, she collected her paints and brushes from the concierge and roamed the wooded banks of the Seine, looking for another scene to paint. She climbed a small hill to get a good view of an old, thatched farmhouse when she came upon Sebastian again. It was a warm morning and he was lying on the hillside in the sun, reading.

He must have heard her coming, because he spotted her before she'd had time to turn around, and waved to her.

'*Bonjour*, Mademoiselle Dupuis.'

'*Bonjour*,' she replied shyly. And then, because she was a little nervous of him, she felt her cheeks warm and she could not hold his candid gaze.

'I did not mean to interrupt.'

'No, of course not. Where are you headed?'

'I wanted a view of that farm house down there.'

He looked in the direction she pointed, and his eyes crinkled. 'That would be here, then, I suppose.'

She smiled, her eyes meeting his fleetingly. 'I can find another vantage point. Perhaps over the farm gate, if there are no dogs roaming free.'

'Please, it would not trouble me to have you painting here. I would like to get to know you. But perhaps that is not how you like to paint, with curious strangers asking questions.'

Genevieve braved another look at Sebastian. His eyes were the same colour as the crisp blue of the autumn sky above them. 'I wouldn't mind,' she said, feeling her blush deepen.

She set up her easel nearby. It was a strong little affair that could be folded very small and hidden in her suitcase, and made especially for her by Henri, who owned the cabinet-makers across from their doll hospital in Paris.

'Are you going to paint the farmhouse?'

'*Oui*. It is very sweet, and has all the grass and flowers that one could hope for from a painting set in Giverny.' What she would really like to paint was Sebastian as he was now, lying back on his elbows with his hair falling over his forehead and looking like the actor Jean Gabin. She would save the picture in her mind for when he wasn't watching her.

'What are you reading?' she asked, fitting a small, cheap canvas into the clips of the easel.

'It's called *Act and Being*,' he replied, frowning slightly at the book he had laid by when she'd come upon him.

'What's it about?'

'Well, I suppose it's about the responsibility we all bear towards our family, our community, our ethnicity, our nation.' He looked up ruefully and smiled at her, his frown evaporating and replaced by a youthful grin. 'Too serious a book for a sunny day in the French countryside.'

'We French can be serious, too. You are in the home of Descartes, Voltaire and Proust.'

'*Pardon*,' said Sebastian, giving another of his funny little nods. 'I stand, or lie, corrected.'

'I think a sunny day in the French countryside is the perfect condition for discussing philosophy,' said Genevieve, an eye on the farmhouse below as she sketched in her painting with a charcoal pencil. 'One cannot argue too fiercely when the sun is softening your emotions. And so,' she smiled at him as she looked over the narrow selection of colours that were all she had been able to afford, 'there is more philosophy and less arguing.'

Sebastian laughed, the sound warm and mellow like the sun. 'I don't know if any contribution from the philosophers could improve on such a sentiment.'

~

They became something of a mismatched pair. Sebastian would read, or sometimes write, while she painted, and when she was finished they would walk back to the hotel together. He was unlike anyone Genevieve had met before, and as the week went by, she overcame her nervousness and a real friendship started to grow between them. He was courteous and interesting, and always insisted on getting her opinion of the topic at hand, and would not let her deflect when she became embarrassed by the gulf between their ideas. He was searching, he said, looking for the girl behind the canvas and the curls, whatever that meant. And he was a nice distraction from the messy, anguished affair playing out between Amelia and John.

By the end of the week, Genevieve had spoken a grand

total of two minutes with her father. They dined each night with John, her mouse-haired, bristle-moustached, nervous father. He seemed more scared by Genevieve than interested in her, and after the first evening, she wasn't required for conversation by either him, or Amelia, anymore. Amelia had her own plans where John was concerned, and Genevieve had a very minor part to play in them. That first evening Amelia had set to work drawing him back into her web, and it seemed to Genevieve that he crawled in willingly, despite the existence of a wife and son.

And now it was their last night at the hotel by the river, and Genevieve was wearing her first ever evening gown, watching the moon rise over the river as the rest of the hotel guests waited for the dancing to begin. She had John to thank for the beautiful new evening dress. Whether he was to become a fixture in their life in Paris for a time, or whether Amelia had some other plan, Genevieve couldn't tell. Usually the addition of one of Amelia's lovers to their home in Paris annoyed Genevieve. The frantic pace of eating out, shopping, dancing all night, fighting all morning through their hangovers, making up only when Amelia had more funds to go shopping, and repeating the same mad program all over again, was exhausting. It was left to Genevieve and her aunt Marie to keep the doll hospital going until Amelia had tired of her current interest, or spent all his money.

'You look beautiful tonight, Mademoiselle Dupuis,' said a deep voice, breaking in on her reverie.

She turned, and Sebastian, who looked very handsome in his black dinner jacket and bow tie, was standing behind her. They were out on the terrace, and the band that had been engaged for the night was warming up their instruments inside while the cocktails were passed around.

'I've been painting the scene in my head,' she said, and then felt herself blush, because it wasn't strictly true. She was painting the scene, not as it was, but as she wished it to be. And as though in answer to her longing, here he was, on the terrace with her, in the silver glow of the moonlight.

'I hope you are the focus of your masterpiece, because it would be a shame to leave you out, in such a dress.' He took her hand and gave her a twirl. The white silk of the skirt flared at the bottom, and the delicate white chiffon sleeves fluttered in the night breeze. The back of the dress came to a v just below her shoulder blades, and the bodice was tailored to shape her breasts and accentuate her small waist. She felt elegant and grown up, and now that Sebastian was looking at her with such obvious admiration, she felt, for the first time in her life, beautiful too.

The band struck up a waltz, and Sebastian took her champagne glass from her and sat it on the balustrade of the terrace. Then he pulled her into his arms and she thought for a moment he was going to kiss her, but then he started to move and she realised he wanted to dance with her. But she crashed right into him.

'I don't know how to waltz,' she said, stepping back from him because the feeling of having his arms about her was flustering her more than her embarrassing dancing. The silk of the dress was very thin, and it felt as though his hands had been touching her bare skin.

'I apologise,' he said, also embarrassed.

She picked up her champagne glass, and Sebastian lit a cigarette and then offered her his case. She took one and he lit it for her, and they leaned back on the balustrade together and watched the couples moving about the dancefloor inside.

'I could teach you to waltz, if you like,' Sebastian offered after a moment.

'No, that's ok. I prefer to watch. Your mother is a beautiful dancer.' The golden-haired baroness was gliding about the room in a fawn-coloured, open-backed gown of satin that reached the floor in a sweeping hem, held in the arms of a besotted dark-haired youth.

'Yes.' Sebastian did not seem interested in his mother's dancing. He signalled to a passing waiter and got them both another glass of champagne.

'The thing is, mademoiselle,' he said, putting his glass down and turning to face her, 'you are leaving tomorrow.'

'Yes, that's right.'

'I will miss you,' he said simply.

'But you hardly know me,' said Genevieve, looking at him in surprise. He was looking at her intently and a little crooked smile showed briefly.

'Yes, and I find that leaves me— restless. I would like to know you better.'

'By waltzing?'

He chuckled. He had a lovely laugh; it was at odds with his often-serious expression, a warm, round laugh.

'No, that was merely a ploy. I wanted to kiss you before you go.'

'But not without waltzing first?'

'It seemed more polite that way.'

'I don't mind if you want to kiss me without waltzing,' she offered. 'This dress was made to be kissed in.' She gave a little twirl and looked over her shoulder at Sebastian. He smiled slightly but shook his head.

'Would you walk with me instead?'

Genevieve hesitated, Amelia's scathing warning from earlier in her mind.

'What do you want to waste your time on that idiot of a boy for?' she'd asked Genevieve while they were dressing. 'He's not the sort to make it worth your while.'

Genevieve, who'd been feeling rather pretty in her white dress, and excited at the thought of what Sebastian might think of her in it, had turned away from the mirror and poured herself a brandy. She'd learned early from Amelia that the best way to tell between what was real and what she wished were real, was to numb herself and see what remained in the morning. And since what was left over never felt like enough, she made up the differences in her paintings.

'Has he tried anything?'

'No,' Genevieve had said, deliberating over the question of ice.

'No?' Amelia had looked up from the complicated application of makeup and stared at Genevieve in the mirror. 'What have you two been doing all day when you disappear into the woods? Talking about poetry?' She'd snorted and gone back to rubbing powder into her cheeks.

'That, and literature and music and philosophy.'

Amelia had laughed again, cawing like a crow in moult. 'Please, child. You're talking to someone who cut her teeth in the *Années Folles*. There's only one reason men quote poetry. If you let him get you pregnant, I'll have nothing more to do with you, d'you understand? So don't be a little fool. I can imagine the baroness will be simply delighted to welcome you and her bastard grandchild to their *schloss*. She'll dress him up specially to take to all their Nazi rallies and you'll be lucky to get a job scrubbing the kitchen floor.'

∼

THE BRANDY, together with the champagne she'd had since coming downstairs, fuzzed the edge of Genevieve's thoughts. Amelia's words echoed in her mind as Sebastian stood with his hand out, taking her answer for granted.

'Mademoiselle? What's the matter? Are you unwell?'

'No, I'm perfectly fine. I don't know that I feel like a walk.'

'Genevieve, what is it? What has happened to put you

against me?' Sebastian put his glass down and took her hand in his.

She didn't know how to explain to him that it was she who had changed. Because of Amelia's influence, she hardly knew how to be the girl he'd liked out on the hillsides. That girl was an illicit fantasy she played out in the privacy of her solitary painting rambles.

'I don't think we should make too much of tonight,' she said, letting her hand lie in his but overcoming the urge to hold tightly to him, and to the girl he saw her as. 'Tomorrow you will never see me again, just as last week you had no idea of my existence. It has just been a little wrinkle in time, but next autumn you won't even remember my name.'

'You forget that you have given us your painting.'

Genevieve shrugged and drew on her cigarette. She told herself that she had given it because she couldn't risk letting Amelia see it, but the thought of sending Sebastian home with a reminder of her had been an impulse too strong to resist.

'Can I see you on my way back through Paris? I'm leaving before my family; I have to go back and complete my military service. I will be some hours in Paris waiting for my train.'

Involuntarily, Genevieve's hand tightened on Sebastian's. Already the list of things she could fill those hours with was writing itself in her head: a stroll through Parc Monceau, croissants on a café terrace, hot chocolates on the Île Saint-Louis.

Sebastian stepped closer to her. 'Is that a yes?'

'Monsieur,' she said, pulling her hand away, annoyed at her own lack of willpower, 'what would be the point? It would just prolong the inevitable fact that, after next week, we will never see each other again.'

'I was hoping you would allow me to write you.'

Genevieve gave a dry laugh and shook her head. She could imagine Amelia opening Sebastian's letters and reading them aloud in that awfully patronising tone of hers. She would take his beautiful words and make them ridiculous.

'I don't think that would be a good idea.'

She needed him away from her before she infected him with her poison.

He looked at her a long moment, his face pale in the moonlight, and a small sigh escaped him. He pulled a pocket-book from his coat pocket, wrote on a piece of paper, and handed it to her.

'This is the direction for my train. I leave it to you, mademoiselle, whether this is *au revoir* or *adieu*.'

CHAPTER 3

PARIS

Genevieve came back to Paris alone. Amelia and John had disappeared somewhere together and Genevieve wasn't given any information as to where they'd gone or when to expect them back.

Though she had a purse bursting with the notes that Baron von Mylius had given her for the painting of his family on the Seine, she walked from the Metro, hauling her suitcase because she didn't want to waste any of the precious money, the first she had ever earned. She also wanted to say hello to Paris. She missed the city terribly whenever they were on holidays. Missed her cranky, tangled streets, her large, smoke-grimed buildings, her wide swathes of parkland. So she walked slowly, smiling into the brightly lit shopwindows, and at the rushing, pale-faced, elegant people. She loved that she was one of those people, belonging to a little shop in one hidden pocket of the city. Her story was written in with the rest of the lives that inked the history of this beautiful, complicated city.

It was coming on lunchtime when she walked through the narrow alleyway that led into the passage where she lived and worked with Amelia and her aunt Marie.

The Paris Doll Hospital was one of an enchanted, forgotten cluster of buildings in the Passage Lhomme, off the rue de Charonne.

Lining both sides of the narrow passageway were the shop fronts of artisans most thought had disappeared from Paris forever. There was an enameller with low, wide windows and blue geraniums growing in a pot by the door, and a French polisher with a battered metal sign that looked as though it had been hung in the Middle Ages. A coppersmith's workshop, with a bright red door and white wisteria growing up the walls, sat next to Henri the cabinet maker's shop, and immediately to her right, tucked into the corner at the beginning of the passageway, was a wooden shop so wrapped with vines that it looked more like an abandoned house in the woods than a Parisian shop front.

A wrinkle in history.

'Marie, it's me,' she called out, walking into the shop dragging her suitcase behind her. Marie was behind the counter, serving a middle-aged man in a brown herringbone suit and with an impatient lift to his shoulders.

Genevieve passed through the workroom, past the cabinets of dolls' heads that stared as you walked by, and the drawers filled with arms and legs and glass eyes. For the bigger dolls, whose body parts would not fit in the narrow drawers of the chest, a rail ran the length of the ceiling, with the limbs suspended like some macabre horror house.

She dragged her suitcase up the three flights of stairs to her little room under the sloping roof. This part of the building was not as old as the rest. It had been burnt down last decade, and rebuilt with more modern comfort but less of the nostalgia that imbued the older part of the shop. Sensing her disappointment about this, Marie had papered one wall of her room with an old newspaper she'd found in the basement when she bought the place. It was from the

Belle Époch, and had dozens of articles to each page, crammed with tiny, cramped typeface. Genevieve had spent her life inspecting every one of those articles, and her favourite was the society article about the fairy-tale marriage of the hat maker and her handsome patron. They'd wedded in Notre-Dame, under the glow of the rose window, a sliver of sunlight bringing jewelled colours down from the heavens to bless the happy couple. It had been Genevieve's favourite daydream as a girl to imagine herself as that bride. One day, when she could do it justice, she would paint that picture.

She dropped her suitcase on the ground and climbed over her bed to open the small window that looked out onto the clutter of rooftops that stretched behind the doll hospital towards rue de Charonne.

The smell of varnish and sawdust that rushed into her room was as much home as the grey streets and the evening crowds on the Métro. She sat on her bed, looking out at her rooftops, trying not to regret her abrupt goodbye to Sebastian that morning. She'd been too scared to say goodbye properly, lest he guess how deeply his kindness and interest had affected her.

A footfall sounded on the stairs and Marie's head appeared around the door.

'You had a good holiday, then?'

'My father was there.'

'Ah. I wondered what had Amelia in a spin when she dragged you off to Giverny at such short notice. She's gone off with him, then?'

'Yes. I don't know where.'

Marie sighed and came to sit next to Genevieve on the bed.

'How was he?'

Genevieve picked up her purse; a silver-beaded, little clutch that was fat with the notes Baron von Mylius had pressed upon her, and tried hard to remember what her impression of her father had been.

'Did you know John? Before?' she asked.

'No. I heard about him afterwards. If it makes any difference, I think he may be the one man she has ever really loved.' Marie sighed again. 'She will be at her worst when she comes back.'

'Maybe she won't come back.'

'She will. He may be the love of her life, but his wife Sunday is the love of his. He won't forsake her, not even for Amelia.' Marie smoothed the quilted bedcover with her needle-roughened hands, her skin catching on the fibres of the quilt. 'Well, we will have a few weeks' peace before we have to worry about that. A holiday of sorts.' She smiled at Genevieve, her face clearing to its usual smooth whiteness framed by her rich brown curls. 'You should spend it painting.'

Genevieve smiled and looked back down at her silver purse, which also housed the note Sebastian had written to her with the time and platform of his Paris train on it. She traced the beaded pattern with one finger, conscious of Marie watching her.

'And?' prompted Marie.

'And what?'

'Do you think I need to be told when my niece has met someone? You're as coy as a chorus girl. Out with it. Who was he?'

Genevieve felt herself blushing, and she closed her hand around her purse.

'His name is Sebastian. He's German, and his family was staying at the same hotel for the week. He asked to write to me.'

'Of course he did. You said yes?'

'No.'

'You're worried about Amelia?'

'I didn't see the point. I'll never see him again. He has me confused with some dream girl that was conjured up by the sunlight and the setting and the lack of constrictions. What would I say to him? I'd only disappoint him. Better to keep the dream than be shattered by reality.'

'Oh, child, what sort of talk is this? The man just asked to write you a letter. There's no need to write a tragedy about it. Maybe he wants to practice his written French. Goodness, what a lot of fuss.'

Genevieve stood and unbuttoned her coat and hung it on the hook behind her door. It did seem silly standing here in the light, cosy little bedroom that Marie had made her, with Marie's kindly face smiling at her as she chuckled about her strangled thoughts. Genevieve laughed uncertainly.

'You think so?'

'I know so. If you're going to ask what the point of everything is, you'll be an old woman before me. What's the point of life, if it comes to it? Do you know?'

Genevieve shook her head and lifted her suitcase onto her bed.

'Love, *ma chérie*. That is the point of life. And maybe this Sebastian will just be a very good friend, but you can love your friends, no? You have a lot to learn about everything love has to tell us. You're starting further behind than most.' Marie put a gentle hand on Genevieve's shoulder and gave it a quick squeeze.

'Give this boy a chance. Enjoy yourself.' She planted a kiss on Genevieve's unruly curls and then left, pausing at the door.

'And if you are worried about Amelia finding out about your correspondence, have the boy write to you courtesy of Madame Pushkina at *Bistrot* Russe. She's Russian, she lives for intrigue, and she can't stand Amelia.'

So, three days later when Sebastian's train from Giverny pulled into Gare Saint-Lazare, Genevieve was waiting on the platform in a new, slim-waisted blue dress with puff sleeves. He must had spotted her from the train, because he strode right up to her, looking taller than she remembered, and dropped his suitcase before wrapping her in a warm, tight hug.

'Genevieve,' he said, letting go of her, 'you don't know how good it is to see you. How it has tortured me not knowing if you would be here.'

Genevieve, pushing her curls back from her face, smiled shyly at him. 'My aunt made sure that I was. She said I was being silly with my worries.'

'A thousand thanks to your aunt,' said Sebastian cheerfully, while giving her a searching look. 'Let me get my suitcase in the care of a porter and then, mademoiselle, I am in your hands.'

On the steps of the station he took her hand and pulled her arm through his and they stood there a moment, looking at the people and cars as they bustled along rue d'Amsterdam. Yesterday, she had been just a girl who lived in Paris, and today she had her hand tucked into the arm of a handsome man who was overjoyed that she had met him at the station. Today, she and Sebastian were one of that most permanent of Parisian fixtures, a couple.

She took him first to the Musée Jacquemart-Andre on the boulevard Haussmann, and showed him the paintings that had taught her everything Amelia had forbidden her from learning. Then they strolled, still with Sebastian holding her close to his side, along the walks of Parc Monceau, the tree branches thinning of their yellow leaves, while dodging the nurses with their prams and the housemaids exercising overfed dogs. And they talked, as though to make up for all the moments of quiet they had shared together in Giverny. Sebastian told her about his home, the grand estate in the Black Forest that would be his fate to manage one day. His family had been the principal family in the region for four hundred years, and Sebastian confessed, as they stood at the edge of the lake in the middle of the park watching small children prod their boats along with sticks, that he found the legacy heavy to bear.

'Is that why you look so serious all the time?' she asked, pushing her curls back so she could see his profile clearly. He looked surprised.

'Do I?'

'Surely you knew that?'

A reluctant smile crept out and tugged at his mouth and his brow cleared. 'Would you think me an idiot if I tell you I thought I was doing a rather good job of hiding my anxieties under a cloak of gaiety?'

Genevieve laughed. 'You're not being serious.'

'No, well, perhaps not gaiety exactly. Calm detachment.'

'When Tabitha first saw my painting, do you know what she said about you?'

'That I was very handsome?'

Genevieve rolled her eyes. 'Before that. She commented on how well I'd captured you. She said you had a way of holding your head forward as though you were thinking very heavy thoughts.'

'Oh dear. Not so detached then.'

'Surely it's your father's responsibility for many years yet. Why do you worry so much about it?'

'I am not sure that Father understands the choices that may be forced upon us. In the past, if you were a man of honour, you did your duty even when it was hard. Going forward, it might not be so clear. Our duty, as it has been laid out for us for the past four centuries, may not be enough to guide us in the new Germany that is being forged without the understanding, or consent, of the German people.'

'How will your duty change? Surely right and wrong cannot be re-written?'

'I suppose what worries me is that doing my duty by my family and the people who depend on us, which has always been the right thing to do, will be at odds with doing the right thing by Germany.'

Genevieve frowned at him, trying to make out his meaning. His light-blue eyes were clouded, and even though they stood in one of the prettiest parks in Paris, she knew he was seeing the woods around his *schloss*, and the people there who depended on his family.

'I don't really understand you,' she said eventually. He shook himself out of his reverie and smiled down at her, and her heart skipped a beat to see the warmth that came into his eyes.

'No, why should you? It's all dreary politics that even we Germans don't want to know about.' He consulted his watch and tightened his hold on her hand.

'We've just two hours left. Where to now, fair guide?'

'Now I will take you to have the best hot chocolate in Paris.'

They took the Métro to Île de la Cité and walked slowly past the graceful towers and spire of Notre-Dame. They had slipped back into their habitual silence as they walked along the side of the cathedral, past the spiderwebbed structure of the north rose window, and Genevieve thought of that enchanted wedding of twenty-five years ago as her hand tightened on Sebastian's arm. They crossed Pont Saint-Louis and Genevieve took Sebastian to a little café tucked away on the island, with plump cushions on the wooden banquette and hot chocolate served in silver spindle-legged teapots.

'I have a ritual,' said Genevieve, pouring the thick liquid into a small white porcelain cup for Sebastian, 'where I must come here the first day of autumn every year. And then as often as I can afford to after that. I even come sometimes in the summer, if I am feeling sad.'

They clinked their cups together, Sebastian's cup very small and fragile in his large hands, and then drank in silence. The pot gave them two cups each, and they drank them slowly, as though by dragging their feet they could slow the hands of the clock that moved heartlessly towards the moment of their parting.

'I thought about what you asked me,' she said, when she could not make her second cup last any longer. 'About whether you might write to me. I should like it.' She lifted her eyes to meet his and felt the colour heat her cheeks. 'Only, I think it best if you send the letters care of this lady.' She passed him a folded note with Madame Pushkina's direction on it. She had thought seriously about spraying the note with perfume as they did in the novels, but had felt a bit silly, and so settled on spraying her wrists generously before she wrote down the address.

Sebastian's lips twitched. 'This is quite the intrigue,' he said.

'Yes, well Amelia can be unpredictable, so I think it better if she doesn't know anything about it. She's quite capable of stealing your letters, if she takes a turn for the worse.'

'I see.'

Sebastian paid and they walked slowly back to Gare du Nord together. Genevieve's heart felt heavy and strange, and she could not see clearly past the moment when Sebastian's train would pull out for Berlin. A crushing sadness came upon her and she felt terribly bereft all of a sudden.

She wanted to tell him that she didn't want him to go, but she felt silly even for thinking about it. What would he think of a ninny who came undone when they parted at the end of a perfectly lovely day? So she hitched a cheerful smile to her face instead and started to prattle about the new brushes she planned to buy with the money his father had given her for the painting. Sebastian listened in silence, and she was so afraid of the need opening up in her heart that she talked right up until they were standing outside the door to his first class compartment.

'Genevieve,' he said gently, breaking in on her desperate ramblings. 'Thank you for meeting me today. I will miss you more than ever after this wonderful day we snatched together.' He took both her hands in his and rested his forehead on hers. Her heart, which had been hammering nervously in her chest, seemed to stop. 'I shall write to you as soon as I get to Berlin, and I will be impatient for your reply. You can finish telling me all about your new brushes and all those other strange sounding objects you were talking about just now.'

'Yes, of course.' Her voice was a little breathless and she swallowed, and tried to sound less ridiculous. 'And perhaps I could get dancing lessons, and next time I can waltz with you.' She smiled up at him, but he did not smile back and she felt her cheeks heat. Was she being too forward?

He touched his lips gently, and far too briefly, to hers. 'Only if you promise to waltz with me in the moonlight.'

CHAPTER 4

*P*aris always put winter on in a sulky way. It was as though autumn stretched too thin and simply faded into a season with no colour and no light. The trees were bare, the skies grey, the weather miserable and damp in a misty way that rarely settled to rain. It suited Genevieve, who felt in-between herself. She had not expected to wake up the morning following her day with Sebastian to find the strange hollow feeling still in her heart. She had not expected to live each moment of her day thinking about what Sebastian might be doing, and whether or not he might be thinking of her. But that became her existence.

She fell to the only thing she knew would relieve some of the heavy melancholy that had settled on her, and spent a portion of her money on some new canvasses, brushes, and paints. She painted Paris in the winter; not the sullen Paris they all lived with at this time of year, but the softer, warmer Paris of fire-lit shop interiors and couples pressed close together in cafés and bars to keep their hearts and their bodies warm. She painted herself into the pictures, always on the outside, in the cold, looking in at the happy couples. She tried, once, to paint Sebastian, but she could not capture him the way she remembered him in Giverny. Her failure frustrated, and scared her.

Amelia had still not come home when Sebastian's first letter arrived as promised, posted soon after he'd arrived at the military training camp. Madame Pushkina stopped her when she headed out to run some errands for Marie and handed her a wonderfully thick envelope.

'*Merci*, madame,' said Genevieve, barely able to tear her eyes away from his firm handwriting. Madame Pushkina, her grey hair escaping from the bun she always wore it in, smiled mistily and sighed. Genevieve held onto the letter throughout the morning as she crisscrossed Paris, visiting numerous warehouses looking for the right materials to match the repairs they were doing on a difficult commission that had come in while she'd been away. It was a very old doll they were working on, and something about this particular doll affected Marie greatly.

'He's written, then?' said Marie, a small smile on her pale lips when she joined Genevieve in the kitchen for their lunch. 'Goodness, what an assortment of pages.'

'Yes,' said Genevieve, unable to stop the smile that was spreading across her face. 'He started on the train, because he said he was missing me before the train had even reached the outskirts of Paris. Then he's just been adding to it with whatever was to hand. He has lovely handwriting.'

Marie laughed. 'Gracious, you've got it bad. But don't stop, tell me all about this wonderful man with the lovely handwriting.'

'He's had to return to Germany to do his compulsory military training, and he says they've got them camping up in the mountains and it's freezing. What? Why do you look like that?' Genevieve asked, as Marie pursed her lips.

'Military training for the army they're not supposed to have. He's up to something, that funny little Austrian.'

'You're not worried they'll attack France again?'

'No, I don't suppose so. Perhaps he has a mind to get Austria and Hungary back together and rebuild the empire.' Marie screwed her face up as though she had tasted something nasty and gave her head a little shake. 'Let's not talk about such things. I have a proposition for you. I saw the paintings you've been doing when I went up to your room this morning. They are very good, *ma petite*. You are growing into your skill, I see.'

Genevieve blushed and hid behind her wayward curls. 'Amelia will be furious.'

'Amelia is not a part of this conversation. Your paintings gave me an idea. I would like to commission you to paint some scenes for the front windows. There is a quality to your pictures that leaves one longing for more, and that is exactly what we need out the front to urge people through the front door. Mending dolls is a slow business. We need to sell more of our creations if we are to keep ourselves comfortable. The big commissions are slowing up. I find fewer people are interested in protecting the past.'

'Marie, do you mean it?'

'Yes, of course. I was thinking a woodland scene for one window, and cannot decide for the other if I want a ballroom, or a theatre, or what. Some sort of interior.'

Genevieve thought about it for a moment. 'Perhaps a sitting room for the interior picture? With a well-to-do family seated around a fire. It's not grand, but it has in it everything people really want, and it's inviting.'

'Yes, perfect. I knew you would excel at this. I will pay you one hundred *francs* per window, plus materials costs.'

'Marie, you don't have to pay me. You house me and feed me as it is.'

'And you work for me for nothing. This I will pay for, and if you won't take the money, I will find some other artist who will.

CHAPTER 5

One afternoon in the middle of November Genevieve was in her room, painting a miniature scene of the hot chocolate shop she had prepared as Sebastian's Christmas present, when she heard the front door slam open in a way that seemed to make the lamps dim. Amelia was home.

Hastily gathering up the painting things she had bought with the money from Baron von Mylius, Genevieve tumbled them all into a wooden box and then opened the little window and tucked the box away on a ledge under her window. Then she crept downstairs and stood outside the door of the workroom to listen.

'You have not tired of betraying me, I see.' It was Amelia's voice, soft and poisonous as ever. Genevieve did not hear Marie's reply.

'I didn't want her to paint. It was a very clear wish. Why, Marie? Why this need to continue wounding me?'

'It's good advertising,' Marie said, her voice wavering. 'We're losing custom, Amelia, and if something doesn't change we will be forced out. Genevieve's paintings have generated a lot of interest.'

'I don't want to hear your excuses.' Amelia gave a short, hacking cough. 'Where is she?'

'In her room.'

Genevieve opened the door to the workroom, and the two women swung around to stare at her.

'Hello, mother,' she said. Amelia was wrapped in a new sable coat and her hair had been fashionably set in waves off her high brow. Her dark eyes were bloodshot and rimmed with red.

'You've disobeyed me.'

'Yes.'

'You will be sorry for it.'

'I don't think so.'

Marie drew in her breath with a hiss as Amelia took a step toward Genevieve and stared at her, her curled fingers twitching with anger.

'What happened to John?' Genevieve asked. 'Is he back with his wife and prodigy of a son?'

Amelia's clawed hand flashed out and caught Genevieve across the cheek, the twisted fingers scratching and drawing blood.

'I tried to save you from this, brat,' Amelia said, her breathing fast. 'You're not so wonderful, you know. I know how intoxicating the first admiration for your work can be. But it's all empty praise, building an ego that is only going to be your ruin. The only thing you have going for you is that you are young. But you can't paint, you're nothing to look at, no man has ever been interested in you, and no one cares for you. And when you realise that, the misery will rob you of your youth and then you will be just like the rest of us.' She smiled grimly, her teeth prominent in the light thrown from the chandelier above her giving her face a strange, misshapen look. She turned on Marie. 'Get back to your dolls, and let me worry about the finances. Genevieve, take down those paintings from the window and burn them.'

~

LIFE BECAME VERY GREY. Sebastian's letters were like a golden thread running through the dull canvas of Genevieve's days now that Amelia had returned. It was always like this after one of her affairs ended. She came home like a wounded bear and was more impossible than ever. Genevieve stopped painting, as Amelia watched her too closely and kept her too busy. The one small mercy was that with all the errands Amelia had her running day and night, she had every opportunity to stop at Madame Pushkina's to collect Sebastian's letters.

It was December when they stopped coming.

It was as though Amelia's power was strong enough to affect even Sebastian; solid, warm, uncomplicated Sebastian, all the way off in Germany. A kernel of doubt had begun to grow in Genevieve's heart all through November. His letters lost something of the confidences he had shared with her, and began to read more like tourist pamphlets extolling the virtues of the regions he was stationed in and the strengths of Hitler's Reich. She began to fear she was losing him, and then he fell silent.

Christmas came and went with no snow and less cheer. Genevieve left the miniature she'd done for Sebastian in the box under her windowsill and could not bring herself to go back to the café on the Île Saint-Louis. Her chest felt hollow and barren, her mind withered, and she didn't even mind not being able to paint anymore. She revelled in the grey gloom of Paris and the miserable faces of her fellow Parisians, and she avoided the brightly lit shop windows, decorated in warm, inviting colours to cheer the lives of the frozen passers-by. She didn't want their cheer. She would hold tight to her misery, the one thing that couldn't be taken from her.

~

'THERE's someone who wants to speak to you,' said Marie one day in mid-February when they were seated at the work bench together. Genevieve was piecing out the silk she had cut to recreate a dress for Marie's complicated commission. The fire warmed their backs as the snow drifted down outside.

'He noticed your paintings in the window, and he wants to see more of your work.'

Only a few months ago news such as this would have filled Genevieve with excitement, but now she saw only problems. 'I don't have anything to show him, even if I could get past Amelia.'

'We will think of something. I didn't recognise his name, although he seemed to expect me to, so I asked Pierre. I must say, for an enameller tucked away in a small street, that one seems to know everything. Anyway, he said that Monsieur Read is a serious London art critic. This is your chance, *chérie*.' Marie put down her embroidery frame and arched her back, her fingers working at her lower spine. 'We could arrange him to see your work as before, in the front window. We'll set it up as an exhibition space, and hide it behind a false back so that Amelia doesn't see it. Then we'll arrange for him to come, and if she's out, so much the better, but if she's not, all he has to do is stand in the street and look through a shop window.'

CHAPTER 6

As Genevieve walked back to the doll hospital after a delivery that evening, she realised that Marie's excitement had gotten under her skin. The snow still sat in drifts on the rooftops and windowsills, and the city had a calm magic about it, like the stroke of midnight on Christmas Eve, when all dreams had a moment to be realised.

Perhaps she could paint in secret on the roof outside her room, where the fumes would not attract Amelia's attention. Marie had said that Monsieur Read had hinted at another big-name art dealer that he wanted to show her work to. If she really could make enough money, Genevieve would take Marie and leave, and they could set up a shop in some other part of Paris.

For the first time in months, the grey gloom shifted a little so that it didn't fit so snugly around her. She even glanced at a couple of warm shop windows on the way home, her mind searching out colours she could put on her palette for a picture for Marie.

That was how she saw him, seated in Madame Pushkina's *bistrot*.

The front table at Madame Pushkina's was in a little bow window that had old, stippled lead-lined glass. So she thought it was a trick of her wretched mind when she saw Sebastian sitting there, watching her pass. But then he lifted a hand to wave at her, and she stopped on the uneven cobbles of Passage Lhomme and stared.

'Don't stand there waiting for your mother to spot you. Inside, quickly,' hissed Madame Pushkina from the recessed doorway.

Inside, the place was warm, and steam rose off Genevieve's coat where the mist had settled on the wool.

'Come, out the back, I'll bring him through,' said Madame, giving a sniff.

Genevieve waited in the dim little office off the kitchen and soon Sebastian walked in, his hat in his hand, his coat over his arm.

'Genevieve,' he said, giving her a half smile, looking unsure of himself. He was pale and had aged in the few months since the autumn. He was thinner, too, and there were dark shadows under his eyes.

'What happened to you?' asked Genevieve. Her first instinct had been to run to him, but then she remembered the curt, formal tone of his last letters. She stood irresolute, holding her coat firmly about her middle.

Sebastian frowned.

'I stopped hearing from you. I was worried... after my last letter I didn't know if someone had paid you a visit. I was a fool, I shouldn't have put it in writing, only I was worried that you wouldn't have understood why my previous letters were so distant.'

'I haven't had a letter from you since November,' said Genevieve staring at him. His face paled further and he wet his lips and looked towards Madame Pushkina hovering in the kitchen outside.

'Madame,' he commanded, in a tone that didn't sound anything like the Sebastian Genevieve remembered from the autumn.

Madame Pushkina shuffled into the room, looking uncomfortable.

'What happened to my last letter? Why was it not given to Mademoiselle Dupuis?'

Madame Pushkina was gripping a sodden tea towel and grey water dripped from it onto the flagstone floor. She looked imploringly at Genevieve.

'Answer me, woman,' barked Sebastian.

It was not the sort of voice that could be disobeyed. Madame Pushkina dropped her eyes to the growing puddle at her feet and said miserably, 'It was Madame Dupuis. She guessed, and she took it from me. She threatened me. You know what she can be like, mademoiselle. I wouldn't for the world have betrayed you. I don't know how she found out.'

'It's alright, Madame Pushkina, I understand,' said Genevieve. She smiled at Sebastian in relief. She'd been a fool not to think of it for herself. It was inevitable that Amelia would find out. She was like a bloodhound on the scent of Genevieve's happiness. She would track it to its source and devour it.

'I thought you'd tired of me,' she said simply. To her horror, she felt tears pricking the back of her eyes. She blinked rapidly and hunted in her coat pocket for the handkerchief Marie had given her. She blew her nose, and when she looked at Sebastian again she found he was smiling at her with a tenderness that threatened to melt her joints and leave her helpless.

'Can I take you to dinner, and tell you just how wrong you were?' he asked.

'Oh, yes. I would like that very much.'

～

GENEVIEVE SENT Madame Pushkina to make sure Amelia wasn't home, and then she ran back to the doll hospital and quickly changed into the white gown she'd worn in Giverny. She retrieved the painting she'd done for Sebastian's Christmas present and met him where Passage Lhomme met rue de Charonne. Sebastian was quick to put his arm around her when she came towards him, wrapped in the only coat she owned. She'd flirted with the idea of stealing Amelia's sable, but she didn't want any part of Amelia mixed up with this evening.

'I want to get you somewhere warm,' said Sebastian, his face close to hers. 'Where to?'

'Away from here,' she said. 'Somewhere across the river.' Sebastian hailed a taxi and held on tightly to her hand as the taxi carried them away from the 11th, across Pont d'Austerlitz to Montparnasse. Not until they were seated side by side in the deep curve of a private banquette did he seem to relax.

'Genevieve, I missed you very much, you know,' he said, looking at her with his old intensity. 'The thought that something might have happened to you has been a torment to me. You don't know what it means to me to see your beautiful smile again.'

Genevieve smiled shyly. She didn't know how to be beautiful. All she had learned from Amelia was how to repel. She reached up and gently brushed her fingers along the frown that was furrowing his brow.

'What was in your last letter?' she asked him.

He stiffened and looked behind them at the couple in the next booth. He shook his head slightly.

'There's so much I have to tell you, and something serious I need to ask you, but not tonight. Tonight I would like to just watch your face and catch up on everything I missed over the past few months.'

'Well, here is something you missed out on,' she said, pulling the miniature from her purse. 'It was supposed to be your Christmas present.'

Sebastian unwrapped the painting from the tissue paper and smiled at the picture. 'It's as though you've painted my memory. I thought of you and those hot chocolates often while up in the mountains this winter.' He smiled at her. 'Tell me, what of your other paintings?'

'That's the last painting I did. Amelia came home just before I finished it, and I've told you her position on my painting.'

'It makes no sense to me,' said Sebastian. A waiter came over and showed them the menus, and they were some time discussing what to eat.

'What happened to your mother to make her so resentful?' Sebastian asked when the menus were cleared.

'She got polio just after I was born. It crippled her hands and she hasn't been able to paint since. She was the best of her generation. Everyone was very excited about the rules she was breaking and all that, and then overnight she was done. I think she tells herself she's sparing me a similar disappointment, but Marie says it's just jealousy.'

'What do you think?'

'A bit of each, probably. It was a struggle both emotionally and financially when her livelihood was taken like that, but she has a very unyielding disposition, so she's not grown accustomed to her disappointment with the passing of time. It's grown, and now her mind is as twisted as her hands. She's jealous and paranoid, and obsessed with the purity of her legacy. I'm not sure what she fears more; that her daughter's paintings become known and are substandard, or they become known and eclipse her own work.'

Another waiter appeared with the wine list, and Genevieve made the selection for both of them. She handed the menu back to the waiter, watching Sebastian as he stared at a family seated in a booth opposite. He looked sad and worried.

'How is your family?' she asked, following his gaze.

'Fine, thank you.' He smiled at her and squeezed her hand so that she would know that he wasn't brushing her off. Beneath the warm glow that had enveloped her since first seeing him in Madame Pushkina's, a current of unease rippled. He had changed since the autumn. There was that voice of command that he had used so easily and to such effect on poor witless Madame Pushkina. Then there was his reserve, which was now bordering on secrecy. And he was not quite at his ease, as though he were waiting for something to go wrong.

'So,' he said cheerfully, but still with that watchfulness in his eyes, 'will you give in to your mother, or will you find a way to paint?'

'I was on the verge of giving in,' she said, glancing at him from under her lashes. 'After those last, strange, formal letters, and then your silence, I didn't know what to think. I found it very hard to care about anything, even painting.'

His large hand squeezed hers again, and she smiled gently at him and rested her head on his shoulder.

'But then today, Marie told me of a crazy plan she has to show my work to some serious critics at the start of spring, and for the first time in weeks, I thought about painting again.'

'You'll do it? You'll take it up again?'

'Yes, I think so.'

'Good.'

Genevieve studied him from where her head rested on his shoulder. He had an arm about her and his eyes were shifting over the people seated at the other tables. His mouth was firm and pressed in a straight line.

'Why does it matter to you?'

He looked down at her, surprised. 'Because the only time I've seen you truly happy is when you're painting.'

'Oh.' He knew her so little and yet saw so much.

Their wine came, and then the food. They talked then fell silent, then talked again. Genevieve tried to distract Sebastian from whatever thoughts were worrying him. She was in a kind of daze, feeling beautiful and sophisticated in her white dress, eating at *La Closerie des Lilas* with Sebastian, who she thought had taken her heart and left it somewhere in the woods in Germany. Yet here he was, distracted and worried, but smiling like a schoolboy every time their eyes met.

It came to her with the dessert.

She was three courses and two and a half glasses of wine in, when she realised, suddenly, painfully, that she was in love.

The realisation made her shy, and she could barely lift her eyes to the chocolate board that Sebastian was urging her to choose from.

'Genevieve, what's the matter?' he asked, putting his lips close to her ear.

'Nothing,' she said, afraid to look at him. She selected a chocolate at random and put it in her mouth.

It tasted bitter and dry and stuck to the roof of her mouth. So she took a large sip of cognac to wash it down.

'Genevieve?' Sebastian tilted her chin so that she had no choice but to look him in the eye, and he saw everything. His own eyes darkened, and a muscle in his jaw quivered.

It felt like they stayed that way for an eternity, searching each other's souls.

'Can I see you tomorrow?' asked Sebastian in a low, urgent voice.

'Yes, of course. I'll get Marie to send me out early and she can cover for me.' She reached a hand up, hesitated, and then gently stroked his cheek.

'I wish you would tell me what is troubling you.'

'I don't want to worry you with it tonight. But tomorrow...' He sighed. 'Tomorrow I would like to go for a long walk. I have a lot I want to talk to you about. I need your opinion.'

'My opinion?' She was surprised. Nobody had ever asked for that before.

'Yes, my sweet one.' He smiled and then checked his watch. 'I ought to get you home.'

Genevieve nodded, though she was disappointed. She did not want to say goodbye to him again.

They rode back to Passage Lhomme in near silence, their hands intertwined tightly. Sebastian kept the taxi waiting for him as he walked Genevieve back to the doll hospital, and Genevieve was relieved to see that all was in darkness.

'You still owe me a waltz you, know,' Sebastian said, holding both her hands and looking down at her in the glow of the gas light that hung from the arch leading into the passage. Genevieve gave him a shy smile, and suddenly she couldn't bear to wait another day to feel his lips on hers. With her heart beating in a terrifying manner, she stood on her tiptoes and pressed her lips to his. He wrapped his arms around her and, holding her close, kissed her deeply.

CHAPTER 7

Genevieve crept up the dark staircase towards her room, her cheeks, lips, and heart aglow with love. When she got to the first floor landing where Amelia's room was, she tiptoed silently across the landing. A dark figure rose up at her out of the gloom, and she uttered a shriek before one of Amelia's clawed hands fell on her face.

'Shut up before you wake that fool Marie,' Amelia hissed, her voice husky with the cold. 'Where have you been?'

'Out,' said Genevieve, her chest rising and falling rapidly as she tried to catch her breath. 'With Pierre and some of his friends.'

'Liar,' snarled Amelia. 'You've been with that Nazi boy. Do you think I'm blind as well as crippled?'

Genevieve didn't answer.

'You're not to see him anymore.'

'He won't be here for long.'

'He won't be here,' Amelia stamped her foot, 'at all.'

'Why do you care?'

'Because it's my duty to care.'

Genevieve clutched her purse, and the glow from Sebastian and his nearness cooled. Her enthusiasm for Marie's scheme ebbed, and she pushed past Amelia to go up to her room. Why did John have to be such an inconstant lover? Why hadn't he kept her for just a few months longer?

'I know all about your pathetic lover and his traitorous ideas,' called Amelia to her back with relish. 'His family would not be pleased to hear what he's been so foolish to put into writing. I wonder what they'd pay to get it back? You silly fool. Of all the idiotic men in the world you could have thrown yourself at, you had to go and choose a German. Don't you know what your father suffered at their hands in the war? Get rid of him, do you hear? Or I send his letter to the German High Command.' She broke off, assailed by a coughing fit, and Genevieve stopped on the stairs and frowned down at Amelia, bent double in her thin, expensive silk nightdress.

'Why would they care?' she asked.

Amelia's eyes gleamed at her in the darkness. 'He hasn't told you then, about his squeamishness when it comes to the way things are done over there?' Genevieve couldn't see Amelia's face, but she could tell she was smiling. This was the sort of sport she lived for.

'They don't like that sort of talk in Germany, so I've heard. They've built special camps for dealing with dissidents. Your poor little Nazi boy would find it a treat, to get his hands dirty for once and learn what real work is like. Of course, I'm not sure that his little sister will take to it as well, but perhaps it would be better for her to have an early death and avoid what's coming to Germany.'

'Don't be ridiculous,' said Genevieve, but she was uncertain. Sebastian's worried look, his nervous behaviour all lent credence to Amelia's wild talk.

'Talk it over with lover boy,' suggested Amelia. 'You'll see he agrees with me.'

The floorboards creaked and Amelia turned away.

'You won't have me paint, you won't have me love,' said Genevieve down into the darkness. 'What is your plan then, Mother? What's the point of this existence?'

'I'm glad you've come so far,' said Amelia. 'There is no point. The sooner you come to terms with that, the easier your life will be.'

∼

GENEVIEVE MET Sebastian on the quai Saint-Bernard and they walked in the cold along the Seine together in the direction of the Sorbonne. Sebastian did not look like he had slept well; his face was pale and lined and his eyes were rimmed with red. Genevieve wanted to ask about things Amelia had mentioned, but she felt shy of saying them out loud. Sebastian was very proud of being a German, and it seemed absurd to suggest anything else.

The day was bitterly cold, there was a promise of more snow in the air, and Genevieve's shoes were not made for long walks in the freezing cold.

'Sebastian,' she said after they had passed Pont de Sully, 'where are we going?'

He slowed and looked down at her. His thoughts had been carrying him away and he looked surprised by the question.

'I'm sorry, Genevieve,' he said, stopping and brushing a mitted hand across her frozen cheeks. 'You're chilled to the bone. Shall we get hot chocolates?'

'Yes, let's.' She said, barely able to keep her teeth from chattering. 'And as we walk there, please, Sebastian, tell me what is going on.'

It was like the lancing of a wound as he described horror after horror that he had witnessed in his training. The dehumanisation process that was being visited on the young men that were being put through Germany's top military programs. The rounding up of people described as Genetically Defective. First it had been their political opponents, then the Jews, and last November it had been the gypsies. Baron von Mylius had intervened for the gypsies that camped on the von Mylius estate every summer. They were as much a part of the estate as the house and the generations of workers—fathers to sons, mothers to daughters— that had called it home.. His intervention hadn't done the gypsies, or the baron, any good. He'd been taken away for questioning, and had been very ill ever since.

'He is dying, Genevieve. Whatever they did to him, it is killing him. I don't think he'll see another summer.'

'Sebastian!' Genevieve stopped and looked at him in horror. She could not imagine the large, burly baron from last autumn now on his death bed. Behind Sebastian, the Seine tumbled along hungrily and the sky was grey and low.

'Mother will re-marry as soon as she can,' said Sebastian evenly. 'She's been unfaithful to Father for some time. Her lover is prominent in the Nazi party and the whole family will be expected to fall into line. I won't let them get their hands on Tabitha and Max. If father dies, I become their guardian.'

They walked on in silence, and Sebastian's strides lengthened in response to his agitated thoughts.

'Sebastian, please, slow down,' said Genevieve, struggling to keep up. He stopped at once and pulled her arm through his.

'We will have to leave Germany,' he said.

Genevieve watched his profile, the taunt lines of his face. Her heart grieved for him.

'For how long?'

'We will have to prepare for the fact that we may not be able to return.'

'Oh, Sebastian, I am sorry.'

He nodded, but his mind had already moved on. 'That letter I sent, the one you didn't get, I outlined much of this to you in that. If it got into the wrong hands, they would probably shoot me. Perhaps for Mother's sake they would send me to a camp rather than kill me outright, but that doesn't worry me so much as the fact that they will use it to force the children into their youth programs.'

Genevieve thought of Tabitha, all innocence and enthusiasm, now caught in the darkness as the world unravelled around her. And Max, so full of bravado, so desperate to prove himself, what would the German military do to him?

'Back to the usual for the hot chocolates?' Sebastian asked, breaking in on her anxiety.

Genevieve took him instead to a small place nearby, and they sat by the fire in the wood-panelled room and drank their hot chocolates and nibbled at hot pastries.

'Genevieve,' Sebastian said, when they had finished. 'There's something I want to ask you. God knows it's not for the world how I wanted to do this, but if I don't speak now, I don't know if I will have the chance again.' His light-blue eyes were clearer now that he was not hiding things from her, and he was looking at her with a fierce love. She dropped her eyes to the table and balled her hands into fists in her lap.

'I want you to marry me. I don't have a home to offer you, or even a good name. I'll be stateless, jobless, and have two children in tow. If I knew I could be sure of seeing you again once we flee, I wouldn't ask you now, but I didn't want to leave Paris without you knowing just how much I love you.'

Her knuckles were white with the effort of holding herself back. He loved her. And now she had to break his heart.

'I... can't.' she said hopelessly.

'Genevieve—'

'Amelia read your letter. If I agree to marry you, she'll send it to your officers. She only let me see you today to say goodbye. For good.'

Sebastian's face paled, and he set his mug of hot chocolate down on the table abruptly.

'What's to stop her using it once we've parted?'

'Her love of power. She won't relinquish such a weapon easily.'

Sebastian pulled his cigarette case from his pocket, his face carved into deep creases.

'I don't want to leave my father in their power. I won't flee while he lives, but the moment he—' Sebastian broke off, the hand that was trying to light his cigarette shaking. Gently, Genevieve took the lighter from him and lit the cigarette for him. Neither of them spoke for a moment. Genevieve lit her own cigarette and watched the first flakes of snow come down outside as she drew the smoke into her lungs.

'It won't be more than a couple of months,' said Sebastian at length, his face drawn, and his thoughts hidden from her. 'Then I'll come back to Paris with Tabitha and Max, and your mother won't have any further power over us.'

Wouldn't she? Genevieve exhaled, sending a cloud of smoke over her shoulder, imagining Amelia's fury if she found her married, happy.

'It's too dangerous, Sebastian. She'll be watching me, and she'll have you handed over to the police and sent back to Germany.' She took another deep draw on her cigarette, wishing they'd ordered something stronger than hot chocolates. Then she straightened in her seat, smiling blandly, and drawing on all the tricks she'd seen Amelia play off over the years.

'We are like autumn leaves, you and I. We've worked so

far only because the light has been right. It comes in gently from underneath and shows us to best advantage. But our time is up. The light has paled and now the leaves must wither and die. We were not meant to stay together forever.'

'But Genevieve—'

'I can't even picture it, you and me marrying. Who should we ask to witness it, your mother or mine?' She gave a tinkling laugh, like the sound of breaking crystalware.

'Please, Genevieve—'

She could not look at him; pale with distress, his eyes searching her face, looking for the truth. She turned her head away and looked out the window at the empty terrace tables. She took a breath, keeping Amelia's venomous face in her mind's eye. She needed to give him something he would believe, something that would keep him away from her. She would not risk his life to Amelia's whims.

'Besides, Sebastian, what about my painting? You said yourself I'm never happy without it. How can I paint if I'm on the run with you and your kid brother and sister? This Monsieur Read is my big chance, perhaps the only one I will ever get. And you ask me to throw it away?'

Sebastian was very still, his dear, clear eyes fixed on her, but she could not meet his look.

'No, Genevieve. They were not mere words before. I love you. I would not ask that of you.' He took a handful of *francs* from his pocket and dropped them on the table. Then he got up and giving Genevieve one of his formal, funny little bows, he left the café, walking alone out into the snow.

CHAPTER 8

Genevieve did not hear from Sebastian again after he'd left her sitting alone at their table the day he'd proposed, and Amelia did not give her the letter. She said it would keep for now, in case Genevieve got any ideas about starting to paint or write to Sebastian again.

It was Marie who had suggested the way out.

They sat together late one night stitching the satin dress for Suzette, the doll Marie had become obsessed with. The lamps were all ablaze, and Genevieve's back and fingers were sore from the hours she'd spent hunched over her embroidery frame. A fire crackled in the grate, the smell of applewood sweetening the air of the workroom. It would have been cosy had not the shadow of Amelia hung over the place like a fog.

'Do you know why I stitch these little hearts into all my work?' Marie asked as she loosened the doll's petticoat from her frame.

Genevieve shook her head.

'It is so that, if one day he sees one of my creations, he will know that it was I who made it, and that I still think of him.'

Genevieve stared at Marie, her needle mid-air, green thread taut.

'Who?'

'The man I loved. That I still love.'

'What happened?'

Marie lifted her eyes from the cloth she was holding. 'Amelia.'

Shocked, Genevieve bent back over her embroidery, unable to face her own heartache reflected in her aunt's face.

'He was from a grand estate near the village where we grew up. We met through the church, of all places. He was overseeing the distribution of goods we had made and collected for the poor.' Marie stopped, her cheeks flushed.

'He complimented my sewing and asked if I could make some items he had noticed that many people in the parish were without. He was odd, for a man, in that he noticed things like that. We worked together all through the winter, and we fell in love.'

Marie shook out the petticoat and then fitted it carefully onto Suzette.

'What did she do?' whispered Genevieve, looking up from the vine she was stitching.

'Amelia? She went to his mother, told her that I'd been compromised, and that we wanted compensation or marriage. I hadn't...we hadn't.' Marie's colour deepened and she wouldn't meet Genevieve's eyes.

'I don't know what she paid Amelia,' she continued, 'only that it was enough for her to come to Paris and pay for the art school she'd always dreamed of attending. She didn't even tell me what she'd done. I found out after weeks of silence, when I finally worked up the courage to go to the manor house and ask for him. He'd been sent away, and the scorn with which those servants treated me...' Marie stopped and closed her eyes, pressing a trembling hand to her breast.

'It seemed such a dreadful thing at the time. I was young and much too sensitive. I should have insisted on seeing the family and finding out the truth. But I was too timid. And I have paid for that with a lifetime of loneliness.'

She put Suzette down and turned to Genevieve, the tremors gone from her hands. 'Tonight I see the worth in my suffering. It is something if I can prevent you from making the same mistake. Start painting again. You can make a decent living with the skill God has given you. Don't waste it. And when your man with the beautiful handwriting is safely out of Germany, then you go to him. Amelia can't hurt you if she can't find you.'

'And if she finds out before he leaves Germany?'

'You cannot get the letter from her,' said Marie slowly, 'she keeps it on her always. I have seen her taking it out and looking at it, gloating at her power. No, you will have to be careful. But you can work, even in a small way, and start saving for when he returns. And we should not abandon hope in Monsieur Read. He may have the power to make you a wealthy woman. One of you ought to have a little money, before you run off into the world together.'

'I don't think he will come back after the things I said to him.'

'Maybe not, but it is best to be prepared, just in case.'

∼

As a rule, Genevieve didn't go into *Magasin Sennelier* on the Quai Voltaire because it was known as the best art store, not only by reputation, but also by price. It was the sort of place where Picasso came to get his colours hand mixed. There was no pricing anywhere in the shop; you brought your selection of items to the wooden counter with the gilt cash register, and the superior looking girl added them all up according to some mysterious pricing guide known only to her.

It was a small tube. Perhaps it wouldn't be too terribly expensive. Genevieve looked down at the cool little tube of paint that lay in her palm, the colour vibrant.

'Is there a problem?' the girl behind the front counter asked, her brown eyes pinning Genevieve to the spot and, Genevieve felt, doing an expert analysis of her financial situation.

'No, *merci*,' said Genevieve, placing the tube of paint on the counter.

'65 *francs*,' said the girl, wrapping the paint deftly in crisp white tissue paper.

Genevieve went cold. That was a huge chunk of the little money she'd managed to make with the sale of her illicit paintings. But she needed this paint if she was to make the sort of impression she was hoping for. The secret exhibition for Monsieur Read was only four nights away. Genevieve thought of her painting, sitting unfinished in the box under her window; good, but lacking the depth she'd been hoping for. Lacking the vibrancy from the french vermilion paint in the girl's limp hand. She took a deep breath, opened her purse and handed over most of her money.

~

Very carefully, Genevieve squeezed a drop of the vermilion paint onto her palette and, holding her breath, dipped the tip of her paintbrush in the mixture. She stood back a moment, and looked at the painting she'd done of the view outside her window. She'd painted it at half moon, a hazy semi-circle almost lost in the misty winter night sky. It was mostly rooftops, the chimney pots of course, the hidden windows, and a slice of the lives lived behind them.

Genevieve leaned into her picture, done on an offcut of plywood donated by Pierre, and added a thin layer of paint to the chimney pots closest to the window. She stood back and chewed the inside of her cheek. The effect was instantaneous. She kept working, touching up the picture with the new paint, adding colour to the rooftop windows, the street lamp in the bottom corner, and lastly to the lamp that burned in her own bedroom window. When she'd finished, she set the picture by the window and stood back. Her fingers tingled around her paintbrush as she looked at the painting, and she smiled. The balance was perfect. The paint added life to the picture. It not only drew the eye, but endowed the shadows with more intrigue, so that it was not just the rooftops the viewer saw, but in their mind's eye, the room behind the window, the occupants, and their lives. The vibrancy of the vermilion paint became the passion of the observer. You were transported into a little rooftop Parisian apartment, and the warmth of the colours pulled you into the painting, inviting you to stay, so that you felt bereft when you had to look away.

She only hoped the illusion would hold up on Saturday night when Monsieur Read and his buyer came to see it.

~

AMELIA KNEW that something was up. Genevieve could tell from the way she watched her in the lead up to the secret exhibition. She was kept busy all Saturday as they put the finishing touches on Suzette, who was to be delivered for a birthday party that night. Late in the afternoon she was sent out for more cherry red twist. They'd run out before finishing the flowers on Suzette's skirt. When Genevieve returned to the Passage Lhomme with the twist in her coat pocket, she saw Amelia arguing with Madame Pushkina.

Genevieve didn't know whether to be glad that Amelia had not guessed that she was painting, or terrified that she thought that she may still be in contact with Sebastian. She needed the painting to sell well and replace the funds she'd squandered on the vermilion paint. As soon as she could be sure that Sebastian was safely out of Germany, she would leave. She didn't have anywhere to go, and her only thought was that she would retreat to Giverny, in the hope that Sebastian, if he ever wanted to see her again, would come looking for her where the light and the leaves were just right for each other.

∽

It was Genevieve who got the job of delivering Suzette to the grand house where her owner was celebrating her 70th birthday. It meant that she would miss Monsieur Read, but it was her painting that he was coming to see. She put on an evening gown, the sort of thing she supposed people wore to art exhibitions, in case she should make it back in time. Amelia had gone out in the company of her latest victim, and Genevieve was thankful that this latest distraction had kept her from home so much over the past month and made subterfuge easier.

As Genevieve stepped out into the Passage Lhomme, with Suzette safely packed in a box of wood shavings under her arm, Marie hurried out after her.

'So silly of me, I forgot to include the bill.' She handed Genevieve a fat envelope and then hurried out of the cold. Genevieve tucked the bill in the pocket of her coat and walked quickly to the Métro. As always when she passed Madame Pushkina's, she had to fight the urge to search for Sebastian sitting in the window. It did no good to look for what wasn't there, and if Amelia noticed, it would only get her and poor Madame Pushkina in trouble.

~

Suzette's delivery was more complicated than Genevieve had allowed time for. She'd not bargained on being kept waiting for so long, because the man who had ordered the repaired doll for his mother could not be found among the party guests. When he was eventually found the transaction was very brief, except that Genevieve forgot to give him the bill that she'd tucked in her pocket. When she went back the man had been joined by his brother. She handed the bill to the older gentleman, but it was quickly snatched by the younger, who looked most peculiar. She'd not stayed to hear their complaints over the cost of the work she could still feel in her back and fingers. Let them see the joy it brought their mother first. She hurried back to Passage Lhomme, eager to hear what the art critic and the buyer had thought of her painting.

As she approached the shop, she saw large squares of white paper strewn across the cobbles. She quickened her pace until she reached the first piece, picking it up with horror. They were pages from her notebooks, her sketches muddied and torn from being trampled into the street. A man in a long coat and a dark trilby leaned against the doorway. She turned to him, still holding the page. 'Monsieur Read?'

'He's gone to see if there's anything he can salvage,' said the man, taking a cigar from his mouth. He was French, and spoke with the quick rhythm of the south. '*Such* a shame. He was really excited about this one.'

Genevieve stared a moment at the man's shadowy face, trying to understand. Then she turned to the window.

It was smeared with great streaks of vermilion paint.

'Oh no,' she said, her head swimming.

She stepped closer and peered into the window space she'd set up so carefully after Amelia had left for the evening. Her beautiful, bright, expensive vermilion paint covered everything she'd arranged in the window. The mirror she'd hung on the false back of the window display had been smashed in its frame. The lamp she'd switched on to give a little light was also smashed, and the rickety chair she'd put beside the painting and covered with cushions was overturned and now had only three legs. The cushions had been slit and feathers littered the space, sticking to the vermilion paint in a hundred different places. The effect was almost comical, except that in the middle of it all, propped drunkenly on the desk close to the window, her painting of *Girl in Moonlight* was completely destroyed.

CHAPTER 9

Genevieve stood staring at the carnage, a chill colder than the Paris pavement in winter wrapping around her spine. All her hopes, all her money, gone. Did Amelia even have a lover, or had that been part of her sick game to lull Genevieve into a false sense of security?

'Oh, clever of you, Herbert,' the man in the trilby called.

Genevieve turned around, took a deep breath, and balled her hands into fists.

A tall, thin man was walking out of the doorway, carrying the larger piece of plywood Pierre had given her.

Her heart knocked painfully against her ribs, and her mouth went dry.

'No!' she cried, but the man paid no attention to her.

'Please, no, you can't. It's, it's not finished,' she said desperately, clasping her gloved hands together. The man, Herbert Read she assumed, glanced at her briefly, but paid no attention to her plea. His eyes were glittering as he rested the large picture on the cobbles.

'I hope you haven't been idle, Mademoiselle Dupuis,' he said in his precise English accent, panting with the effort of carting the large picture down three flights of narrow stairs. 'This might just save face for both of us.'

'You can't, monsieur. Listen to me, please don't do this. It's nowhere near ready.'

'Don't be daft, Paul. Get her out of the way, would you?'

Monsieur Read stood balancing the large piece of plywood while the man in the trilby put a strong arm around her.

'Stop it,' she said, struggling, 'let me go! It's my loss for heaven's sake. I don't want that painting shown.'

'Nude self-portrait?' asked Paul with a laugh. He looked like he was considering trying to kiss her. Amelia appeared in the doorway to the doll hospital, standing in an evening dress, and swaying as she gripped the door frame.

'Monsieur, no!' Genevieve cried in anguish, but it was too late. Monsieur Read had turned the crate side around and her secret painting was facing them all, in the full glare of the streetlight.

⁓

THE MEN STARED. Genevieve wrenched free of Paul's grip only to have Monsieur Read grab her elbow.

'Mademoiselle...' His voice was strange, and Genevieve shook his hand from her angrily.

'I told you it wasn't ready. You had. No. Right.' She was talking through her teeth, and the tears she had been fighting for so long started dripping down her cheeks. She saw Amelia advancing towards them. But Monsieur Read wasn't looking at her, or at Amelia. He was staring at her painting.

He breathed out with a low whistle. A smile stretched his lips and the pre-occupied look vanished from his eyes.

'I knew you had it in you, mademoiselle. I knew from the moment I saw those window displays in the autumn.' He dragged his eyes away from the painting and smiled at Genevieve. 'Look at Monsieur Anouilh.'

The man called Paul was staring at the painting, his mouth open, and his cigar cooling between his fingers. He took a step towards the sheet of plywood, his eyes darting over the surface of the picture.

At the entrance to the doll hospital, the door slammed.

~

'I'LL HAVE you know the police are on their way,' said Amelia, her voice rasping, her clawed hands clutching at a sable wrap that was slipping from her thin shoulders. Her eyes were bright and sunken in her sallow face.

'Madame, we mean you no harm,' said Monsieur Read in his stiff manner. 'We are here simply to talk to this young lady about her painting.'

'That painting is not hers to give.'

The two men looked at Genevieve, and then back at Amelia.

'The girl's aunt assured me that this is her work,' said Monsieur Read, with an uneasy glance towards Monsieur Anouilh.

'Open your eyes, Herbert,' snapped Amelia. 'Doesn't it remind you of anything? Anyone? Don't I?'

The tall Englishman stared into the gloom, and Amelia took another unsteady step into the light.

'Good heavens, Amelia?' he asked, wonder in his tone. 'I had no idea. Why didn't you say so at once? Why didn't you tell me you were painting again?'

'You worked it out anyway,' said Amelia, her mouth twisted into a scowl.

'This is, quite simply, brilliant. Even more so than your

earlier work. Even old Anouilh's excited by it. This is going to put you back on the scene in a big way, my girl.'

'You can sell it?'

'Sell it? It will send the auction house into a frenzy.'

In the weak light of the gas lamps, Genevieve saw Amelia's eyes gleam. Genevieve's stomach clenched, and her mouth stung with the taste of bile.

'Shall we discuss it over dinner?' Amelia asked, pulling herself up straighter.

'Absolutely,' said Monsieur Read, and Genevieve saw then that he was an old conquest of Amelia's.

'Wait here then, boys. Genevieve, follow me.'

Neither of the men would look at her as she gave her painting another glance, her tears still damp on her cheeks. She reached out and touched the painted sunbeams that danced through the stained-glass window and filtered down through the soaring columns of Notre-Dame to light the couple being wed in the little side chapel; a man, tall with broad shoulders, and with a distinctive tilt to his head, as he watched his bride, who was small and dressed in white with tousled blonde curls escaping her veil.

'There's something a bit off about the rose window, now that I look at it,' said Monsieur Anouilh coming up behind her.

'It's not the rose window.'

'No, I can see that. What is it?'

'It's the harvest moon.'

'Genevieve!' Amelia's voice was sharp from the doorway, and Genevieve turned quickly and followed her mother.

'Give me the letter,' she said, speaking quickly before Amelia could confuse her with her hate. 'Give me Sebastian's letter, and I'll let them all think the painting is yours. I'll never paint another thing if it keeps your treachery secret, as long as first you make Sebastian safe.'

Amelia, pulling on a large fur coat, started laughing; a thin high-pitched sound that ended with another coughing fit so violent that she had to grab the back of a chair until it subsided.

'I've known Herbert Read for longer than you've been alive. Do you really think he'll listen to you? Besides, I've already sent the letter to Germany, after I saw that boy lurking around here yesterday. You little fool. Did you really think I wouldn't? I know all about his plans to meet you here after that pathetic showing you and Marie cooked up. You'll have a merry time of it, I'm sure. All of you.' Amelia smirked, and then turned and went up the stairs to get her purse.

Genevieve stood a moment in the dark of the shop, feeling emptier than after a week of no food.

Sebastian was back in Paris.

She sank against the counter and looked over at paint-smeared window, staring at the debris inside the display space. Was he on leave, or on the run?

Voices sounded outside, and then someone came into the shop, pausing on the threshold in the gloom.

It was Sebastian.

'You told me you couldn't even picture marrying me, the idea was so absurd,' he said, walking towards her when his eyes had grown accustomed to the gloom.

'It's not what you think,' she said desperately, as he took a step towards her. His foot stepped on the splayed spine of one of her destroyed notebooks, and he looked down, seeing the destruction all about them for the first time.

Frowning, he knelt on the ground beside her and gathered up the pages from her notebook. She stayed still, watching his strong, brown hands, illuminated by the moonlight that snuck through the window, cradling her sketches, she remembered what it was like to have those hands on her skin, in her hair; those fingers tilting her chin towards him, his lips consuming her. She closed her eyes again, her heart aflame with the agony of having to push him away a second time.

There was an almighty crash from upstairs, and Genevieve's head lifted with a start. Sebastian was looking at her, his blue eyes bright in a face that was, now that she dared to look at him, was swollen in parts. He looked as though he had been beaten.

She gave a little cry and reached out a hand to stroke his swollen jaw gently.

'What happened to you?'

'I disobeyed a commanding officer. Hush, don't look so worried. I was lucky not to be shot on the spot.'

'So you're not on leave?'

'No,' he took one of her hands in his. 'I'm on the run. It happened sooner than I was prepared for.'

'Are they looking for you? What happens if they find you?'

'I'll be sent back to Germany for trial and execution I imagine. But they won't find me, nobody knows I am here.'

Another crash sounded above their heads. Sebastian frowned at the ceiling.

'What was that?'

'Amelia.'

He handed her a sheaf of her notebook pages and she crammed them into a drawer under the counter, her heart pounding.

'Sebastian, Amelia saw you here yesterday. She sent the letter to Germany, and she knows you're going to be here tonight. She's called the police. Do they have the power to send you back to Germany?'

Sebastian wet his lips, his hand tightening on hers.

'They could. There will be pressure from Germany to

send me back when it becomes known where I am. It might become politically expedient to send me back.'

'I've been so terribly afraid she would do something like this.'

Sebastian looked at her keenly. 'Is that why you spoke to me the way you did when I asked you to marry me?'

Genevieve stared miserably at him, not wanting to hurt him any further, but aware that by giving him hope, she was encouraging him to put himself and his family in danger.

'Why did you come back, Sebastian?'

'Because I love you, and I could not keep away.'

∼

'WELL, THAT'S A SHAME,' said Amelia, giving a wheezing laugh from where she stood with difficulty at the bottom of the stairs. Her face was mottled and purple, and she clutched at the banister with her paw-like hands. 'Because once your superiors receive your letter that I sent off this afternoon, I'm afraid you'll have to keep away for a very long time.'

Sebastian stiffened and Genevieve, fear enveloping her like a blanket heavy with rain, clutched at his arm. He took his arm from her and stepped in front of her, protecting her from Amelia.

'You should know, Madame Dupuis, that my intentions toward your daughter are honourable. I have asked her to marry me.'

The gaze from Amelia's dark-rimmed eyes darted between them. She smiled in a snarling sort of way and then spat in Sebastian's face, a globule of wine-stained phlegm landing on his cheek.

'She'd be a widow before the month is out,' she said, her eyes bright in her gaunt face. 'They're coming for you. There's not much time left, poor Romeo.' Her eyes slid to Genevieve, held back by the arm Sebastian had thrown around her when Amelia spat on him. 'Now it is your turn to find out what it is to have everything taken from you at once. Now, daughter, we are even.'

∼

GENEVIEVE AND SEBASTIAN fled the Passage Lhomme via the back door of Pierre's workshop. They saw no sign of any policemen, but Genevieve could not be easy. She and Sebastian walked the softly lit streets of Bastille until they arrived at the banks of Canal Saint-Martin. They had not said much to each other.

'What will happen when your letter gets to Germany?' Genevieve asked as they walked by the water, listening to the faint strains of music coming from somewhere along the canal.

'My guess is my new stepfather will make it all disappear.'

'Your new...? Oh, Sebastian, no. Your father?'

Sebastian hung his head and didn't say anything for a moment.

'Two weeks ago. Mother was away in Berlin. She came back only just in time for the funeral.'

'Max and Tabitha?'

'Are following me as soon as their passes can be arranged. For now, they are in the care of an old family retainer.'

A barge docked at the edge of the canal had lights strung up over the deck, and a band was playing while beautiful couples danced. Sebastian paused and took Genevieve's hand in his.

'I couldn't disappear without trying once more to convince you of how much I love you.'

She looked up at him, at his dear, handsome face, and at the eyes that still knew how to search in wonder despite everything that had happened to his family and his country in the past six months.

'You took a foolish risk,' she said, whispering, not feeling quite safe, even out here.

'It would have been more foolish to lose you.' He bent down and touched his lips to hers, and she caught her breath, her heart and her head taken up with the intoxicating dizziness he always caused in her.

'There's something I have to show you,' she said when the band started another song.

She led him out from the shadows beneath the naked branches of the plane trees and shrugged her coat off, revealing an elegant navy-blue silk evening gown that hugged her frame and left her arms and back bare in the moonlight. Then she stepped closer to Sebastian and slipped her hands under the lapels of his greatcoat, easing it from his shoulders before tossing it on the ground with her own.

He closed his warm, strong fingers over her hand, and his other hand rested on her lower back, causing her to shiver as he pulled her into a waltz. She rested her head on his shoulder, and he kept his eyes on her, their faces almost touching.

They waltzed in silence until the end of the song, and then as the band started up its next number, Sebastian held her at arm's length and smiled down at her, his beautiful blue eyes twinkling.

'Anybody would think that you'd been waltzing your whole life.' He kept looking at her, and his smile faded and a frown creased his brow again.

'Do you remember telling me that the reason the autumn colours are so beautiful, is because the light comes from underneath the leaves? That in any other season they would be duller or wrong?'

Genevieve looked past him to the floating fairy dance on the lake. She didn't want to think about that day right now.

'Stay with me, Genevieve. This is important.'

She brought her eyes to his face and gave in to the intensity of his gaze. She shivered, though she had not been cold before, and felt a fire flicker in her chest.

'Do you not wonder,' Sebastian said, 'that autumn leaves don't colour at any other time of year? That the light and the leaves come together at the exact time to bring out the best in each other? Apart they are nothing remarkable, there's something off, even, but together they are magic. Because they were designed that way, made for each other.'

The music dipped to a softer tone that floated over the canal. Laughter came with it, and behind Sebastian's head, three brave stars shone brighter than the Paris lights.

'The leaves will brown off and die,' said Sebastian, watching her closely, 'and the light will fade too, and disappear into winter. But next season, they will both reign again, and so it will be until the end of time.'

A bang sounded from somewhere on the canal and Genevieve jumped, and Sebastian held her close in his arms. A shower of sparks lit the sky and a cheer went up from the barge. Genevieve's heart was thumping in her chest, and she was shaking from the force of it.

'I'm really asking you this time,' said Sebastian, brushing her wild curls back with his warm, gentle hand. 'If you send me away this time, I can't come back. I have to join Max and Tabitha. We are all three of us going into hiding. I don't have much time if the police are already on the lookout. I don't want there to be any trace of us, in case anyone from Germany comes to settle a score. We'll be cut adrift, and I won't be able to reach you. I shall be a dull autumn leaf out of time and season.'

'No, Sebastian,' she said, reaching up and brushing the tips of her fingers against his lips, 'you could only ever be the light.'

He closed his eyes and rested his forehead on hers.

'Is that a yes?' he asked quietly.

She hesitated. Under the lowering strains of the music she could hear the water lapping against the side of the canal.

'What are you afraid of?' he asked. 'I thought perhaps it was to protect me that you sent me away last time.'

'Yes, that's right.'

'But now?' He opened his eyes and looked at her closely.

'I'm afraid of destroying you.'

'Because of your mother?'

Genevieve nodded. 'I've seen the way she loves. Her infatuations are poisonous, but when she loves it consumes people until there is nothing left. What if I am the same and do that to you, and we don't find out until it's too late for you to escape?'

'My darling,' said Sebastian, cupping her face in his hands and frowning at her. 'I don't want to escape you, ever.'

'But what if we fight? What happens when we scrap and you can't walk out on me. What then?'

'Then we get angry at each other, we calm down, we forgive each other, we compromise. And it might be hell, but we'll get better at it. We will have the rest of our lives to practice.'

'Sebastian...' Genevieve closed her eyes and took a shaky breath. 'That painting tonight, it wasn't me imagining us marrying; it was me imagining what sort of person I would have to be to make such a fantasy possible. The bride in that painting, she doesn't exist. She's pliable and delicate and feminine; full of hope, rather than fear. Her heart is a golden ball rather than a twisted knot of thorns.'

'Genevieve, listen to me. I don't want some imaginary version of you. I want to marry you, my wonderful darling. Do you love me?'

'What?'

'It's the only thing that would stop me from marrying you, if you didn't love me.'

Another shower of fireworks exploded behind Sebastian's head, the green and purple lighting their faces briefly and showing the strain in his eyes more clearly. Genevieve curled her hands into fists where they were resting against his chest.

'Yes,' she whispered. Another firework exploded and hissed in answer to her words, and Sebastian crushed her to him in a sudden, fierce hug.

'Oh, my darling,' he said into her ear, and the passion that was unchained in his voice made her knees go weak. She had not realised how much he had been holding back from her, waiting to know how she felt. His arms tightened around her, and he kissed her forehead and then her eyebrow, and then her cheek until his lips found hers. She thought that if his hold on her had not been so strong, she would have fallen for want of support from her legs.

He pulled back and looked down at her in the moonlight. 'You will marry me, won't you?'

His face was drawn and white, and as she looked at him, all her fears crowded in on her. But Sebastian was warm and holding her tight, and the darkness of her mind was not proof against the silver light that bound them both together at the side of the canal.

'Yes,' she said, tears gathering in her eyes. 'If you're sure.'

He laughed and kissed her again, and she felt the fear that had haunted her at the thought of marrying Sebastian drain out of her like poison wicked from a wound.

'Will you meet me at Notre-Dame first thing in the morning, say eight o'clock? We'll find a priest and see what it will take to get us married as soon as possible.' He took her hands in his, brought them up to his face, and kissed them. 'I don't want to walk away from you again. I want to be bound to you for the rest of my life, starting tomorrow.'

CHAPTER 10

Genevieve stood in Parvis Notre-Dame at a quarter to eight, her mouth dry. The early morning sunlight filtered down through the mist still left over from the night-time, bathing the entrance to the cathedral in a shaft of golden light that was straight from a Monet.

She paused on the edge of the sunlight, and looked about for Sebastian. He had taken rooms in a small hotel in the Marais, just over the river. He was probably inside already, waiting at the chapel she had painted for them.

She stepped into the sunlight, and her soul lightened further as she walked through the glowing motes that danced in the morning breeze. She walked alone and happy to the entrance of the most wonderful church in Paris, and passed inside to meet her fiancé.

But he wasn't there.

So sure had she been that he would be early, that the bare pews took her by surprise.

At fifteen minutes past eight, she began to grow cross at his tardiness.

At half past eight she was anxious.

At eight forty-five she walked around the whole of the cathedral, in case he was waiting in a side chapel.

At nine o'clock she knew something terrible had happened.

Was it Amelia's doing? Had his government the means to get to him so quickly, even here in Paris?

She sat in a hard pew in front of the high altar, the wood cold at her back. A headache, just a dull throb left over from the exhaustion of the night before, took hold of her. It beat at her head until she thought her skull would break with the pain. A lump grew in her throat and became unbearable, and her eyes strained with the effort of not crying.

She stood unsteadily and left. Outside the sun was warming more of the square, and people were smiling in the warmth.

One weak-willed tear escaped and slid down the edge of her face.

The sun was nothing but a liar.

∽

THERE WAS a large crowd gathered in Passage Lhomme when Genevieve returned. She wondered if Madame Pushkina had had too much of her home-made vodka and was dancing on her tables again. But it wasn't Madame Pushkina. It was Amelia. She was dead.

Two men in cheap suits came out of the doll hospital, covering their noses and mouths with their handkerchiefs. The people of this district did not need infectious disease spelled out to them. It had been stealing their family members all their lives. They stepped back as one, and Genevieve was left alone by the front door.

'Spanish 'flu,' one man was saying glumly to another. 'I knew it'd come back.'

'That's poor Monsieur Read done for,' muttered Pierre, who had come over from his shop to slouch by Genevieve. 'She was kissing him last night, after they'd started on the gin. Looked like she was going to suffocate the silly dog.'

'We'll have to tell the authorities,' said the other cheap-suited man, looking annoyed at the bother. 'They'll probably want to shut down the street.'

Genevieve made her way to the edge of the crowd before either of the men could notice her and lock her in with Amelia's infectious corpse. She saw clearly in her memory the purple-streaked flecks of spit splattering Sebastian's face.

~

THE ADDRESS SEBASTIAN had given her the night before turned out to be a fussy little hotel in the Marais with a façade that was painted bright blue. The corridors were busy as the guests went down to breakfast or came back to grab coats and bags before heading out for a day in Paris. Genevieve didn't look at anyone, but let the residents past as she searched the numbers on the doors. Memories of the blueish tinge on Amelia's face were merging with the pale, lined look that had been on Sebastian's towards the end of the night. Why, oh why, had she taken Sebastian's coat off him last night? Why had she kept him dancing in the cold so long?

She reached Sebastian's door and opened it without even thinking of knocking, so sure was she that he was on his death bed. She walked into a small, warm room to find Sebastian standing, swaying, by the bed, with one hand gripping the bed head and the other shielding his eyes from the light. He had his suit jacket on over his pyjama shirt and his feet were sockless in his brogues.

Genevieve closed the curtains and crossed to Sebastian,

where he was all but falling over. She put her arms around him.

'Sebastian,' she said softly, 'you don't need to go out. I've come to you. You can rest now.'

He took his hand from his eyes, and she was shocked by the blue tinge of his skin.

'You came? I'm late, Genevieve. Please don't go. I don't want to be late, but I can't find my pants. You said you'd marry me, but you won't if I'm late.'

'Of course I'll marry you. You don't need to worry about your silly pants. Hop into bed and rest now.' He collapsed down onto the mattress.

'Yes, that's right, like that,' she said, as she struggled against his bulk to take the suit jacket off him. His head was restless on the creased pillow, the horrible blue colour of his skin intensifying. His breathing was slow and laboured, rasped out with great effort.

She found a flannel in the bathroom and soaked it under the cold tap, then laid it on Sebastian's brow. 'There, rest now,' she said gently.

'I'm late,' he muttered.

Genevieve moved to the telephone and picked up the receiver. 'Yes, this is Monsieur von Mylius' room. We need the doctor urgently. Monsieur is having difficulty breathing.'

~

THE DOCTOR, wearing a worn black coat and a tired expression, came in carrying a large black bag.

'Monsieur von Mylius?' he inquired, stepping up to the bed. His trained eye ran over Sebastian's gaunt face and cyanotic colour and the seemingly habitual frown he wore deepened.

'When did the illness come upon him?' he asked.

Genevieve told him briefly about Amelia and her encounter with Sebastian the night before. The frown on the doctor's face smoothed out, and he assumed a blank expression that was worse than the frown.

He proceeded to examine Sebastian. Genevieve waited by the window, her hands knitted tightly together. The day was warming up outside, the terraces of the cafés were filling up, and laughter, birds, and the occasional horn could all be heard from the street below as people went about their day with no idea of the lives that were unravelling three floors above them.

The doctor straightened and came over to Genevieve by the window.

'I am afraid it is quite serious. We cannot have him in a hospital. The risk of spreading the infection is too great and he must stay here. There is not much to do in these cases anyway,' he said, shrugging his heavy shoulders. 'It's a matter of watching the patient, and waiting for them to decide whether they live or die. Are you capable of nursing him, mademoiselle?'

'I am if you tell me what to do.'

The doctor nodded once. 'You must sit by him until he is well. Keep him cool and keep him quiet. Give him as much water as he will take, and try, if you can, to get him to take a little broth. He will be stronger for the fight if he can take some broth. But really, it is up to him.'

'Is there no medicine you can give him?'

The doctor looked back at the bed where Sebastian was kicking at the bedclothes with restless legs.

'No, I'm afraid not,' he said. He picked up his bag. 'I will be back this afternoon. Good luck, mademoiselle.'

SHE WOKE some time later to a room that was brighter, and quieter. Sebastian's breath wasn't rasping anymore, and she turned quickly to check him. His pale-blue eyes were wide open, staring at her. Her heart froze, and she sat up quickly, panic overriding the fog in her head.

He blinked, and she gasped and then let out a shaky breath.

'Sebastian, oh my goodness. I thought you were dead,' she said, pressing a hand to her chest, to still her thumping heart. 'How do you feel?'

'Awfully thick in the head,' he said, his voice croaking. His eyes followed her as she got off the bed and went and refreshed the flannel and then poured him a glass of water. His eyes were troubled and there was a frown creasing his brow.

'Genevieve, what happened? I don't remember meeting you this morning. I thought I'd missed you, but then here you are.'

'You've been unwell. Terribly so, in fact. I was worried—' She hitched a wobbly smile to her lips. 'Anyway, you came through it. Gosh, you gave me a fright, staring like that.'

'I was trying to remember.'

'What's the last thing you remember?'

Sebastian did not take his eyes from her face. 'I remember dancing with you, and you telling me you loved me. And we were going to get married. And I've been dreaming ever since of trying to get out of this room to get to you, but no-one will let me.'

'You don't need to worry about that anymore. I came to you.'

Sebastian's eyes clouded and he reached out a still-weak hand to grasp hers. 'You will still marry me, won't you, Genevieve? I didn't dream that part?'

'Let's worry about you getting better first,' she said,

smiling at him, and kissing his forehead, 'Then we can talk about all that when you're well.'

'Genevieve—'

'I'm going to call the doctor and get him to have a look at you,' she said brightly.

~

WHEN THE DOCTOR RETURNED, Genevieve went down to the café across the street and ate a plate of sandwiches for lunch. By the time she arrived back at the hotel, the doctor was standing in the corridor outside Sebastian's room, a deep frown on his face as he scribbled on a note pad.

'Doctor?' she asked, his posture alarming her, though she couldn't say why. He looked up, and the frown vanished as his blank, professional mask re-appeared.

'Mademoiselle,' he said, nodding at her.

'Is everything alright?'

'Monsieur von Mylius is with a priest now.'

'A priest?' Genevieve felt her stomach drop and her ears rushed with a static white noise. 'But he was fine when I left for lunch. What happened?'

The doctor detached the hand that gripped his jacket sleeve and frowned at her slightly.

'It is on the request of Monsieur. He wanted some advice. But, also as a precaution I think it is a good idea.'

'Why?'

'Monsieur is not out of danger yet, mademoiselle. This disease I have seen once or twice before. The patient recovers, and you think the worst is over, then two days later, poof, they are dead.'

The hotel wallpaper, which Genevieve had not noticed before, was patterned with a tangle of little vines, entwined in a diamond pattern reaching along the corridor. Every now and then, nestled in the design, a little peep of colour and a bud could be spied hiding among the foliage. She felt as though she and Sebastian were the little buds, twisted and strangled by events out of their control.

'But Sebastian, can you tell if this will happen to him?' she asked, working hard to keep the rushing noise down.

'There's no way to tell. This disease makes up its own mind. In two days, if he is still alive, then he will be through the worst.'

'And if he starts to get unwell again, is there something you can do for him?'

'I have left a medicine.' The doctor shrugged. 'It is mostly to bring him comfort. It is his body, his own strength that will be the best medicine.'

∼

GENEVIEVE COULD BARELY LOOK at the priest when he came out of Sebastian's room, like an aged grim reaper. She felt that by giving Sebastian the last rights, he was signing his death warrant.

Sebastian was sitting up against the pillows when she went to him, looking pale and drawn, but like his old self.

'Genevieve.' He smiled, and the old warmth was there. He held out his hand to her. 'Don't look so afraid, my love. I'm not done for yet.'

'No, of course not,' she said brightly, hating the stupid cheerfulness in her voice. 'How was the padre? Did you get his blessing to go to heaven?'

'I didn't ask him that. I asked him about getting married.'

'Oh.' Genevieve looked down at her hand enclosed in Sebastian's. The white noise rushed upon her again.

'Genevieve...' Sebastian touched a hand to her cheek, and she forced herself to look at him.

'I thought we would have more time,' he said gently. 'I wouldn't have had it this way if I'd had any choice, and I'm sorry to ask it of you, but it seems that it has been taken out of our control. You saw Doctor Gustave before you came in?'

'Yes.' Genevieve focussed now on the carpet, dark-green flecked through with brown, like the leaf mould on a forest floor.

'He told you of the danger I'm still in?'

Genevieve nodded.

'I've had a telegram sent to get the children out of Germany. They should, God willing, already be on a train to France. Max is of an age to make his own decisions. If he does not want to stay in France, neither I, nor you, can make him. But I don't want to leave Tabitha without anyone to look after her. If I die tomorrow—'

He lifted a hand at her moan. 'Hush, just listen please.' He leaned back against the pillow and took a few deep breaths with great effort. 'If I die tomorrow, without a wife, she and Max will revert to my mother's custody. Don't give me your answer now, but the padre will be back tonight after Vespers to marry us, if you agree.'

Genevieve didn't know what to say. The idea that she was fit to look after a child was laughable.

'It wasn't a very attractive offer when I was sure I was going to live. Now you risk an early widowhood.'

'Don't—'

'Shh.' Sebastian reached up, and she could see the effort it cost him just to lift his hand to her cheek again. 'I love you, Genevieve. But I can't make you promises now. It's no longer in our hands.' He dropped his hand and his colour faded.

Genevieve looked at him hopelessly. When did he need her answer? The reality of the situation would not change. She was inadequate to take care of Tabitha with Sebastian alive. As his widow, she would be worse than his mother.

'Go for a walk, Genevieve. Enjoy the sunshine. If you can face it, come back this evening at eight o'clock. Father will be waiting. If not, then this is goodbye, my darling. For the last time.'

Genevieve held tightly to his hand, not able to meet his look. She ought to be protesting with tears in her eyes that she would walk through fire and face endless illness for him, but she couldn't. She didn't want to lie to him anymore. Instead she kissed his hot head and refreshed his face flannel, and then left him to his rest.

CHAPTER 11

Back at Passage Lhomme, there was a light burning in the front windows of the doll hospital. The place looked warm and inviting and Genevieve, coming through the entrance way from the rue de Charonne, stopped and realised, for the first time that day, that Amelia was really gone. She ought to have felt sadness, or at least relief, but she just felt adrift. For better or worse, Amelia's malignant presence had been the one constant in her life; through the smoke-hazed childhood of artistic salons, the cheap-spirited poverty of the depression, and the warmer, uncomfortable gentility of the last few years. She'd never had to worry about who she was because Amelia had always dictated.

The shop floor had been re-arranged, and a fire was burning in the dusty grate, the sweet-smelling spice of apple wood filling the shop. Marie was seated in a chair by the fireplace, wearing a soft pink cardigan Genevieve had never seen before and working her needle in and out of a piece of fabric, transforming it into a spring garden. She startled as Genevieve walked into the shop and Genevieve saw the spot of red bloom on her finger where her needle had dug in.

Was she really so like Amelia?

'Peace, it's just me. She's not come back to haunt you.' She seated herself in the armchair that Marie had placed on the other side of the fire and watched as her aunt's needle set to work again.

'I suppose they've taken her away?'

'Mm,' said Marie, peering closely at a stitch that had gone astray.

Genevieve stared at the logs burning brightly in the grate. The sparks floated about in the warm air and were carried away up into the dark recess of the chimney.

'Monsieur Read came by today,' said Marie, her voice muffled. 'He said that the other man didn't believe that Amelia had painted your picture. They want to talk to you about your paintings. You've made a lot of money, *chérie*. They're coming by tonight to see you.'

'Tonight?'

'Eight o'clock.'

Genevieve laughed, a dry sound that made Marie look up.

'Sebastian has asked me to marry him at eight o'clock. It's rather funny, don't you think?'

'Do you want to marry him?'

The simple question was so unlike anything that Amelia would say that Genevieve looked up from her contemplation of the fire and stared at her small, defeated aunt.

'He's dying,' she said shortly, unable to say more.

'Ah.' There was so much sadness and knowing in that small sound that Genevieve could barely stand to sit still.

'Well,' she demanded, 'what do you say I should do?'

'I?' Marie looked searchingly at her.

'Yes. Should I plight my troth to a man who may be dead in the morning, and saddle myself with his siblings, or should I stay and woo Monsieur Read and his influential friend, and make a place for myself in the world?'

Maire did not answer directly. She plied her needle rapidly, in time Genevieve supposed, to the agitation of her secret thoughts. At length she looked up, and her mild, brown eyes did not flinch from Genevieve's look.

'You have a chance, my niece, to do some real good in this world. To ease the last moments of a dying man, and to make a difference to his brother and sister by being in their lives.'

'How do you know I would make a difference for the better?'

'If this boy has asked you, he knows it. He did not strike me as the sort to make idle decisions.'

Genevieve watched the needle go up and down, darting all over the material in a complicated little pattern.

'Why did you never marry?' she asked Marie abruptly. 'Why live here in Amelia's shadow?'

'Because I was not as strong as you.' The needle slowed and Marie looked at her. 'But you, my love, are not weak, and God knows you are not foolish. What does your heart tell you is the right choice? The deepest part of you, down below all the worldly considerations. That, *chérie*, is the right path.'

As she spoke, the moon rose over the back of the courtyard wall and a finger of moonlight crept into the workroom. Genevieve brushed at her rumpled, stained skirt, and took a deep breath as tears gathered in her eyes.

'I don't really have anything to wear that I could get married in,' she said, peeping through her tears at her aunt.

'That, *chérie*, is but the work of a moment.' Marie was wreathed in smiles, and Genevieve, her heart suddenly glowing within her, burst into tears.

∽

SEBASTIAN'S BREATHING had worsened by the time Genevieve arrived at the hotel at seven forty-five. She walked into the room, wearing the dusk-pink satin Lanvin gown that Marie had unearthed from a locked trunk in the basement. It was simple and elegant; sleeveless, with a square collar and an intricate pattern of silver beading over the bodice and the front of the skirt.

The curtains had been drawn, and Doctor Gustave stood at one end of the room while Sebastian conversed in short, excruciating sentences with the priest.

Doctor Gustave frowned heavily at her and then looked down at the green and brown carpet to avoid meeting the eyes of the dying man.

She breathed deeply, and clutching the snowy white handkerchief with the inevitable heart embroidered on it that Marie had pressed on her as she was leaving, she stepped up to Sebastian's bedside.

If she lived to be two hundred years old, Genevieve did not think she would experience a more pure happiness than in that moment when Sebastian, struggling to breathe and blue around the lips, saw her coming towards him.

'You came,' he said, and the wonder in his voice smote her heart.

'Yes, my darling,' she replied, as tears gathered in her eyes, 'for better or worse, I am here.'

'Please,' entreated Sebastian, looking at the padre, 'open the curtains and turn out the lights.'

And so it was that Genevieve and Sebastian were married in a darkened hotel room, lit only by the generous light of the full moon.

∼

When the padre left, Doctor Gustave came and examined Sebastian again. His breathing was more laboured and he had relapsed back into semi-consciousness.

'The night will tell whether he lives or dies,' Doctor Gustave said quietly. 'May God be with you Mademoiselle—pardon—Madame von Mylius.'

Genevieve felt the heat rush to her cheeks. 'Is there any hope, Doctor?'

Doctor Gustave, in the fussy manner of some middle-aged French men, pulled out his handkerchief and mopped his brow. It was an ancient handkerchief, white linen yellowed by age and use, with a faded pink heart embroidered in the corner. Suddenly Genevieve knew where she had seen him before. He was the son of the woman who owned Suzette. The one who had looked so strangely at Marie's bill.

'Mademois— Madame, there is always hope. But your hope is no longer in me, but in God.'

He rose to leave, but Genevieve, her eyes on the yellowed handkerchief clutched in his fist, put out a hand to detain him.

'Doctor,' she said, looking him full in the face, 'Are you Gustave Aubert from Auvergne?'

He frowned slightly and nodded.

'Then I ought to tell you,' she said, smiling slightly, glad that someone might have the chance at happiness out of tonight's dealings, 'that Marie Dupuis lives at the doll hospital in the Passage Lhomme, and has never given up on her love for you.' She gave him a sad smile. 'Do with that what you will. I know what I, given the chance, would choose at this moment.'

~

DOCTOR GUSTAVE LEFT and Genevieve was alone with Sebastian, her husband. He had smiled at her once since they had sworn to stick by one another, in sickness and in health, and then he'd fallen into a restless semi-consciousness that it was her lot to relieve or manage as best she could. As the moon rose higher in the Paris sky, she refreshed his flannel, did her best to induce him to drink, and pleaded with a silent God to spare his life.

At the midnight hour, Sebastian stilled his tossing and fell into a deep and silent sleep. Genevieve knew from Doctor Gustave that this sleep would either cure him or be his last. She looked on him, on his dear, kind face, smooth beneath the bruises in its resignation, and brushed a dark curl from his brow.

Then she took off the Lanvin, and in the rose-coloured silk chemise that Marie had given her, she pulled back the covers and slipped into bed beside her husband for the only night they may ever have together.

CHAPTER 12

GIVERNY, AUTUMN 1936

High on the bank, Genevieve sat with her easel trying to capture the last of the evening sunlight. It was the dying moments of the golden hour and Max and Tabitha were down below on the Seine, Tabitha sitting in the back of the boat like the Queen of Sheba, with Max pulling her to shore like a young slave. Genevieve's heart was smote every time she focussed on Max. He was filling out now, approaching the adolescence that Sebastian had been in full possession of when they had met in this same spot months ago. Genevieve considered her palette and selected a light bronze to wash over the form of the Max she was working on her painting.

As the light dipped below the tree line and the shadows took over from the golden light, Genevieve packed up her easel and trudged down the bank to meet her young brother and sister. They were an odd group; she the supposed matriarch, and they the unconvincing subordinates, all three of them running wild in this playground of light and colour, and making the most of the last days of warmth.

'Did you see, Genevieve, did you see us? Look at the fish we caught!' shrieked Tabitha, almost upsetting the boat.

'Steady on,' said Max, laughing at her. 'You'll send it back into the river at this rate. It was quite a fight,' he said to Genevieve, and she was not fooled by his quiet modesty.

'What a fine dinner you've caught for us,' she said warmly, and was rewarded with seeing Max's ruddy complexion deepen in colour. 'I don't suppose you know how to cook it?'

'Not a clue, but Giovanni at the hotel knows all about it, and promised to show me. He said he'd cook up anything I caught today.'

Tabitha came up alongside Genevieve and wrapped her small arm about her waist, as was her want. 'How was your afternoon? I still think you would have been better to have come out with us.'

'It was lovely. I climbed up the bank and had the most splendid view. I started painting again.' They were small words, but they cost her a lot to say. Max looked at her swiftly, almost as Sebastian might, and Tabitha skipped awkwardly in her step, not taking her arm from Genevieve.

'Did you paint *us*?' she asked excitedly. 'Did you?'

'Yes,' said Genevieve laughing, 'but you cannot see it until it's finished.'

'Oh, how long will that take?' said Tabitha impatiently.

'As long as it takes,' Genevieve replied, her eyes on the terrace of the hotel above them. Now that the sun was down, the romance of the region gave way to shadows and mists, and most of the hotel patrons had retreated to the warmth provided by the large open fire inside. There was one lone figure out on the balcony, watching them all climb the gentle slope to the hotel gardens.

'What's he doing outside?' Max muttered.

'He can't help it,' said Genevieve, even though she privately agreed with Max. She lifted her hand and waved at Sebastian, hoping he would still be able to see them through the gloaming.

IN THE LOUNGE of *Maison de Repos* Tabitha and Max were much petted by the older patrons who had read of the terrible things happening in Germany, and had decided to make projects of the little refugees.

Since this left Genevieve and Sebastian to enjoy some moments every evening alone in each other's company, they let it go on, even though, it was spoiling them terribly.

'I heard you started painting again today,' said Sebastian, his arm around Genevieve, holding her close. She pressed herself tightly against him and rested her head on his chest.

'I did. It wasn't complete without you, though. Max is getting older, he reminds me of you when we first met.'

'Time marches on I guess.'

'Not without us though, thanks be to God.'

'No, not without us.' Sebastian looked down at her and smiled tenderly. 'I love you very much, my darling wife.'

She smiled up at him, her lips quivering despite her best efforts. 'I love you too, husband.'

He leaned down and kissed her, wrapping his arms about her and pulling her onto his lap. Some of the old matrons spied them and tsked in their direction, but Genevieve snaked her arms about his neck and kissed him back, revelling in the smell of him and his closeness, and the fact that he was warm beneath her touch. He was here and hers. And they were bound together forever. For better or for worse.

THE END

THE SPARROW AND THE TIN MAN

By Nancy Cunningham

CHAPTER 1

PARIS, OCCUPIED FRANCE, WINTER 1944

A small sliver of light fell between the blinds. Therese Lambert hadn't expected this. And she'd never expected it would be *him*. William Bartlett—his name a familiar reminiscence from a past she'd left behind. But was it him? His blindfold masked his face, and in the weak winter light seeping in through the window she couldn't make out his features.

'Who's there?' He shifted and struggled against his bonds. 'You're not a Nazi, are you? I can smell you. Sweet, flowers.'

Therese let out a laugh. Underlying any remnant scent of perfume, how could he smell anything pleasant when the overarching stench of this room was of sweat and torture?

'Speak for god's sake!' He followed the demand with a stuttering laugh. '*Êtes-vous française?*'

His French was guttural, like most of his Canadian countrymen.

Four days had passed since Therese had witnessed his arrival. The Germans, losing the war, were desperate for information, their methods growing ever more brutal. From the shadows, she'd watched the process of his mistreatment, unable to intervene. Her role was to spy, interpret, report.

Like any good soldier, the captain had followed protocol: name, rank, serial number. But unlike the countless times before, when all Therese had done was pass on information, Jacques had told her if she had a chance, she must free this prisoner. And now was the time.

'You need to be quiet, Captain. Otherwise, I cannot help you,' she whispered in English. The soldiers, despite the urgency of defeat, had grown fat on the delights of Parisian life, and become negligent in their duties. They'd left the airman unguarded—but only for a moment. If she didn't act now, they would come for him and move him under the jurisdiction of the *Bande de la Rue Lauriston—Carlingue*—the French Gestapo. Collaborators, brutes feared and loathed in equal measure.

'You're English? Where the hell am I?'

'You're in Paris.' Therese wanted to add—far from the markets of Les Halles, where she'd first met him in 1935.

'Are you a friend or a foe?' he said. Therese removed his blindfold, and he blinked several times. His face, gaunt and sharp, a sickly pale haze against the dark background of black walnut furniture.

'Stop asking questions and listen.' There was little time to move. The soldiers—torturers—would return soon. She could kick herself for agreeing to this. Should she risk her carefully crafted cover built up over years, and future work for this one man? A risk that also placed in jeopardy news of her brother Freddy's whereabouts. Two months she'd waited for a letter. Anything to say he was safe and well.

She cut his ties and loosened his hands, but instead of shaking free, he grabbed at her, his grip clamping around one wrist like a vice despite days under debilitating torture. 'Who are you!'

Therese let out a grunt and plied his fingers away with

her other hand. 'I'll tell you who I am, but you need to follow me. They'll be here soon.'

'French Resistance?'

'*Oui.*'

Therese wasn't French Resistance, but he needn't know that. She was working with the French though, playing informant. Now they'd caught a lucky break in the Gestapo's focus on the prisoner. A door banged, and the sound of male voices raised in laughter further heightened her senses. Time was precious.

The captain staggered to his feet, and she let him fall against her, resting his arm around her shoulders. She might be short and spare, but she could support a heavy weight for a time. Underneath the lingering scent of sweat and blood, he smelled of wood smoke.

They stumbled into the hall and headed towards the bathroom. He nodded to the other end of the hall. 'The stairs are that way. We're going the wrong way.'

Therese opened the hatch to the nearby dumbwaiter with a free hand. 'We're going the right way to escape. Now get in. I'll call the dumbwaiter down using the controls in the kitchen.'

He grunted as she pushed him inside the small space. She could only surmise that the pain came from his ribs—bruised, maybe even broken. Shutting the hatch with a dull thud, she ran down the stairs.

Therese stopped on the landing near the first floor. German voices carried from inside a front room on the floor below, and a door jarred open in a single whoosh. A soldier emerged and looked up at her, his gaze narrowing. '*Fräulein*, what are doing here? You should be gone by now.'

'Yes, monsieur, I forgot my bucket.' She looked down at her hand. The captain's blood was a bright crimson smear across her knuckles. She withdrew it inside the cardigan's sleeve to cover it, the stain now engulfed under a thick cable knit.

His thumb ran across his bottom lip. 'Where is it then?'

'Where is what?'

'Your bucket...'

'Oh!' She carried no bucket but quickly retorted, 'I *thought* I forgot my bucket, but Madame Joubert must have picked it up.'

He joined her on the landing, placed a finger under her chin and tilted her head up so their gazes met. His eyes were a brilliant cold blue that matched his stare. 'What is your name? How old are you?'

Therese swallowed the lump in her throat. 'Therese... Soulier. And I'm fourteen, monsieur.'

His unwelcome stare travelled down Therese's body and studied her bound and flattened chest. He bent his head to the side and examined her scuffed, worn shoes and thick stockings and moved back up to her hair. Her unruly dark bundle of curls she kept dyed mouse brown and braided— and today—rolled it into a bun at the nape. Therese's cover was that of a teenage girl, an easy disguise for someone so slight. It had gotten her far.

He jutted his head towards the hall leading to the kitchen. '*Geh raus, mädchen.*'

Therese blinked several times, pretending not to understand.

'Go! Get out of here, girl,' he said in French this time.

She ran down the stairs and towards the kitchen, slamming the door shut, and her heart thumping hard in her chest. The morning staff had yet to arrive, and she had the kitchen to herself. She pressed the button to the dumbwaiter several times, as if doing so would have it magically appear before her. A clunk and a whirr signalled its descent, and she opened the hatch to find the captain passed out inside. She shook him. 'Captain, wake up.'

His eyes fluttered open, and he stared at her, a deep furrow forming along his pained brow. 'You're a child.'

Therese took his hand and helped him from the dumbwaiter, steadying him as he stood. 'No, I'm not a child, Captain.'

'Who are you?'

She reached for her bulky gabardine wool coat draped over a nearby chair and wrapped it around his tall frame. 'I am The Sparrow. Come fly away with me.'

CHAPTER 2

A warm, damp sensation passed over Will's nose, and rivulets of water washed into his eyes. He blinked them away, conscious of the body next to him. 'Who are you?' He took a long look at the girl—no, woman—who wiped at his brow. 'You look familiar.'

She let out a low laugh. 'I hope so. I dragged you over a mile after helping you escape from a secret Nazi torture chamber.'

'Secret Nazi torture chamber?' He reached out and touched the braid cascading over her shoulder, but she brushed his hand away and it fell limply on the bed next to him. He looked down at his bare torso. Was he naked? He reached his hand down. His belt was gone but he still wore pants. His stomach lurched. 'I don't feel so good.'

'I'm not surprised, Captain Bartlett. They've kept you awake for days. Slapped you, poked you, prodded you, beaten you. I can't feel any broken ribs, but you're going to be very sore. It's their method to get what they want from you. You're lucky you didn't end up in Fresnes Prison.'

Captain Bartlett? Now he remembered. 'They never got a thing,' he said. Not even his actual name. Although he had been on the brink of telling them everything. After all, there was only so much a man could bear before spilling his guts to his torturers. What they really wanted he would not give them. But his mind was hazy on what that was exactly. Plans of some sort—plans for the liberation of Paris? Was that it? He remembered the plane falling, he remembered... he remembered...

The ache in his chest passed, and he leaned into the soft touch of the cloth on his cheek. That was sore too.

'You're feverish, and not out of the woods yet,' she said. Her voice was soft, lyrical and light.

'It won't be long, you know. Paris will be free and back in Allied hands,' he replied. He would be part of the engineering of it.

'So, I'm told. But until the Germans stop goose-stepping down the Champs-Élysées, and the government collaborators release their iron grip on order, we are still under occupation.'

Will reached up and clasped her upper arm in an uncontrolled, feverish move. 'Paris will be free. You will be free.' He'd forgotten in his stupor that the girl wasn't French, or maybe she was. But her accent was English. She had a pretty beauty spot under her right eye and her eyes were as large as... as large as... the moon. He collapsed back on the bed and expelled a large gulp of air from his lungs.

'Are you sure you're not a doll? Only dolls have eyes like yours,' he said weakly.

She snorted a laugh. 'What are you talking about?'

He lay a hand on the back of his neck and rubbed. Despite a dizzy, spinning fog in his head, he lifted it to peer around the room. He found it paid to be observant where he could. 'A basement?' In one corner sat a marble topped vanity, and next to it a tap and a bathroom sink. A round window above it bathed the space in a shaft of winter light despite a clump of dirty snow pressed against its pane. Sooty black marks coated the walls as if a fire had once gone through. A small table and two chairs sat against one wall and, above him, a bunk. The blanket and starchy clean linen covering him had a faint scent of lavender. Above the table a long shelf reached from one corner to another, laden with canned food, plates, bowls, and cups. On another shelf, board games: Ludo, Monopoly, Snakes and Ladders, and a set of dominoes sat stacked against a—birdcage? His eyes fluttered and narrowed for a better look, but everything blurred.

'Lay back, Captain. You'll only make things worse.'

He had a vague memory of having trudged through snow, of voices, German and French, and leaning on the woman as they walked. He'd laughed at a stony-faced bald man at the threshold of a door before passing out and waking up here.

The room was littered with toys, vast numbers crammed into a small space. 'Have I died? Is Heaven a toyshop? Are you a living doll?'

A crease had formed between her brows, and she placed the back of her hand against his forehead. 'You're burning up.'

'I feel like utter shit. Excuse my... French. My leg hurts, too.'

'When the Germans brought you in, you had an injury. But you walked here with me. What's wrong?'

'Are you a doctor as well as a living doll? It just bloody hurts, alright?'

'Alright.' A look of concern crossed her face, and she pushed the blanket down over his legs.

He regretted his harsh response, but the pain overcame him in waves. She was only trying to help. But where the hell was he? Who the hell was she?

She stared at the button on his trousers as if deliberating and shifted her gaze to his bare feet before shucking up his trousers and examining his legs. 'Your ankle is swollen,' she said and crossed to the small sink. The tap squeaked followed by a spurting sound, as water hammer reverberated through the room. She returned to his side and laid a freezing-wet cloth over his foot.

He stuttered an intake of breath as she wrapped it around his ankle. 'Oh, hell. That's woken me up.'

Her gaze skittered over his naked torso, lingering on his upper chest before looking away.

'Like what you see?' He said, half delirious and laughed.

Her gaze returned with an unfriendly stare. She poked at his chest, her fingers skirting the bottom rib. 'Definitely not broken.'

He flinched. 'Feels like it.'

'Only badly bruised.' She sighed. 'We won't be able to move you yet.'

'I need to get to the coast. Back to England, or to Ireland at least.'

'Our people have organised everything. I'm merely a cog in a wheel. You'll just have to wait until others arrive tomorrow.' She stood and plopped the cloth back in a bowl and rubbed a hand over her face. 'Damn!'

'Who are 'our people' and others? Resistance?'

'Yes.'

'But you're English.'

'And you are Canadian.'

'I—' Will expelled a cough before he could finish, the fit tearing at his chest and wracking his torso with convulsions he couldn't stop. He sat up, and the cough eased in intensity then passed.

She retrieved something on the table—a jug— and turned back to him, cup in hand. 'Here, drink this.'

He took it with a shaking grip and drank. A mixture of water and something stronger burned in his chest but soothed his parched throat. It dribbled down his chin onto his chest and he shivered.

She took the cup from him. 'Please, lay down.'

Too weak to disobey or do anything other than listen, he surrendered to her command. She brought the blanket up to his chin. 'What's your name, Sparrow?' He'd remembered that part of the escape at least.

'My name is—' She paused her lip quivering as if deliberating. 'Therese.'

'Please to meet you, Therese, I'm Will.'

The skin crinkled at the corner of her eyes. 'I know you are. Captain William Bartlett of the Canadian Air Force.'

'And you are Therese of?'

'The toy shop.'

He laughed, but a jolt in his side stopped him. 'You are Saint Therese of the toy shop. I like that. *Sparrow. Doll.* Which nickname do you like best?'

She was silent, although she appeared contemplative rather than angry. He scratched absentmindedly at his cheek, the bristles sprouting on his face causing sudden irritation. 'You can call me—'

'Tin Man.' She turned to a poster of *The Wizard of Oz* on a nearby wall. 'He's a woodsman, a lumberjack. Aren't Canadians famed for such exploits?'

'Yes, I suppose they are.' He'd seen the film once. He'd taken his mother to the Tivoli Theatre in Richmond Street, back in Toronto, a week before Canada joined the war. 'But I have a heart, Sparrow.'

Therese's brow raised. 'Do you?'

He laughed and gave in to the sudden fatigue that made his eyelids heavy. He dozed, the fever sending him into a nightmare—the plane falling from the sky, tainting his nose with the smell of burning oil and flesh. He couldn't escape the vision of the man at the controls lying bloody and skewered to his seat by a shard of metal.

What a bloody mess. But he did what he had to do.

He must have completely blacked out as he woke in a darker room with only subdued light radiating from a small oil lamp. His eyes blinked partway open. Therese stood in the lamp's glow, half undressed and uncoiling a roll of material from around her torso. The fabric had pressed so tight he could see the indentations against her translucent skin. He'd always found a woman's form bewitching, and his gaze, still in a half stupor, remained trapped on the swell of her breasts before travelling to the soft, feminine skin of her shoulder blades. She leaned down and pulled on a camisole and then a shirt before turning towards him, fastening the buttons. He snapped his eyes shut. It was beneath him to act this way, even if he had the excuse of a restless fever.

'It's alright, you can open your eyes now, I'm dressed.'

His cheeks blazed hot, like a chastened schoolboy. 'How did you know?'

'I've been in Paris for a while. Watching my back is a natural reflex.' She crossed to the bed and reached for his forehead, frowning. 'How are you feeling?'

'Like a battalion of Germans stomped all over me.'

She gave a small smile. 'Try to rest, Captain Bartlett.'

'Will. Call me Will.' He let the fever grip him again. Tomorrow he'd apologise for staring.

CHAPTER 3

Therese looked pleadingly at her Resistance colleagues, Charlotte and Jacques. 'Please tell me you're joking. I'm not a nurse. I report information, I interpret, I spy. I don't fight and I certainly don't nurse Allied soldiers.' A sudden draft blew through the door of the hidden part of the basement. She tucked her hands under her armpits and glanced at Will. He remained sleeping, as he had for the last two days. 'He's been half delirious with fever. Is he even who he says he is?' It had been the main reason she hesitated when he'd asked her name. 'Who do you think he is?'

'Why do you say this? We had it plain from our operatives on the coast. He is Captain William Bartlett,' Charlotte said.

Therese sighed. 'I've met him before.'

'What? When?' Jacques demanded.

'On my first trip to the Continent nine years ago. I was a naïve seventeen-year-old, travelling with my tutor. We met Captain Bartlett in a café.' Therese closed her eyes, recalling the cocky, twenty-two-year-old rookie pilot with the dazzling smile. 'But this man looks—different from my memory. There's something not right.'

Charlotte reached out and stroked Therese's chin. 'You know me. But nine years ago? A lot has happened since that time. I'm not the frail little mademoiselle from Verdun I once was. And you? I know your family's tragedy plays out every day in your head. But you need to trust us, trust our sources. We have orders, and we don't question them.'

'Perhaps you should, like I should have questioned my involvement in this escape.' Never in the entire time she'd been in Paris had her superiors asked her to do anything like this. 'I only agreed because I saw...' What had she seen? The captain's name gave her a yearning for a past long gone, a past when Paris was free, and she was happy. 'I'm just not sure he is William Bartlett, the man I met so long ago.'

'You can't leave, Therese,' Jacques said and looked with hooded eyes from Therese to Charlotte. Therese stopped cold. Something was off. She'd known Jacques and Charlotte since they'd saved her from an over-friendly gendarme, a little over two years ago. They usually kept nothing from her.

'Why can't I leave?'

Charlotte nodded towards Jacques. 'Show her.'

Jacques pulled out a sheet of paper and handed it to her. Words in ominous thick black ink sat stood out against the grimy yellow colour of the paper.

Gesucht, Recherché, Wanted,
Therese Soulier also known as 'The Sparrow',
Five-feet two, medium length pale brown hair (worn back),
Age: fourteen years or older.
If seen, report immediately to your local police station.

Underneath the words was a handsomely drawn and extremely accurate likeness. At least they didn't have her real last name.

'You must stay here, Therese. You don't have a choice.

The flyers are strewn everywhere.' Charlotte said and pointed towards the captain. 'And pictures of him too.'

'When he's better and able to move, you can accompany him to the coast,' Jacques said. 'Return to England.'

'To England?'

'Orders. You're to leave Paris.'

'Jacques, no, I—'

'Orders, Therese. You cannot stay here now.' Jacques's voice was low and gruff, and he shook his head in warning. 'Don't.'

'Orders from who? I don't answer to you. You are not—'

He grabbed Therese by the shoulders. 'Enough! You'll do as you're told. These orders come from the British. Your Special Operations Executive. You're to return to London. Ruben has his eyes peeled for trouble above in the shop. *Merde*! Be grateful we can keep you safe—for now.'

Therese shrank at his touch but held her lips in a defiant grimace. Jacques had never lost his temper with her before. He had at least three days of stubble and a haggard look in his eyes. But then, they all had that same haunted look, and Therese was sure she was no picture of feminine beauty. The unrelenting brutality of their existence had etched deep furrows in all their faces. Therese couldn't remain posing as a teenager for much longer at this rate.

Charlotte spoke more softly,, a smile playing across her full lips. 'Therese, please, just do as ordered. I'd hate for you to get in trouble.'

'I'm not worried about getting into trouble.' Therese pulled away from Jacques's grasp. 'Don't you think it odd?'

'Odd?' Charlotte said.

'That I'm compromised after this man escapes?'

Charlotte's eyes softened. '*Cocotte*, your cover was always at risk. Always. And now that you yourself have disappeared...' She shrugged her shoulders.

'So, after two years of cultivating this disguise, my cover is now in ruins.' Therese couldn't keep the bitterness from her voice. *Fool.* 'I would never have agreed to this if I'd known.'

'Whoever this man is, he was a prize prisoner and we've jumped right into the middle of a storm. One that's worse than this winter,' Jacques replied. 'He could be the King of England himself. I don't care.'

'He's Canadian.' Therese waved a hand flippant in her response.

'Putain de bordel de merde!' Jacques cursed. 'Why do you question everything?'

'Because you usually tell me what I need to know, and suddenly you're leaving me in the dark? None of it makes sense.'

Jacques shook his head and stormed out, shouting instructions to Charlotte as he ascended the stairs.

'Why is he so steamed? I'm the one stuck here. I'm the one with the blown cover ordered to leave France,' Therese said, indignant that they would have the gall to order her back to England. She'd been an effective operative, an accolade hard earned by her reckoning.

'The increased patrols have him on edge.'

'No, that's not it. It's something else.' Therese couldn't put her finger on it, but she'd seen Jacques unfazed in the face of ten German soldiers and a *Milice* Officer. She'd lost more than one friend to their traitorous collaboration with the Germans.

Therese stared towards the stairs. No matter Jacques's directive, or how foolhardy she knew it to be, she couldn't leave Paris or France. Not without news from her brother. She'd promised herself if she hadn't heard from Freddy within the next week, that if he weren't safe back in England in their Tonbridge cottage like he promised he would be, she'd look for him. Even though she wasn't sure exactly where to start. 'Is there any mail for me?'

Charlotte shook her head. 'I don't know. We can't get near Madame Joubert's. The Germans have been there since sunup going through your things.'

Therese's shoulders slumped. Still no word. Freddy had written regularly, and as Therese boarded with Madame Joubert under the guise of being her niece from the country, his letters always found their way. An involuntary shudder travelled through her, stopping in her gut, she prayed for Madame Joubert's safety. The canny old woman would play the Germans for fools, and likely escape scrutiny. A good thing too that Freddy's letters were always in code, in the strange language they'd invented as children, just the three of them, she, Freddy, and Maddy. Where was Freddy now?

'When Captain Bartlett can move and it's safe, you can leave,' Charlotte reiterated.

'That could be a week or more!' Therese declared. How could she look for Freddy while stuck in here?

'Then it's a week or more,' Charlotte said and shrugged. Her hand went to Therese's hair, playing with the mousy dyed braid. 'You may have to disguise yourself. Wear boys' clothes, or I could get you some blonde hair dye.'

'I have to get out. I have to find...' Her jaw hurt from clenching, and a wave of exhaustion came over her.

'Therese, you are tired,' Charlotte said. 'I'm sure there is a letter from Freddy waiting for you right now. Madame Joubert would have hidden it. We'll make sure you receive it. There's no need to be worried.'

'Then I have no choice. Look after the airman?'

'*Oui*. Ruben is solid and loyal, no one will get past him. He'll remain upstairs and will make sure there's enough to eat. I'll drop by next week with some travelling clothes. After all this excitement has died down.' She rubbed Therese's shoulder. 'Get some rest.'

Charlotte left the basement room through the hidden entry. Ruben had instructed Therese to stack boxes against the opening once someone had left, but she walked around the room rubbing her arms instead. A cold air sifted in from somewhere. She put on another layer of clothes from a bag Charlotte had left, sat on a chair and sighed. She needed to be out doing her duty. She needed to be out there fighting, not cooped up in here. She needed to look for Freddy. Her stomach curdled at the idea her brother might lay injured somewhere. But Charlotte was right. If every German soldier and gendarme had Therese's picture, she wasn't safe. They'd uncovered her code name.

She shot a glance at the captain and gritted her teeth. *'Merde.'*

Her nose itched at the room's stuffiness. The stench of the Germans' ill treatment wafted off her patient. The metallic scent of blood underlined a hint of sandalwood from the soap she'd used to wash him when they'd first arrived.

Pulling a chair close, she leaned in to stare at his face. Soft breaths emanated from his mouth, and his eyes fluttered as if dreaming. He was alive where Freddy could be dead. She murmured close to his ear, 'You don't remember me, do you? I remember you. Well, I remember your name. If you're him, you were all silken words and dashing presence. And Angelique was in love with you. I might have been too.'

She leaned down to pick up her knitting from the bag, and as she raised her head, the captain's eyes stared wide open at her. She gasped.

He sat up and groaned. 'You remember me?'

Therese attempted to compose herself, but lost for words, she remained silent. What had he heard her whisper?

'Where is Angelique now?' he asked.

Gone was any embarrassment at admitting her girlish crush from ten years ago. What had happened to Therese's old tutor stabbed at her chest and she stared down at the ground. 'She's gone missing. I tried finding her, but everyone said...' Therese's voice stilled and she swallowed. 'Angelique's family is Jewish.'

'These are dangerous times, Sparrow.'

'Who are you really?' she said, staring back at him, the back of her throat stinging with a hoarse whisper. Her eyes welled with recollection. 'You're not the same man I remember. You're—' Her throat closed.

Had her memory played such awful games with her? She remembered Maddy and mother, their bodies covered in dust and her father, nowhere, as if he'd evaporated in a magician's puff of smoke. She remembered saying goodbye to Freddy. She remembered the night sky over London like a fireworks display, the colours so vivid, so real. But she could barely remember the man in front of her, even though she should. The Will Bartlett she remembered had no heart. Therese stifled tears and turned her face away as the memories of love and loss burned across her consciousness.

The captain touched her cheek and turned it to him, his hands rough and clean, his eyes a tawny sparkle. 'I'm your ally, Sparrow.'

Therese brushed his hand away and wiped her face with the back of a sleeve. 'You aren't Will Bartlett, are you?'

He stared at her and shifted. 'How long have you been in the field?'

'Two and half years.' She answered his question even as he evaded hers.

'And you haven't been back to England in all that time?'

'There is nothing for me there,' she replied. Only a house full of memories of people she'd loved and lost. 'Only reminders that the world is on fire.'

'So, you stepped into that fire. Did you think you could remain untouched by the flames?'

An unsteadiness claimed Therese's limbs, but she stood anyway and went to the makeshift kitchenette. Pulling down two plates, she took a baguette and ham from a brown bag, cutting the bread into slices and smearing them with butter. 'Whoever you are, the Germans are looking for you. We can't leave Paris yet. Not until you can travel.'

'The Germans know who you are. I overheard that much,' he replied.

Therese paused, placing her hands on the counter. She was still reflecting on what that meant. 'Yes, it appears they do. But if I can't be the Sparrow, perhaps I can be something else.' She turned and stared at him pointedly, then handed him a plate.

'Black market ham?' He tilted his head and her cheeks warmed as he studied her. 'Have you always dressed as a child?'

'Not a child.' A strange mirth tickled her throat. Perhaps his fevered delirium was catching since she'd gone from the edge of tears one moment, to contemplation the next. Now a well of bubbling nervous giggles waited to erupt from inside. 'A teenager. Un-endowed mademoiselles garner little attention. You go unnoticed—mostly.'

'And you know how to take care of that? I saw your binding.'

The laughter fell out of her. Sometimes it was good to laugh. She'd done little of that of late. Charlotte was right again. Therese was tired, no, exhausted, was a more apt description. The laughter ceased as quickly as it had come and she sat, staring at her plate.

'That's a wonderful sound, your laughter. I miss... I miss laughing.'

Therese concentrated on eating, conscious that he was

observing her. The only distraction was the food on her plate, and like a beggar at a banquet, she began salivating the longer she stared at the ham. She devoured it and licked her fingers after. Closing her eyes blocked out everything except the salty meat on her tongue. It had to be delirium. She placed her plate down and picked up her knitting.

'You'll come with me?' the captain asked.

'Yes. When you're out of danger and can walk the streets,' she said without looking up. *Knit one, pearl one...*

'Therese...'

She lifted her head and hummed an acknowledgement.

He wore a serious crease on his brow. 'You're in as much danger as I am.'

CHAPTER 4

Almost a week passed, and Will, able to bear the pain and weight on his ankle, could walk and his body no longer rattled with fever or shakes. He was healing, thanks to the French Resistance and the Sparrow. She was one of many unconventional warriors of Special Operations Executive—the secretive SOE—carrying out espionage, sabotage and reconnaissance for the British throughout Europe. He paced the room and watched her covertly. Over the last seven days, when they weren't sleeping, they'd played checkers and chess, Monopoly and dominoes. When he rested, he watched her. This petite woman never stopped moving. Even as she sat, she knitted or hummed. She kept house. He snorted a laugh. Or 'kept basement', in this instance. But now, on the upper bunk of the bed, she laid still, face towards him, one hand tucked under her head. Asleep.

She'd known he wasn't Captain William Bartlett, having met the pilot years ago. But he couldn't let her know who he really was. Not yet. Not while the Germans stalked the Paris streets looking for him, and for her. Not while he couldn't trust his rescuers. His cover had saved him from a worse fate, and there was no need to reveal all.

In the dim light of the room, he took in her features. Lord, how on earth did the Nazis ever think she was a child? Braids, bound breasts, and freckles aside, she had maturity to her face, a trim nose, and long dark eyelashes to go with her endlessly brown eyes. Her hair looked unnatural, a mousey brown dark at the roots.

One of her legs had slipped out from beneath the cover and he stared at it. Her leanness, likely from years of rations, had an attractive shape to it. The curve of her well-defined calf tapered down to her compact foot. His mind skated around thoughts of other girls, ones he'd loved and left behind, ones that never quite lit a fire inside of him, the ones he had used to dull the hurt. They were lovely, but never extraordinary.

'Oh, for God's sake, Will,' he hobbled over to the bunk and pulled the blanket over her bare leg.

His movement was enough to make Therese stir. She moaned, and the sound went straight through him. This was not the time for such thoughts. Trapped in an icy basement in a toy shop of all places.

She sat up and stretched so alluringly that Will almost fell off the chair when he sat.

'Good morning, Sparrow.'

'You're up? How are you feeling, Tin Man?'

In a brief space of time, he'd grown used to that friendly moniker. 'Still dizzy, but I'm much better, thank you.'

'You have more colour in your face. If we get the all clear, we can move soon.'

'I'm glad to hear it.' He grinned and tottered to the cupboard in the tiny kitchenette. 'Coffee?'

'Coffee. What is life without coffee?'

'It's the best medicine.'

Her light laugh thrummed through him. She'd grown more relaxed—rested—as the days passed, particularly those first couple where tears sat on the edge of her every word. 'You really shouldn't be walking around.'

'I'm fine.' He stood next to the almost boiling pot and swivelled his head toward her. His eyes travelled to her legs as she pulled on her thick ugly brown stockings. What a shame to cover them. When she lifted her skirt higher to clip the stockings into place, he glimpsed her thigh. Heat rose in his cheeks and he looked away to pour the coffee.

He passed her a cup, and she let her dowdy brown skirt fall to her knees. Damn war, it was so devoid of anything remotely colourful. Hopefully in a few months from now, things would be very different for the people of France. Colour and light would return. How devastating would Therese look in a floral dress? He'd be on his knees for sure.

'Tell me, Sparrow. The SOE. I've heard about the things you've done. Brilliant.' Few had lasted as long undercover as she had. He'd known of the Sparrow's exploits.

How she relayed information to the Allies: troop movements, valuable prisoner locales, stockpiles of German munitions, and where German units lay in wait for unsuspecting Resistance fighters. Her eavesdropping as simple as if Hitler himself sat on a park bench and fed her breadcrumbs. Her hands cradled the cup, her index finger tapping the side. 'You've heard of me?'

'You sound surprised. If the Germans know who you are, why wouldn't the Allies?'

She shrugged. 'Nothing I do is common knowledge. Not even with the Allies.'

'Word spreads.' He let out a small laugh. 'What do you do when you're not rescuing dashing airmen from interrogations?'

'You make it sound as if I do that all the time. You're the only one I've ever rescued.'

'Really? I've heard you have had a lot to do with helping Allied airmen escape.'

'Well, it depends on what you mean by help. I've relayed where they're imprisoned. Infiltrated several civilian holding cells in disguise. But involved in an actual escape? You're the first. Look where it's got me. Stuck here and ordered back to London.'

Will laughed. 'Can't be that bad? Stuck here with me. Then going home.'

She sent a pained expression his way. 'It is, actually. Worse than bad.'

Silence fell over the room, and Will sipped his coffee. What deprivations had she gone through? What losses had she faced? He had a sudden need to know.

'I knit. I read. I practise my Russian, is what I do when not rescuing idiotic airmen who get caught,' she snapped.

'Russian? Do you know something I don't, Sparrow?'

'I don't know, do I?' Her gaze focused on his, unblinking, those deep brown eyes like an alluring puddle of dark chocolate.

With the settling of the coffee in his stomach and the thoughts of chocolate, he ached for an accompaniment. 'You don't have any cigarettes, do you?'

'No. My mother...' She paused.

'Your mother?'

'My mother thought it a filthy habit. I happen to agree.'

'I suppose it is. Still, can't help but crave it.' He ran his thumb over his lips. 'Where is your mother now? Does she miss you?'

She trailed her delicate fingers down the side of her face. 'She's dead. Along with my father and my sister. They died in an air raid.'

'I'm sorry.' That's where the tragic air and sudden tears

had come from. He could sympathise with memories that tore at you and caught you unawares.

'You have nothing to be sorry for. You weren't the one over London bombing us to hell and back.'

'All your family, I can't imagine.'

'Not all, my brother... my brother might still live.'

'You don't know?'

'The last I heard, he and his unit were to travel from somewhere in Greece to Gibraltar. They were to fly to Lisbon, then to London. He promised he would write to tell me he was safe, like he had many times before. But I've not heard anything.'

A tingle shot down Will's spine. He had flown from Gibraltar to Lisbon. The night before departure, he'd drunk with a unit of British soldiers travelling from Greece and flying out at the same time, but only half had made it to Lisbon thanks to a German ambush. From what he understood, the injured soldiers had remained in Italy with the Americans.

She tilted her head, her eyes narrowing. 'Where were *you* flying from when you were shot down?'

'How many languages do you speak?'

'Stop evading my questions. Where were you flying from?'

'Lisbon.'

She stared at him and placed her cup down on the floor. 'I speak five languages. French and German, of course. Italian and Spanish, and now Russian. Poorly, I'm afraid.'

'Why learn Russian?'

'You'd have to be living in a cave not to know the Russians, British and Americans are bouncing off each other. If you don't think they'll be fighting one another for the spoils of war when this over, then you're an idiot. Are you an idiot, Captain Bartlett?'

'Will.'

'Ah yes, "Will",' she said, a small smile curling the edges of her mouth. 'Why won't you tell me who you really are?'

He coughed and looked around the room. In one corner was a shelf stacked with toys, and underneath the pile a wooden box of dominoes, and a Spear's family board game of Snakes and Ladders. The bright green of a cartoon snake slithered cheerily along the side of the box. He walked over and removed it from the shelf, placing it on the table. 'How about we get to ask one question if we land on a ladder, and we must share a fact about ourselves if we slip on a snake?'

She looked at the box, then back to him and bit her lip, her teeth sliding on her wet lips. His heart did a small flip in his chest at the gesture. 'Alright. It has to be facts, though, *Will*.'

He lifted his finger. 'If we ask a question, you can only ask once. And not a double-barrelled one.'

'Certainly,' she said.

Will laid out the board. Instead of dice, there was a cardboard wheel with an arrow that you flicked with a finger. 'Ladies first.'

Therese's first move was to the base of a ladder. She smiled smugly. 'What's your name?'

'William, or Will for short.'

Her mouth opened into a gape. 'I said truth. What's your full name?'

'You've had your question.' He replied and waggled his finger.

Her smug smile disappeared. His turn—he landed on an empty square and Therese on another ladder. 'Who do you work for?' she asked.

'The Royal Canadian Air Force, on secondment to the British government,' he replied. No need to reveal his surname or that he worked for British Security Co-ordination and Project-J.

She hummed sweetly and nodded.

He landed on a snake. 'I have three brothers, all of them older than me.'

She blinked and landed on an empty square. He landed on another ladder.

'Tell me the names of your family, Sparrow.'

'My parents, Genevieve and Henry Lambert. My sister,' she paused and gulped, 'my sister, Madeline, and my brother Fredrick.'

Will sat back in the chair. 'Your last name is Lambert and your brother is Fredrick Lambert?'

'I knew it. You know him?' Her voice cracked, the tinge of urgency unmistakable.

'I don't know him but...'

'But what...'

'I know his name.'

'I don't want to play this stupid game.' She stood and reached for her coat, fumbling through the pockets. Gone was the tearful Sparrow who flitted from smiles to sadness. She pulled out a knife, flourishing it towards him. 'How do you know his name? Who are you? Tell me!'

Will put his hands out. 'I'm not here to hurt you. Trust me, Therese.'

'Why? You won't even tell me your actual name. I'm going to tell Jacques and Charlotte. I'll call Ruben right now!'

'I'd rather you didn't.' He rubbed his face and began laughing. 'Besides, that would have to be the bluntest knife I've ever seen.'

'Don't laugh! It's not funny!'

'But it is, Sparrow. Hilarious. I'll tell you anything you want to know. I promise, and I'm not lying. My name *is* Will. But who I really am—it's not safe to tell you here.'

She inhaled deeply and lowered the knife. 'I've known you barely a week. If you lie to me...'

The bookcase suddenly shifted aside, and she had no time to finish her ultimatum. A pale Charlotte and Ruben—his bald head furrowed with lines—poked their heads through the opening.

'Therese! Captain! You must leave. Now!'

CHAPTER 5

'Is everything alright?' Charlotte asked, advancing into the room.

Therese's hands quivered as she held the knife, and as deftly as she'd revealed it, she tucked it away. The idea that she could persuade this man by wielding a weapon, threatening that if he didn't tell her all she'd use it, had a sudden witless air to it. She had never needed to exercise her weapons training. His joking aside, she would make him tell her who he was and where Freddy was one way or another. 'The captain and I are just playing games. Aren't we?' She looked to Will briefly and then turned to Charlotte and Ruben. 'Why must we leave *right* now?'

'We've distracted the searchers. They're heading south, following a false lead. We need you both out now. Here are some clothes.'

Charlotte passed over a hefty suitcase. Before Therese had time to rummage through the contents, Charlotte stepped behind her and tugged on her braid. She cut it off in a swift action then brandished it in front of Therese.

'Interesting,' Will said.

Therese scowled. He appeared awfully calm even with a

panicked Ruben rubbing his hands together at the basement entrance, and sending "hurry up" glances towards them every minute.

'Sit,' she said. 'Quick, I'm going to give you a haircut.'

Ten minutes later, Charlotte handed her a mirror. Therese bobbed her head, the weight of her thick hair gone. She squinted. The ends were still that awful pale brown colour, but the cut was that of a young woman, her curls set free mid-neckline and the front pinned back off her face. She tingled at the sight. Seeing her reflection with this new hairstyle made her long for something other than a dreary and cold winter, something other than war and the surrounding brutality. But the face she wore was a stranger's.

'I like it,' Will said. 'It suits you.'

Therese's gaze flicked to him, pretending she was indifferent to his compliments. He'd changed out of his clothes so fast she hadn't noticed and now wore a simple pair of trousers, shirt, and knitted vest. They'd given him a cane, as if he were an old man.

'Your turn now, Captain,' Charlotte said.

'Mine?' he said but sat obediently as Charlotte dabbed something at the sides of his hair then passed him the mirror. He turned his head from side to side and hummed. 'I have a look about me now. Like that of a life well lived. Old and wise.'

Even with the grey, his eyes twinkled like a mischievous youth. 'Age and wisdom are quite separate things, Captain,' Therese said.

'As long as the right one arrives ahead of the other,' he said and grinned. 'But you, Sparrow, you have a blush to you. No one could mistake you for anything other than a beautiful young woman.'

Heat rose from her chest and flushed her neck and face.

'On that,' Charlotte opened a palette of makeup and

dabbed face powder and pink rouge on Therese's cheeks. She passed her a stick of bright red lipstick. 'Get dressed. You're to play father and daughter.'

Will frowned, and Therese couldn't help letting out a laugh.

'Father? That's disappointing. Can't we play older distinguished gentleman and his younger, exquisite wife?'

Charlotte laughed. 'Why give Therese a husband? Men are too stupid for her to marry. The young ones have temperaments that could get them killed. The older ones expect you to cook, clean, and lie with them.'

'And that sounds divine.' Will said and smirked. 'What about the men in between?'

'They're busy fighting and dying,' Charlotte replied soberly.

'Then here's to fighting and not dying, then,' Will replied and the smile faded from his lips.

Therese uttered a silent prayer for Freddy. Will stared at her and the smile returned to his face. Her face flushed hot again.

'Put your coats on.' Charlotte passed her an envelope. 'Read it now quickly. Instructions for once you're out of the city. You need to memorise it and destroy it as soon as possible.'

Therese ripped open the envelope her gaze running over the name of every Resistance safe house between here and Houlgate, six in all. She had a method and soon as she'd committed the houses to memory, she handed it back to Charlotte. 'Done.'

'Use the phrase, "I'm afraid I've lost my way to the train station" at the safe house. You can rest during the day and travel at night. Bicycles, horse and cart, but not a car or motorbike or anything that would draw attention.'

Therese nodded. 'These safe houses, need I...'

'Do you remember the *Les falaises des Vaches noires*? And the fisherman's shack nestled off the beach?'

'Yes. I remember the summer we spent there.'

'Head there from Houlgate. When you arrive, wait for us. Jacques will know what to do.'

She didn't like the sudden trust Charlotte had in Will. Nor for the trust she expected Therese to have. Yes, she wore the vulnerability of a teenage girl as part of her disguise, and although she was far from defenceless, anyone could see the strength in Will's arms. He could overpower her, he could...

Therese paused her panicked thoughts as Will took Charlotte's hand. *'Merci beaucoup.'*

'Ruben and I will travel several hours behind,' Charlotte said.

'And Jacques?' Therese asked.

Charlotte paused for a moment and looked at Will. She smiled, but the smile was aloof and wavering. 'He will be there. Stop chattering. Go.'

Therese pulled on the new green coat and pocketed the lipstick. Will offered her his arm, and she hesitated. 'More for me than for you, *ma fille chérie.*'

'Oui, Papa,' she replied and took his arm in hers. As they exited the toy shop, Therese whispered low into Will's ear. 'You will tell me who you are. That's not a request, but a demand.'

'I stand by my promise.'

She nodded, satisfied, and they trundled off down the street and into the night.

CHAPTER 6

Will and Therese walked in silence, avoiding patrols where they could. They crossed the Seine several times and were well into the countryside before reaching the first safe house. They had little banter between them, both on high alert. Will was glad of it; he wasn't quite ready to speak and tell all. Who knew how she might react? Should he even tell her at all? But he'd made a promise and he would follow through.

They arrived at a well-appointed farmhouse sitting behind an immense stone wall just before seven o'clock in the morning. The sun had not begun to rise, but a dim light on the horizon cast a grimy yellow into the sky. Despite his bundle of clothes, the early morning air caught in his chest. They both wore thick gloves and hats, but it wasn't enough to keep all the cold out. The overweight farmer let them in with Charlotte's code phrase and showed them to a storeroom on the northern side of the house. Inside, two mattresses nestled in under shelves of fruit preserves and a barrel served as a table for an oil lamp. A scent of damp, wet earth infiltrated the room along with wood and cork. A sweet scent too, from dozens of preserves, all lined up in neat rows.

'Looks comfortable,' he said. 'And warm.'

'Anywhere is better than outside. Why Charlotte made me wear this silly dress is beyond me. It's not as if I'm going fashion shopping,' she replied. 'Perhaps now we are warming up you can tell me—'

Before she could finish, the farmer's wife, rake thin compared to her stout husband, popped her head around the door and offered them a basket of food: A baguette, something akin to chutney, and a pot of *fromage*. Will smiled at her and her thin lips twitched. She nodded to an open bottle of wine on a shelf in the corner.

'*Merci, madame,*' Therese said as the three stood awkwardly in the small storeroom. '*Bonsoir.*'

The woman eventually got the hint and stepped back out through the door. Will sank to the ground opposite Therese and leaned his back against the stone, warmed from the fire inside the farmhouse kitchen.

'What's the time?' he asked.

Therese looked at her watch. 'Just after five o'clock.'

Although his stomach growled from hunger, he took two bites and closed his eyes, too tired to partake of anything else. Not even his throbbing ankle could stop him from falling into slumber. But Therese would not let him rest just yet.

She kicked him in the shin and he startled from dozing. 'What was that for?'

'You promised me you would tell me who you were.'

'Will, but not Will Bartlett.'

'I gathered that,' she said impatiently.

'He was the pilot. When the plane crashed, there wasn't anything I could do for him. But there was still something left he could do for me.'

She crossed her arms. 'Go on.'

'I swapped my tags for his, and his jacket, and his papers. Made sense. Because if I got caught...'

'You took a dead man's identity to save your skin. How very heartless of you. Tin Man without a heart, I knew it. Why?'

'Because if they knew who I was, you would never have needed to rescue me. They would have shipped me off to Berlin. Or Poland, or whatever horror of a camp they take important Allied soldiers. I would never have lasted the week there.'

'Important? But what is your—'

'No. No more questions, no more answers for today,' he said holding back a smile. 'We have an entire journey ahead of us. You tell me something now, Sparrow. How did you know Will Bartlett?'

She narrowed her gaze and folded her arms across her chest. 'It was ten years ago, in Paris. I was with—'

'Angelique. That's right you were both in love with me.'

Therese's cheeks coloured to an attractive shade of pink. 'Very funny.'

'Tell me—I want to know a little more than just your companion's name.'

'I was on exchange, seeing the Paris sights, and we met him and his air force friends at a café. Angelique had one of those faces that stopped men in the street. He charmed her, and me. No one really paid me attention. I was only fifteen.'

'You've filled out since then,' he said, letting his mirth bubble to the surface.

She ignored him, but the glint in her eyes told him she held back amusement. She wrapped her coat around her tightly. 'He was charming. He charmed the pants off Angelique, literally. A week of romance where I was a mere voyeur. And then he left. Angelique was distraught. We went back home to England, back to Kent. And Angelique became quite despondent. I didn't understand why. But later Maddy told me she'd fallen pregnant, to Will Bartlett.'

'Oh, I see.'

'I was angry at you, sorry, angry at Will Bartlett. But when I saw your name on the list of prisoners, I didn't feel angry. I remembered how the three of us walked along the banks of the Seine. How we stopped at cafes and looked at famous monuments. He made me laugh.'

'What happened to Angelique's baby?'

'She went away for six months. When she came back—no baby. Nice Jewish girls don't have babies out of wedlock. Mind you, that same view applies to most women.'

Will's lid grew heavy. 'Thank you, Sparrow, for telling me that story, for sharing.'

'Tomorrow you're going to tell me what you know about my brother, Tin Man.'

He nodded and lay down. Within seconds he was asleep, but even though many hours passed, he woke unrested, as if he'd never slept. Daylight still crept in around the door. It wasn't dark yet and Therese was gone. Filled with a sudden overwhelming protectiveness, he shook to waking and stood.

Low rumbling voices travelled through the gap in the part open door, the farmer's thick and tinged with gruffness as if he smoked too much pipe tobacco, and Therese's soft French vowels. They were arguing.

He exited the storeroom into a shambolic courtyard full of squawking chickens and geese and a pig feeding on swill from the kitchen. Bloody hell, it was cold. He rubbed his hands together. The storeroom had been cosy. He rounded the farmhouse to confront Therese and the farmer. 'What are you arguing about?'

Therese turned to him, her face flushed red in the cool air and a puff of mist blowing from her mouth. 'Monsieur

Gambol has offered his horse and cart this evening. But I don't have quite enough money to pay for his better horse. He's insisting on an old nag, and anyone can see it will go lame the moment we start up the lane.'

Will turned towards the farmyard and in the closest paddock three horses stood near a water trough. 'One of those? They all look fine.'

'He'll let us take his best horse if we take half a cart-full of rutabagas and artichokes to his brother in Irreville. And we won't have to pay any money. His brother will let us stay. But it will delay our trip.'

'Is that on our route?'

'A little off but—'

'There's no problem then. Let's take the vegetables. If a passing patrol stops us, we have an excuse. Don't we, my lovely daughter?'

Therese looked at him blankly, let out another blast of mist from her pursed lips as if if a fast plane was taking to flight. She shook her head. 'Alright then, Papa.'

CHAPTER 7

Therese pushed Will off her. His lean was a heavy burden she could do without. The added distraction of constantly hoisting him upright made her veer the cart to the side of the road. 'Oh, for goodness sake.'

She steered the cart back onto the road and pushed him away from her again. It still champed her at the bit that he had not told her everything she wanted desperately to know. He'd stymied her at every opportunity. She would argue he was stalling, but to what end? It made her nervous. And despite his jovial company, and the honesty she read in his replies, being alone with him had left her with strange feelings. Of longing. Of wanting. And in the pit of her stomach, a desire for a man's companionship. Something she'd actively discouraged since arriving in France. On the night before parachuting into France, her SOE trainer and supervisor had told her not to get close to anyone—right after he'd seduced her.

She shrugged off thoughts of that last night in England, pushed Will off her shoulder once more, and flicked the reins to urge the horse to pick up pace. Travelling at night wasn't much fun and at this rate, they'd not arrive before light. She could see the first rays in the distance. To add to her mild discomfort, like the princess and the pea, Therese could feel the rough, slatted wood underneath the cushioned seat. Three years of part starvation had turned her bottom to skin and bone.

'Damn stupid vegetables,' she said and leaned back to pull up a rutabaga. Why anyone would want to eat these awful vegetables was beyond her. But she supposed it supplemented people's meagre rations. Some of the best cooks were in Paris, and maybe they could make this dull root tasty. It's just she had yet to experience such culinary delicacies.

'What? Where...' Will snorted and woke. His hand went to her shoulder and squeezed. 'Where are we, Sparrow?'

'Only a mile from Irreville and our destination.'

'We've made it this far without—'

Voices carried down the narrowed lane, and Therese's stomach turned to ice. She halted the horse and cart. Even with new outfits and forged papers, she worried they would catch the ire of some German soldiers or local gendarmes. The Germans had most port towns under their control, and their destination, although not a major location, was near enough to Le Havre to make the road busy and treacherous.

'Is that—'

'Shush. Yes. Soldiers or a patrol.'

Voices rose and fell against the surrounding bushes and grew closer. There'd been no snow here to muffle sounds. Therese pulled the horse and cart into a small pass under a leafless poplar tree, avoiding the camber of the bend in the road. There would be no time or place to avoid them.

'I'll get in the back and pretend to be drunk,' Will said.

She looked up at his face, a shapeless grey in the light. 'Alright.'

The patrol rounded the bend, laughing and joking, with cigarettes blazing in the darkened night. Therese pulled her coat around her and grabbed an old sack, hauling it over her legs.

Germans.

Their laughter came to stop as they neared and caught sight of her. She steeled herself for what was to come.

'Fräulein, was machst du hier auf der straße und um diese Nachtzeit?' A young soldier, who couldn't be more than twenty, asked.

Therese understood him, but pretended she couldn't. *'Je ne comprends pas?'*

'What is going on?' The sound of a deep, resonant voice carried and reverberated as a man pushed his way through the soldiers.

Panic thrummed through her. A regular gendarme. *'Oh, monsieur, je—'*

A shout from behind her interrupted her explanation and Therese closed her eyes. Will's voice sung in a raucous French accent from the cart. An old French drinking song.

> *'He is one of us.*
> *He drank his glass like the others.*
> *He's a drunk.*
> *You can tell by his face!'*

The best Therese could do was pretend and use her best thespian skills. She lay a hand on her chest. 'Oh, I'm sorry my papa is drunk. I had gone to fetch him from a neighbouring village. I had to rest for a moment, but if I don't return by morning, my maman will be worried!'

Will sat up abruptly, and the soldiers responded by lifting their rifles. He tilted his head towards the gendarme and laughed. 'I have the back teeth that bathe!' he said in guttural French.

Therese froze, the panic reaching her throat. Surely

they'd recognise his pronunciation was not that of a Frenchman. You could disguise an accent in song, but in conversation? Although Therese was English, her French was that of a native Parisian She'd learned the inflections and nuance of the accent to perfection. Will's slurred declaration that he was so drunk that he would vomit was pure Canadian French. She held the gaze of the gendarme, looking for any sign of alarm, and smiled. He laughed and she let out the breath, a cloud of mist rising with the crisp early morning air.

'You'd best get him home. I don't want him puking on my shoes.' He turned to the soldiers and explained in faltering German that he was drunk and to let him suffer la *migraine* for his misdemeanour.

The soldiers walked past, and Therese steered the horse back on to the road, relief washing through her. But she remained uneasy until the men's voices disappeared into the dark.

Will joined her on the seat, his closeness a welcome warmth. 'That was close.'

'Too close. You play the part of a drunk very well.' She laughed, but he didn't join in. 'Not far now.'

'Good.' He put his arm around her and she leaned into him. 'I can see why you have done so well here, Sparrow.'

They arrived at the second farmhouse within the hour. The farmer's brother, a salty looking grey-bearded man, displeased at their interrupting his breakfast before dawn, quietened on reading the letter.

He looked between the two travellers, grunted, and pointed to the stairs. 'Bathroom, bedroom.' His jerked his head behind him. 'Food.'

Therese smiled in acknowledgement, grateful that he'd not quizzed them further than needed.

The farmer stood, pulled his cap onto his head, then put

his jacket on and whistled. A shaggy Briad, which Therese hadn't noticed sitting in the corner of the room, sprang to attention. The farmer nodded and exited, leaving them standing, somewhat bewildered, around the kitchen table.

Will nudged her. 'Normans, hey?'

'*Oui.*'

They ate their fill: coffee, bread, jam, and padded upstairs. On opening the bedroom door to a small spartan room with only one bed, Therese looked to Will and a smile crept onto his face.

'I'm too tired to try anything, Sparrow. I promise, and when have I broken my promise to you?'

'So far, you've never broken a promise. I wasn't thinking...' She stopped and fanned herself, feeling hotter than she had for the last few days.

'Yes, you were. But you wouldn't be the cautious SOE operative if you didn't.'

She slipped past him and his mocking smile. In the bathroom she removed her dress. The awkward cut had rubbed painfully under her arms. She bathed in warm water and revelled in the warmth directly on her skin. A woman's dressing gown hung on the back of the door, but there had obviously not been a woman in this house for a long time.

She returned to the bedroom where Will was already under the thick cover of blankets. Therese joined him saying nothing and pulled a blanket up and around her neck. The day broke, light creeping around the window blind. She turned to face him. The growth of hair on his chin had almost become a beard. 'Are you going to tell me who you are now? And about my brother?'

His smile returned and lit a blaze in his eyes. 'Tell me something about yourself, Sparrow. You mentioned family. I sense you are holding something close. What happened?'

Her heart lurched. He had caught her at a weak moment.

She wriggled, savouring the warmth that both their bodies created. 'My sister Madeline—Maddy—recommended me for a job in the War Office, as a switchboard operator at first, then as an interpreter. We shared a flat near to where we worked. Our parents lived in the country side, in Tonbridge, in a small cottage on the edge of the town. They came to visit to help Maddy with her wedding plans and her trousseau. I went to work and left them; I was to join them for lunch. But they never arrived. The bombers came and went in the early part of the day.'

'I am so sorry, Therese. Is that why you joined the SOE?'

'I didn't know what to do after they died. A man in the War Office came to me, quizzed me on my French, on how good was my German, my Italian and Spanish.'

'How did you learn so many languages?'

'My father was a language teacher, my mother half French.'

'It must have been difficult to lose them.'

'Yes. I was numb for months after their deaths, I didn't know what I was agreeing to do for the Ministry.' She stared into his mocking tawny eyes and wanted to kiss him. Those teasing lips made her body tingle with heat. She wanted to feel something, anything, but she licked her lips and closed her eyes instead. There was no room for desire here, despite the pull of it tempting her to lie against him, to shed every bit of good girl from her cold bones. She needed a diversion. 'Back in the lane, you looked unhappy when I mentioned you made a good drunk.'

He shifted against her and the heat inside her spiked. 'I had a lot of time to study. My father was a rotten drunk. My brothers and I used to mimic him. He was never cruel, not in a conventional sense, but he was always too drunk to be part of our lives.'

'What about your mother?'

'She covered for him. Too much.'

'Please, tell me who you are. Please, I beg you.'

He ran his hand down the side of her face. 'My name is Major William Thomas Crowhurst. Canadian Military, British Security Co-ordination task force out of Camp-X.'

Therese's breath stuttered out of her and she sat up. 'You're an Allied spy! You're the Raven!'

He smiled. 'I like Tin Man better.'

CHAPTER 8

Will's hand stroked Therese's arm. 'We still have a way to go, Therese. We should sleep.'

She lay down, but her eyes did not close. 'What happened in the crash?'

'No idea. I'm not a pilot. There was an almighty bang, and we were flying on one engine. I thought I would die, but after we crashed and I was still alive, I knew I had to hide my identity if I was going to make it out of France. And with the pilot dead and us looking so much alike... It wasn't a simple decision.'

'And my brother?'

'I told you everything I know. He's probably still in a US Army hospital. The safest place for him.' She looked at him, her eyes wide like the first time he'd met her. But this time, unlike the doll soulless blankness, there was deep emotion. He could fall into those eyes and drown.

'Is it very important you return to England? You are going to help free France—free Paris?' she asked.

'Yes. I have information. I couldn't tell you before. I think... I think there is someone in the Resistance feeding information to the Germans or the collaborators. Someone close. It's why I didn't want you to say anything to Jacques or Charlotte.'

Her eyes darted from side to side. 'What? No, that couldn't be. Who?'

'I don't know. The interrogators asked questions about me—about William Crowhurst. They wanted to know where I was. I said he was dead. But they didn't believe me. Betrayal has happened before, Therese. It will happen again before the war is over. People want peace and to live their lives. If they're hungry, they're suggestible, and desperate. If that means trading information to the enemy, it's all they have left. But thanks to you, I am here. I am alive.'

She nodded several times. 'I will get you to the coast, Tin Man. I promise.'

'I know you will, Sparrow.' He inhaled deeply and turned onto his back to stare at the low, thatched ceiling. Therese's breaths became low, steady, and slow. He turned back to her, his gaze traversing the outline of her full lips, the beauty spot, the dark roots of her hair, the line of her jaw. The nearness of her made his heart thump and he swore under his breath. She was utterly breath-taking.

~

'WE SHOULD HAVE BROUGHT that game of snakes and ladders,' Will joked. He pulled Therese in tighter and pressed his back against the stone wall. She didn't complain, instead she wriggled closer like a bird nesting. He liked the sensation of her nuzzling next to him, and he'd grown used to her scent over the last five days, a mixture of lavender and cedar. Better than the smell of this abandoned farmhouse. Hopefully it would be their last stop before reaching the coast.

'We're only an hour away now, I think. I can smell the sea,' she said. The scattered rays of twilight filtered in through the broken window. 'It's almost dark. We can leave soon.'

Travelling only at night and through parts of the countryside devoid of towns, people, and German soldiers, had allowed him a closeness to her. They were soldiers in arms, he and Therese, and he liked that very much. A pang of loss, of the inevitability of their separation, tingled through him. He pushed the thought of it aside. Damn war. 'I can't wait to be somewhere warm.'

'Do you have someone waiting for you? A wife? A girl?'

He paused before answering. There had been a girl. Four years ago, at the start of the war, he'd had a fiancée. But it had ended when he'd returned on a surprise furlough and found her in bed with another man. He had walked, not waiting for explanations or excuses, his heart too full of disappointment, his head too full of rage, and never looked back. Afterwards, he'd joined the program at Camp-X and having a relationship was impossible. 'No. You?'

'I've disguised myself as a teenage girl for two years now.' She looked up at him and laughed. 'What do you think?'

'Maybe someone in the Resistance. Jacques, Ruben... or Charlotte.'

She slapped his chest. 'Honestly. No, I don't fraternise with those I work with.'

He pulled her in tighter, wishing he'd met Therese anywhere but here. A nightclub in Soho, a gathering at a concert, anywhere he could remain close without fear of death dogging their journey. 'Is that right?'

'Yes!' she said and sighed, burrowing in closer. 'I read somewhere that during the Irish Easter Rebellion, young men were too scared to take wives. They feared dying and leaving the hungry mouths of the women and children they loved. I don't know if it's true, but I carried that for a long time, as if those young men's burden was mine.'

Will had done the same, not for fear of dying. He'd told himself if he feared dying he could not live life. He'd let no one get close until now. Five days and he was under the spell of this diminutive woman, of this heroine of the SOE.

'Charlotte and Ruben,' she said and pulled away from him. 'They should have caught up to us by now.'

'Maybe they're already there, waiting for us, with Jacques.'

'Of course, yes. They're freer to travel than we are.'

He hadn't bothered to quiz her further on their destination on the coast, or what route they needed to take other than through country lanes to evade the Germans. Without a care he'd followed her, trusting her implicitly. 'Where is this town where they are to meet us?'

'Houlgate is a small port at the mouth of the Dives River. There are German fortifications all the way along the beach and harbour, but fishing boats can come and go freely. There is scrubland to the east of the town with a rocky feature of large limestone boulders covered in molluscs, so we need to be careful we don't cut ourselves. There's a fishing refuge nestled in between some rocks. We're to meet there.'

'You've been there before?'

'Yes, a reconnaissance disguised as a family holiday.'

A family holiday with Therese sounded appealing. He looked to the window; darkness had crept up on them. 'Let's get out of here.'

An hour on, he and Therese scrambled over rocks and through dense thickets of bushes until they landed on the beach. Waves from a dark ocean kissed the shore and the air pierced through him, despite little wind. Therese pointed up the beach to a small wooden shack, a pale light emanating onto the sand. They approached and Will's chest throbbed, not just with cold but with anticipation. Something was off, but he'd trusted her this far. Outside the huts and along the shore, several small boats, tied to stakes, bobbed with the waves.

Therese was about to open the door, but Will put his hand on hers. 'Let me go first,' he said and cocked his ear. There was the shuffling of boots but no voices.

He opened the door fast. Jacques stood from his seated position at the table. Will's gaze travelled to the blood on his arm and a needle and thread in his hand. He'd been sewing up a cut.

'Jacques!' Therese said and sighed. 'Where is Charlotte? Where is Ruben? Why are you bleeding?'

Jacques shot Will a glance, then a sickly grimace at Therese. 'They're dead.'

CHAPTER 9

Jacques's words slurred as if he'd been drinking.

'Dead? What—what happened?' Therese cried. The sudden knowledge of Charlotte's death hit her in the chest. This brave woman, this almost sister. No, she couldn't be dead.

'They were traitors, Therese. They planned to hand you into the Germans.'

'What? But why wait until now? Why not in the toy shop, where they had us cornered?' None of it made sense. It was inconceivable. Especially Charlotte. She hated Nazis with a fiery passion and fought with the Resistance from the very beginning.

Jacques shrugged and looked at Will.

'What are our plans?' Will asked.

'We stay here until nine o'clock when the fishing boat will arrive and signal us. Then we wait. They'll send a smaller boat to fetch you.'

'Here, let me look at your arm,' Therese said.

Jacques moved it away from her. 'It's nothing. A scratch I got climbing the rocks.'

She nodded and stood closer to Will. Why did she feel

safer with someone whom she hardly knew, with someone who'd taken a dead man's place and lied to her? Will put his arm around her, and she leaned in towards him. Jacques gave her an odd look, then turned away.

Therese ran her hand along the seasoned, grey wood of the fisherman's shack, surprised the building was still standing. A small pot belly stove sat unlit in the corner. The cast iron door had come off its hinges and now lay on the floor. Her bones were so cold that not even the radiating heat Will had shared with her could warm them, but they couldn't risk smoke being seen from the chimney. The light from the lamp was bad enough. A bed with a stained and soiled mattress sat in one corner. Fishing gear, rods, and reels rested against the back of the shack door, and two precariously stacked lobster pots leaned heavily to one side next to them.

Jacques dimmed the lamp and rolled down his sleeve. He'd opened a bottle of wine and poured it shakily into an old tin cup. 'Would you like one while we wait?' he said and nodded to Will and Therese.

Will didn't answer, and Therese shook her head. A shiver ran through her. She did not like the sensation. All her nerves tingled as if the cold had got to them too.

She glanced at her watch. Another hour.

Jacques remained at the table, twitching nervously, and Will, finding an old blanket, lay it over the bed and sat leaning against the wall, one hand behind his head. He beckoned Therese over. She wanted to join him on the bed, lay against him, feel his warmth, and listen to his heartbeat. But Jacques watched her furtively. She refused Will's offer and sat on a chair on the other side of the table, rubbing her arms.

Will's easy conversational tone had ceased the moment they had stepped into the hut. But Therese was not one for small talk, and Jacques, ever-serious Jacques, rarely spoke unless he needed to. So they sat and waited, and Therese let the events of the past two weeks wash over her. Charlotte—dead. A sudden bubble of anger invaded her, her muscles tensing, her arms stiffening. She stood and dragged the chair to the window, looking out for the fishing boat that would come and whisk them away.

A light flashed from the water and remained still. A signal. Morse code.

'They're here,' Therese said.

Jacques stood. 'What? Already?'

She looked at him in confusion. 'You said nine o'clock.'

'Yes, I did,' he replied and shrugged on his coat, patting the pockets as he opened the door.

They poured out of the shack and onto the beach. Will came out last and Therese huddled her arms around herself. A small white boat came into view and as it came closer, she squinted at the single figure gently rowing.

'It can't be...' She gasped as the boat reached the water's edge. 'Charlotte!'

An arm grasped Therese around her neck and dragged her backwards. She scrabbled at Jacques's distinctly ropey hand.

'No, it can't be! I saw you lying...' he shouted.

Charlotte jumped from the boat onto the sand. 'But you never confirmed it. Too busy running away like a frightened rat. But Ruben is dead, and you're a filthy collaborator!'

Will moved towards Therese, but Jacques brandished a gun, waving it towards Will and Charlotte. 'You've ruined everything. The patrol will be here soon.'

'Put the gun away, Jacques. There's no need for anyone to get hurt,' Will said.

'Shut up, you stupid American.'

'Canadian, actually,' Will said mockingly.

Jacques spat on the ground. 'All the same. All you want is power. You are no different to any combatant.'

'Jacques,' Therese croaked. 'They are here to help us, please...'

'Like your English SOE? We have centuries of hate between our countries, little bird. A legacy of war and betrayal. Why would that change? I'll tell you why. Because England wants something too.'

'What do you want, Jacques?' Therese asked, unable to escape his iron-tight grip. Jacques was thin but had a wiry strength.

'Don't hurt her,' Will said. 'It's me you want. The Germans don't want her. They're looking for me.'

'You're wrong. They want you both. And I, and what's left of my family, can take the reward offered for the two of you.'

'How long have you been working with them?' Will asked.

'I don't work for the Germans; I work for me,' he replied.

Therese squirmed, but he held her tighter. She whimpered in pain under his throttling embrace.

'Therese!' Will cried.

'Stay back.' Jacques swivelled the gun from Will to Charlotte. 'Get back in the boat, or I'll shoot you a second time.'

'I can't, Jacques. You know I can't. You killed Ruben. You're a traitor and a collaborator. They know it's you who traded secrets with the Germans.' Charlotte's voice was calm, unlike Therese's heart, which beat like a hundred tiny bird wings.

'*Merde*! You wouldn't know what that means! My parents are dead, and the rest of my family is fighting for a useless cause. We're all going to die, Charlotte, if we don't help the Germans. The Russians will come, and they will kill us. The Germans are only protection against further subjugation,' Jacques said.

'At least when we are free of the Germans, we will have

friends like the Canadians,' Therese replied and looked towards Will. Jacques's grip tightened further, hurting her neck. Her whimper turned into a pleading cry as a sharp pain travelled down Therese's spine.

'Shush, Sparrow. You're a little bird who knows how to keep her beak shut, but you're not a fighter.'

Will stepped forward. 'You're a coward, Jacques. How many did you betray and send to their deaths?'

'It is a pity you are not a woman.' Jacques breathed loudly through his nose. 'Fitting for the Raven to die at Ravensbrück. Yes, I know who you are. I've known from the moment they caught you. Why do you think they allowed your escape?'

'Allowed?' Therese cried. 'You put me up to this?'

'With Charlotte's help.'

'I would never have helped if I'd known what you were going to do,' Charlotte spat.

Will cleared his throat. 'You should never underestimate those around you.'

'I thought Therese would fail, and you would both die. But you were wily, evading every soldier I sent your way. And I had hoped the plan would go smoothly. But it doesn't matter. The Germans will be here soon, and I can leave this hellhole of a country full of weak men and whores. At least the Germans have strength. I'm going to kill this little bird, shoot Charlotte again— I won't miss this time— and I will kill you as well, Major Crowhurst. The Germans don't care much whether you are dead or alive. I will be free, and you will be dead.'

He cocked the gun next to Therese's ear, pointed it at Will, and pressed the trigger. She screamed as it went off. Kicking at Jacques's shin as hard as she could, managing to loosen his grip. She ran to Will, lying on his side in the sand, blood trickling down his cheek. 'No! No!'

She pulled out the useless bread knife and thought of all the lives lost, so many gone too soon. Memories of her mother, father and Maddy flooded back. Of Angelique and her family. Of those who had died in the SOE and The Resistance. And Freddy, did he still lay hurt somewhere?

'Fill your bowl to the brim and it will spill. Keep sharpening your knife and it will blunt.' Therese's furious cry came from deep within. One she held for far too long. She ran at Jacques, and another gunshot rang out in the frosty night air.

CHAPTER 10

Will had found the gun in the second farmhouse they'd visited. The one where he and Therese had snuggled under thick blankets together. He'd hidden it, unsure why, other than he didn't want her to think he didn't trust her. And at that stage, he wasn't sure he could. He had no doubt there was a Resistance collaborator at play.

It had to be one of them—Therese, Jacques, Charlotte or Ruben. But his senses told him it wasn't Therese. His Sparrow.

Therese half collapsed into Charlotte's arms and stared at Will. 'You're alive? How? He shot you.'

He pulled the heavy cast iron door from the potbelly stove from under his shirt and threw it onto the wet sand.

She started laughing and threw herself on him. 'You fool! You stupid Canadian fool!'

Nobody had noticed him pick up the door before they'd left the shack. He'd covered his chest even though there was no guarantee a bullet wouldn't hit him in the head. But it had turned out that Jacques wasn't a sharpshooter and holding Therese had unsteadied him, rendering him off balance.

'*Vive la France,*' Charlotte said and kicked at Jacques's gun.

He lay moaning and bleeding, the sand turning black around him.

Will looked down at Therese in his arms, leaned down and kissed her. He pulled back, but she pulled his face towards her and kissed him again. She broke from him and smiled. 'You are the Tin Man.'

'But I have a heart,' he said and took her hand, placing it on his chest. 'I promise you that. And technically, it's iron. Not tin.'

'Oh, shut up,' she said and kissed him again.

'When you lovebirds...' Charlotte paused and laughed. 'When you're finished, we have to go. There is only a small window of opportunity before this patrol shows up.'

'Is he still alive?' Therese asked.

'Yes. I say we leave him here for his patrol to find.'

Will took Therese's hand and led her towards the boat. 'Follow the yellow brick road with me.'

She baulked and pulled her hand away. 'I—'

'Therese?'

'I can't go with you.'

'But you have to—the patrol—the SOE.'

'*Jacques* said the SOE recalled me. He might have been lying about that. Like he was...' She paused and glanced at Jacques. 'And I can hide. They won't find me.'

'I saw the orders, Therese,' Charlotte said. 'But... I could pretend I didn't.'

Therese's gaze flitted back to Will's. 'I have to stay as much as you have to go. Go, free France, free us, *free me*.'

The bitterness at such a parting sent a tightness to Will's chest. Images of what would come flashed through his mind. The Liberation of Paris would involve everyone: men, women, and children. The ground swell of the Resistance would have their day. Many would sacrifice their lives to free France. He didn't want her to be one of them. 'Therese...'

'I have to find Freddy.'

He took her hand again and drew her close. 'Sparrow. Your brother—if he's with the Americans, he will be fine.' He kissed her hard, savouring the taste of her, the scent of her, the feel of her beneath his hands. He lifted her into his arms. She was as light as a feather—as light as a sparrow. Her lips were warm against his and he'd give anything to spend the whole boat ride back to England kissing her.

'We have to leave.' Charlotte said again.

Will parted from Therese. 'Alright. Stay safe, Sparrow, and don't lose touch. We'll meet again, yes?'

Therese didn't answer him but simply nodded and folded her arms around herself. 'Go!'

Will climbed into the boat, keeping his gaze fixed on her until darkness swallowed her whole.

~

Paris, December 1944

AFTER RETURNING to England and passing on his intelligence to the BSC, Will attempted to locate Therese. She had broken ranks with her superiors in the SOE, and not even Charlotte had knowledge of where she'd gone. He'd even contacted friends in the US Army stationed in Italy, to no avail. He'd looked for her brother too, but the British government, despite Will's status, was less forthcoming on that information.

Therese had haunted him like no other woman had before. He should have forced her to come with him. Then he'd know she was safe. She was with him in spirit in June when, like a good Canadian soldier, he took his place on the beaches of Normandy. He could have sworn he'd caught her scent when he'd walked the streets of Paris on August twenty-fifth, following Charles De Gaulle's impromptu victory march. Paris was free, and the tricolour flag flapped in the breeze. Not even German snipers in buildings above the streets could dampen celebrations for the city's liberation. If only his heart could know such elation.

Among the joyous faces around him, none were Therese. His Sparrow.

Will stood, coffee in hand, at the window of the Canadian embassy, staring down and across the street. A blanket of snow covered the park across the rue de Constantine, the street itself devoid of people and cars. Post liberation, he'd returned to the secretive Camp-X for a brief period before its closure and before his assignment as Paris liaison for the Canadian Military. Officially, he was a diplomat. Unofficially, still a spy.

He turned at a tap on his office door. 'Come.'

A khaki clad secretary entered. 'Sir, there's someone here who wishes to speak with you.'

'Tell them I'm busy.'

'The young officer was very insistent, sir.'

Will sighed. How many soldiers had come through here looking for a brother, father or sons? 'I don't know why they come here. I can't help them. They're better off approaching the Red Cross.'

'He says you know his sister.'

He froze. 'Sister? Do you have a name?'

'He wouldn't give me his name.'

'You better send him in, corporal.'

Will's cup clattered onto his desk, spilling black liquid over a pile of papers. He began mopping it up when the young man entered. He was not very tall, about five-seven, and wearing a British officers' uniform. He was unmistakably Therese's brother. He saluted. 'Major Crowhurst?'

'That's my name on the door. You are Fredrick Lambert?'

He removed his cap; he had the makings of curls in his short hair. 'Yes, sir. Lieutenant Lambert. My sister spoke of me to you?'

He couldn't stop the grin from spreading across his face. 'Yes. Your sister saved my life. You look like her.'

'Oh, she didn't mention she'd saved your life, but then, she doesn't tell me much.'

'It seems we have that in common.' Will's heart began racing. 'She's not with you?'

'No, but she asked me to come here and give you this.' He retrieved a letter from his pocket and handed it over. 'It's for someone named "Tin Man". A code name, I presume. As if she thinks she can hide all this cloak and dagger business from me, but I thought it best that I bring it here straight away. Do you know him, sir?'

'I know him.' Will studied Fredrick's face. Etched in his features, large brown eyes and similarly shaped lips, was a family resemblance so acute it hurt to see it. He'd not had a picture of Therese, but her face, he couldn't forget. 'Are you well, lieutenant?'

'Very well, sir, thank you for asking.' He stood awkwardly. 'If that's all, sir, I must go. I have other duties.'

'Of course, don't let me keep you. But, lieutenant, before you leave, where is your sister now?'

'Staying somewhere in the eleventh arrondissement. Something about living above a toy shop?' He saluted and left the room.

Will couldn't open the letter fast enough.

Tin Man,

I'm here. Come find me. We have a game of Snakes and Ladders to finish.

Sparrow.

EPILOGUE

Therese walked through the streets, still littered with snow. The house where she'd saved Will—the German torture chamber—lay destroyed. How many floors had she scrubbed in that place? She shuddered at the memory. Now when the gendarmes passed, she nodded, no longer worried whether they'd ask for papers or her business on the street that day. But the war was not over yet, and Paris was still dangerous, still mired in the aftermath of occupation. And something was missing. It had loomed large in her heart since that wintery night on the beach.

She rounded the corner and started down the tiny lane. The door to the toyshop hung off its hinges and the building had been looted and partly burned from a fire. The black-charred wooden shopfront appeared almost picturesque against a foreground of white. As if an artist had sketched it that way. She kicked at the snow, revealing a clump of darkened ashes underneath.

'I suspect it's not safe inside, unless you're in the basement,' a deep voice said from behind.

Therese paused and closed her eyes. If she turned, would he be an apparition? Like she'd witnessed disappearing into the dark on that bitter January night? A weakness invaded her limbs, and her eyes burned with hot tears. 'You got my note?' Her voice faltered, and she spun on her heels.

'I looked for you. You made it difficult.'

He looked the same minus the silly grey patches Charlotte had painted on his hair. 'I had things to do.'

'Sparrow...' His voice caught and he blinked.

Therese launched herself into him, her face grazing a button on his chest. 'Tin Man.'

'My Sparrow,' he said, his hand caressing her head. 'I like your hair.'

Therese's hair had remained at shoulder length. But the natural dark brown was now released from its mousy, dyed prison. She released a sobbing laugh and wiped the tears that spilled onto his jacket. Somehow this man had infiltrated every spare thought she had. Dreams came and went, but his face was a constant.

'You missed me, then?'

She stared up at him and nodded. His eyes creased at the corners, and he placed his hands on either side of her face and kissed her.

Their lips met smoothly, and his bottom lip slid between hers, captured. On pulling away, his lips had turned the colour of her red lipstick. And he kissed her again and again and again. He kissed her until her lips burned with more need and lit a fire throughout the rest of her body.

'Let's go somewhere warm,' he said.

'I'm already warm.' She looked around at the debris of the toyshop, the place ransacked and now empty. She took his arm, nestling in close. 'No snakes and ladders, I'm afraid.'

'I'm sure we'll find another way to tell each other everything.'

They walked the quiet streets, and she savoured the warmth of him next to her.

'Does the SOE know you're alive?' he asked.

'I might have mentioned it to someone.' Therese held him tighter, her heart beating fast. If she let him go, he might leave, and she might never see him again. But he hugged her against him as if he held the same thought. 'What about you? What are you doing now that Paris and France are free?'

'Don't you know? You were the one who found me because I couldn't find you. You were my needle in a haystack. Not even Charlotte knew.'

She paused, looked up at him and bit her lip.

'She knew?'

'I'm sorry about that. I asked her not to tell you. There were things to sort out, not just Freddy. But I'm ready now.'

'Ready?'

She leaned up and kissed his cheek, smearing more lipstick across his jaw. 'To get close to someone.'

'Then I feel the wait was worth it.' He took her hand and clasped it tight. 'What became of Jacques? Charlotte says he's in prison.'

'Yes. But given half the police force in France were collaborators, only the worst of the worst will sit in prison for long. I doubt there will be any official repercussions for him. That doesn't mean someone won't find him after he's released and introduce him to a blade.'

'But not you?'

'I've only a blunt butter knife,' she said and laughed.

They entered a small café, warm and inviting, the smell of coffee an endearing scent. They ordered and found a seat in a corner facing the door. Old operative habits die hard. Therese took a sip, enjoying the warmth. 'What now, Tin Man?'

'There's a church around the corner from the Canadian consulate.' His Adam's apple bobbed, and his gaze was soft on hers. He grabbed her hand. 'I know I'm asking a lot from you, but I can't live with the idea of you not being close. Don't fly away again, Sparrow, please.'

Her heartbeat increased, joy causing an unsteady breathlessness to wax and wane in her chest. He was asking her to marry him. 'Will you have to fight again? Put yourself in harm's way?'

'It depends on what you mean by fight. The war is still here and events with the Soviets have escalated. Certain—investigations are required. I'm biding my time here until the end of the war, and then a new will begin. A different sort of war. A man with my skills is a perfect candidate for such tasks.'

She gripped his hand harder and stood to lean across the table. 'Is that so?' She kissed him on both cheeks and then on the mouth, long and drawn out.

He let out a low groan and kissed her forehead. 'Oh, Sparrow.'

'That's a yes, by the way. To the church visit,' she said and kissed him again and sat.

He slapped coins on the table, stood and held out his hand until she joined him. She let out a surprised cry as he enveloped her in an embrace and lifted her, cradling her against his chest, her legs dangling over one arm, his other arm supporting her back.

As he carried her out the door into the cold winter air, she folded one arm around his neck, the other she placed on his cheek. 'It's fortunate, you know.'

'Fortunate?' he asked, as he laid a series of kisses along her jawline and nuzzled his lips below her ear.

'If you need to make enquiries in your investigations...' Therese sighed and pulled away, fluttered her lashes, and tucked an errant strand of hair behind her ear. 'I'm now reasonably fluent in Russian.'

AVA JANUARY

Ava January is a writer living in sunny Brisbane with her sons and a Spoodle named Stroodle.

When she isn't breaking up fights over strangely shaped pieces of plastic, she can be found obsessing over Victorian era fashion (in the name of research, of course!) reading and writing stories with strong female leads.

Her first full-length novel, The Lady Detective - a light-hearted, romantic romp through Victorian England about a Lady Detective and London's most scandalous rake-was released in May 2020.

After embarking on a Bachelor of Creative Arts she fell heavily in love with writing and hasn't looked back.

Her work was longlisted for 2019 Richell Prize for Emerging Writers. The Lady Detective won 1st Prize-Historical - Orange County Rose Prize for Emerging Writers 2020 and was a 2nd round winner in LERA's The Writer competition.

Web: www.avajanuary.com
Facebook: @Ava January
Instagram: @authoravajanuary

CLARE GRIFFIN

Clare Griffin is a best-selling and award winning freelance writer, author and playwright, who will start conversations with "I love your shoes!" – often to complete strangers. Clare writes about strong willed women, past and present, in contemporary and historical fiction. With a love for vintage fashion, her characters are normally quite well dressed at some stage of their journey.

In 2016 she published her debut novel Tumble which became an Amazon best seller. The first chapter won the Freshly Squeezed C1 Blitz and became part of an anthology. In 2017 her 10 minute play The Karma Fairy was runner up People's Choice Award as part of Gemco Players Take Ten Festival. Clare has also published several novellas and short stories such as Happily, Ever After? and The Hunt for Scarlett O'Hara a short story about the night Hollywood found its Scarlett.

In 2020 she curated the historical anthology Easter Promises with four other historical fiction authors and in 2021 was longlisted for the Adaptable prize.

Clare lives in the eastern suburbs of Melbourne in a house full of men in the form of her husband, two sons and a retired greyhound called Gary.

Web: www.claregriffin.com
Facebook: @claregriffinwriter
Instagram: @ClareGriffinWriter

SARAH FIDDELAERS

Sarah is a writer, blogger and mother. She has a deep fascination with history and loves writing stories filled with the intrigue and romance of the past. Sarah was longlisted for the 2019 Richell prize and the 2020 Romance Writers of Australia Emerald award.

Sarah lives in the Macedon Ranges with her husband and five children. *Easter Dawn* in the historical anthology *Easter Promises* was her first published work. *The Secret Artist of Paris* is her second published work of historical fiction.

Web: www.sarahfiddelaers.com

Instagram: @sarahfiddelaers

NANCY CUNNINGHAM

Nancy is a writer, research scientist and mother. Nancy has always loved stories about nature, science, history and love and has endeavoured to weave these into her stories. She writes across genres – including Historical, Romance, Crime and Science Fiction. Nancy has been a Romance Writer of Australia competition finalist and winner (2019, 2020, 2021) as well as a finalist in the West Houston 'Emilys' (2020). In 2020 Nancy's manuscript 'The Bridge' won best adult manuscript (Adult Fiction) at the CYA annual conference.

Nancy lives in Adelaide with her partner and daughter. She has published in Tulpa magazine, Antipodean SciFi, RWA Sweet Treats anthology 'Cupcake', *Easter Promises*. Her story *The Sparrow and the Tin Man* is her third published historical fiction short.

Web: www.nmcunningham.com
Facebook: @NancyMCunningham
Instagram: @nan_writes
Twitter: @Bugsie70

CPSIA information can be obtained
at www.ICGtesting.com
Printed in the USA
BVHW082241020921
615904BV00003B/639

9 780994 533364